THE PLAGUE DOCTOR

OTHER BOOKS BY E. JOAN SIMS

The Paisley Sterling Mysteries
Cemetery Silk
The Plague Doctor
The Paper Detective
The Cradle Robber

THE PLAGUE DOCTOR
A PAISLEY STERLING MYSTERY

E. JOAN SIMS

WILDSIDE PRESS

Wildside Press

www.wildsidepress.com

Dedicated to two fantastic young women who never cease to amaze me with their intelligence, beauty, wisdom and wit—my daughters—Caroline and Polly—with love and joy.

CHAPTER ONE

Six days after Labor Day I bid a grateful farewell to the sultry and oppressive heat of the dog days of summer. In less than a week, the winds blew away the grey cocoon of humid, low-lying air that had trapped the summer's heat to expose the brilliant blue of the early autumn sky. These high stratospheric winds scoured fluffy white clouds into thin wispy ribbons. Mares' tails, that's what my father used to call those high striated clouds. He claimed it was sailor's jargon. I'm sure it was. Sailing was just one of the many things he had loved to do

The summer had been wet as well as hot. The grass was tall and green, and every hillside was brightly decorated with dancing yellow heads of Goldenrod and Black-eyed Susans. Dainty white splotches of Queen Anne's Lace lined the roadsides and country lanes. Dragonflies and honeybees skimmed over the newly mown fields with a pleasant hum, and songbirds were outdoing each other with farewell concerts before heading south for the winter. It was my favorite time of year in Kentucky.

Everything would have been perfect except for the fact that my beautiful daughter, Cassandra, was in love again. The first sign of this emotional turn of events came one evening when she asked if she could raid my closet. She needed something silky and feminine from my past. Another dead giveaway was the fact that she kept bumping into furniture and breaking her grandmother's antique porcelain teacups. And most troubling of all, she had developed a very inconvenient memory loss concerning the care and feeding of her nasty-tempered but adoring Lhasa Apso, Agatha Christie—Aggie for short.

The object of her affections was a nice enough young man. He was not very handsome, but he was not hard to look at in a homely blonde sort of way. He was pleasant and polite, interesting and intelligent, and he enjoyed spending time with the whole family. I tolerated him as politely as I had all of his predecessors.

My imaginary alter ego, Leonard Paisley, the detective hero of my mystery novels, had been instructed by my agent to "get busy or else." The real writer, me, Paisley Sterling, was having trouble getting started on a new book. Lazy Indian summer days on the farm were just too beautiful. I often found myself gazing through the French doors of the library in my mother's sprawling country home instead of conjuring up daring deeds for the intrepid Leonard.

More often than not, after a delightful lunch prepared by my culinary genius of a parent, I would whistle for Aggie and sneak out for a run in the back forty. The dog never tired of hunting things smaller and furrier than herself, and I never tired of just being me and being here.

Meadowdale Farm had been in my family for years. When I rented out my townhouse in New York and came back here to live a year ago, I became a true clodhopper, a mud bud, a lover of all things earthy and fertile. I had also happily forsaken my city persona and burned my panty hose. It was clean livin' in high cotton for me, Paisley Sterling DeLeon, country girl, from now on. Cassie was welcome to anything in my closet. I was through with Gucci and Pucci. My idea of formal dress was a linen jacket over my jeans. If more formality was required, then my presence was not. I kept my unruly auburn hair under bandanas or within the restraint of a ribbon if the occasion called for it. My figure had slimmed to the dimensions of my college days, and my hazel eyes dressed up my freckled face with happiness. I was free of the constraints and demands of city life. I had followed my bliss.

It was ironic, really, if you considered that when I was writing nature-oriented stories, the *Bartholomew the Blue-eyed Cricket* children's series, I had lived in the middle of Manhattan. Now, happily ensconced in my rural paradise, I was writing hard-boiled detective novels set in the tough, dirty streets I had abandoned. Unfortunately, I was about to find out that every paradise has its snake.

The afternoon it all began, Aggie and I took a long, satisfying walk over to the man-made lake at the back end of the farm and picked up a ton of beggar lice along the way. I dreaded the thought of having to comb them out of the dog's thick, soft fur. She was a vicious little mutt and had the bite of a cobra.

We walked for almost two hours before we headed back home. Aggie's tongue was hanging out, and I was really looking forward to a cold gin and tonic on the patio before dinner.

My mother, Anna Howard Sterling, was much more proper, stylish, and, well, much more everything than me. Tonight she was making one of her spectacular dinners for Ethan's birthday. Cassie was creating, or maybe constructing was a better word, her boyfriend's cake. For my part, I had promised to behave myself, comb my hair, and wear a dress—*ergo*, the gin and tonic.

Aggie and I ran the last mile home. We collapsed in a grateful heap on the chaise lounge on the patio in the middle of the big lawn in back of the house.

"There you are, my pretty! I was afraid I would have to drink alone."

Horatio Raleigh, my mother's old and dear friend, came out to greet me with a tray of canapés and two tall, frosty glasses deco-rated with a slices of lime. Horatio himself was tall and lean, and walked with a military bearing. A neatly trimmed white halo of hair circled the sides of his head, and a Van Dyke beard adorned the bottom half of his handsome, roguish face.

He smiled ruefully as he handed me my libation. "I've abandoned the kitchen. Your lovely mother will not even acknowledge my presence when she is in the throes of working her culinary magic. And I was afraid to disturb your daughter. She might make me taste something."

He leaned closer and patted my arm. "Just between you and me, my dear, we'd better find some other outlet for young Cassandra's talents—judging from the looks of her young man's birthday cake."

I took a long, cool sip of gin. "Umm, that bad?"

"Do the words, 'leaning tower of Pisa' ring a bell?"

"Perhaps animal husbandry . . . " I mused.

Horatio nodded at the puppy curled up against my legs on the chaise "Yes, by all means. Let her breed that vicious little mutt."

As if she had been cued by a stage manager, Aggie raised a perfectly adorable fuzzy head and curled her little black puppy lips in a snarl.

Horatio shuddered dramatically and added in a theatrical whisper, "Imagine the savings in our national defense budget. We could kiss the Cruise missile goodbye."

A large and very fat rabbit crept out of the blackberry bushes along the fencerow and munched cautiously on some clover. He must have given a silent bunny signal to his buddies, because a short while later, six more joined him in the picnic. Horatio and I sat very still and watched their antics. When a big groundhog, whom we had named Zacharias, lumbered up from his den under the herb garden, the rabbits respectfully made way for him as he waddled over to the pear tree to dine on the fallen fruit.

I sighed contentedly and thanked God for the one millionth time that my father and grandfather had had the foresight and the vision to buy this place. I was also grateful that the next generation of Sterlings, including me, had held on to it for dear life.

The big old farmhouse had originated as a "four pen" log cabin with no electricity and no plumbing. By the time I was born, that original humble dwelling had become a sprawling country cottage with six bedrooms and seven baths.

We no longer farmed the land. The pretty, white-faced Hereford cattle that we kept in my grandfather's day were long gone. But the fields were still sown with seed every spring and mowed every fall. And according to my father's wishes, we were careful to leave scattered thickets and bits of woods here and there for the abundant wild life.

Horatio leaned back in his rocker and smiled at me.

"There's a bit of gossip in town about this young man of Cassandra's."

"Oh, yeah? Just what has the Rowan Springs Country Club rumor mill come up with this time?"

"Well actually, it's more like the 'spit and whittle' crowd."

"The old coots who spend the day sitting on the wooden benches outside of the hardware store? What in the world does a dapper gentleman like yourself have in common with the likes of them? Were you telling them where they could buy Giorgio Armani overalls?"

"Very amusing, my dear." Horatio paused as he took a drink. "I buried one of them last week."

"Oops, sorry," I sputtered.

Horatio's family had owned and operated the one and only local funeral home since Rowan Springs was a wide spot on the road. He was semiretired now, and only went into the "shop" when someone of importance or wealth passed on and the family needed a bereavement counselor.

"Yes, he continued, "poor old soul. Lived alone with seven hound dogs and a mattress stuffed with hundred dollar bills. He had a lovely funeral. Nothing but the best."

"I bet!"

"Now, now, my pet, mustn't be judgmental. His friends enjoyed it immensely. Catered, you know. He left a will, and I followed his every instruction to the letter. As I was saying, the old coots who attended were all discussing young Dr. Ethan McHenry. They say he is some sort spy for the government. Some claim he was sent here to see if that new African virus has infected the local livestock. Another old gentleman swears he saw the good doctor beam up to a flying saucer the other night out in the middle of Judge Hershey's pasture."

"Wow! Maybe I should visit the spit and whittle for some inspiration for my book. Those old guys have some imagination."

"Perhaps you could just imbibe of the same locally made spirits. You would have similar results, I imagine."

"Speaking of spirits, would you be a dear and fix me another drink while I dash in for a quick shower?" I made a face. "Promised Cassie I would dress for dinner."

He winked back. "Be happy to, my dear. And if that's Dr. McHenry's strange little car pulling up in the drive, tell him to join me. I'll fix one for him as well."

Ethan McHenry was a good bit taller than Cassie, which made him very tall indeed. He was thin, almost gaunt, and bespectacled. His features were regular, with a nice straight nose and a firm square chin, but by no means could he be called attractive.

He would make a funny looking old man. One could imagine him bent over a cane with a long white beard growing almost to the ground. I had seen a drawing like that in a childhood storybook once. I thought of it each time we met.

The best thing about Dr. McHenry was that he considered himself to be the luckiest man in the world because Cassie had agreed to date him. He treated her like a queen. Moms like that. Cassie obviously liked it, too.

As I approached, I could see that Ethan was struggling to get something out of the back of his tiny little car. The vehicle was some sort of old Volkswagen convertible. He called it a Karmann Ghia. I wondered what on earth possessed a man so big and awkward to buy such a small car—and in orange, too, for heaven's sake.

"Afternoon, Mrs. DeLeon. Please pardon my back. Ummmff, ouch. Excuse me, my elbow's caught."

He pulled himself free and whirled around holding a large gallon bucket full of fat, ripe, blackberries. He smiled down at me.

"Found these this morning when I was poking around, ah, out in the woods. Gorgeous, right? Thought Mrs. Sterling could make something terrific with them."

I was mesmerized by his smile. Now I knew what Cass saw in him. His whole face joined in his happiness. His blue eyes sparkled. His firm lips turned up to expose straight white teeth. He made you happy that he was happy. I found myself grinning back at him like an idiot.

"Thank you, Ethan. How thoughtful. I know she'll love them. That must be where you got all those scratches—in a blackberry patch."

The smile vanished. I felt as though I had turned off a warm and comforting light. He sat the bucket down and quickly rolled down the sleeves of his blue chambray shirt. Either his arms were too long or his sleeves too short, because they failed to hide some really deep, angry-looking marks on his wrists and forearms.

"Oh, forget about it," he said. "I'm fine," His face had stained a shade redder than his sunburned nose.

His obvious discomfort aroused my curiosity. I started to make a further comment, but he seemed so uneasy I decided to let it go.

"Well, I'm going to wash up. I'm running late. Cassie's in the kitchen. I'll take the berries. She's working on something she probably won't want you to see yet. Or ever," I added under my breath. I called back over my shoulder as I headed for the house. "Horatio has a drink ready for you on the patio."

Ethan peered over his glasses and went loping off in that direction.

CHAPTER TWO

We had dinner on the back porch. According to my mother, it was simple fare: creamed chicken and wild mushrooms in phyllo cups with warm goat cheese tarts and grilled vegetables. I didn't quite keep my promise to dress for dinner but I did spruce up a clean pair of jeans with a silk shirt in a lovely warm apricot.

I needn't have worried about my outfit—Mother had dressed up enough for both of us. She wore an Oscar de la Renta gypsy skirt and peasant blouse that would have made me look like a bag lady. She looked like a million dollars.

Cassandra wore a simple pale aqua shift that came to the top of her pretty knees and showed off her long, tanned legs to perfection. My daughter, her rich pile of dark hair piled carelessly on top of her head and tied with a green velvet ribbon, was full of smiles and laughter. I found it hard to take my eyes off her face, and so did Ethan. Cassie was so beautiful it was a pleasure just to look at her.

We watched the late September sun go down while we ate what was left of Ethan's birthday cake. Cassandra had been humiliated when the top fell onto the floor as she was bringing it out to the porch. Aggie had immediately jumped into the middle of the sugary, gooey mess and started gobbling. Mother was horrified, and I, of course, started laughing. Ethan saved the day by scooping up Aggie and most of the mess in his big hands. He threw the cake in the garbage on the way to dumping the dog in the nearest bathtub. I mopped up the residue and made Cassie quit sniffling. Then we all sat back down and started over again with the bottom half of what turned out to be a very tasty cake.

Mother patted Cassie on the shoulder. "Never mind dear, you've got down the basics. Next time we'll work on aesthetics. I have a lovely dessert cookbook that tells all. Have another piece, Ethan?"

What a sweet guy! He ate three pieces. Cassie's smile got bigger with each piece. Ah, young love.

We took our coffee and Cointreau out to the patio and watched the fireflies send their little signals of yearning to each other. The moon rose slowly over the trees to illuminate the night garden I had planted that spring. I had taken special care in choosing only flowers with white blossoms. The big silver reflecting ball I had always wanted sat in the middle of the yard on a pedestal and made the whole thing magical. It looked like a fairy garden.

The scene evoked memories of the summer when Cassie was twelve and into crystals. We had taken them all around the yard and hidden them in tree trunks. They were for the fairies and gnomes, she had said. I wonder what had happened to them. I guess the bark grew up around and over, encompassing each little piece of quartz. I supposed they would make a future Sterling pause and reflect someday when he cut down the tree. It had better be a Sterling, after all the hard work we had put into this place.

I was surprised that the young people showed no signs of leaving. Mother was apparently thinking the same thing.

"You children have no plans for tonight?"

"No, Mrs. Sterling. I hope you don't mind if we stick around?"

"Why, of course not, Ethan, dear. We love your company. But how can you put up with us old fuddy duddys?"

"Come on, Gran, quit fishing for a compliment. You know you're about as far from a fuddy or a duddy as they come."

"As a matter of fact I've been looking forward to some conversation with you, young man."

"Yes, Mr. Raleigh?"

"Please, call me Horatio. It seems there are a few rumors floating around town as to the reason for your visit to our little neck of the woods. What does Rowan Springs have that would interest a man of your experience and talents?"

"Ethan, have you been holding back on me?" teased Cass.

It was too dark to see him blush, but I'm sure he did. It was something he did often. It made him look almost handsome—like a young Gary Cooper.

"Your young man here is quite well-known in certain scientific circles, Cassandra. Before he went to work for the Centers for Disease Control, he was in Kinshasa trying to find the original vector for the Ebola virus."

"What's a 'vector', Ethan?"

Horatio went on as if Cass had asked him instead of her boyfriend.

"Let me finish showing off here, my dear. I learned all of this from the Internet this afternoon when my curiosity about this young man could be contained no longer. A vector is the creature, insect or animal, which carries a viral or bacterial agent—an illness if you will—to man. An example would be the mosquito whose bite causes malaria. The vector that causes Marburg Disease, or the Ebola virus, has yet to be identified. Am I correct young man?"

"Right you are, sir. You're a fast learner."

Horatio smiled, obviously pleased with himself. "I also found out that young Dr. Ethan McHenry went into a cave in Africa where the original case of Marburg was contracted. I would say that is comparable to Daniel going into the lion's den."

"Well, it wasn't exactly like that. I *was* wearing protective gear."

"Nonsense, my boy. Daring to enter a dark and dangerous

cavern in search of an unknown entity which causes a deadly untreatable virus—why, I call that damned heroic!"

Ethan laughed, a rich full laugh, and there was that smile again. I saw "son-in-law" written all over him.

"My colleagues called it damned foolish."

"Well, I should say so! I hope you're not doing anything like that now," Cass scolded. "You're not are you?"

"Africa's a long way from Lakeland County, Cassie."

"I know, Mother, but Mabel said . . . never mind," she trailed off.

Ethan reached over and took Cassie's hand in his big one.

"What is she saying about me?"

"Only that you went to see her last week and asked all about her pregnancy. She said you were asking other women the same thing. Lots of other women."

Mabel had been my mother's part-time housekeeper for years. She had confided to me a few months ago that she and her husband were determined to have another baby before she turned forty. She said she could not imagine her home without a little one around to get underfoot and pull the dog's tail. I guess she had told Cassie the good news first.

"Do we have some sort of medical problem here in town, Ethan? Something we should know about? I mean, if you are at liberty to discuss it."

"That's the problem, Mrs. Sterling, I'm really not supposed to discuss it. But I can see that the rumors are flying."

"You don't know the half of it, son," said Horatio as he topped off his liqueur glass. "You're on par with the little green men from Mars."

"I guess I should have gone about this differently, but we usually have more information to go on. Most of the time one of the local docs calls us in. This time the call came from the state, and I came in blind."

"What are you investigating, dear?"

"The truth is I don't really know, Mrs. Sterling." Ethan shrugged his big bony shoulders. "At first I was thinking about bacteria in the water. And then I considered some sort of infection from the local wildlife getting into the domestic animal reservoir—chickens, pigs, that sort of thing. But none of the specimens I sent back to the lab have shown anything unusual. It's like Marburg all over again. A big question mark."

"But what does this unknown agent do? What does it cause?"

"Miscarriages, abortions. There hasn't been a viable baby carried to term in Rowan Springs in the last six weeks."

"You mean they are all born dead?" I was stunned.

"Either dead or dying. But since most fetuses are lost in the first trimester, I suspect we don't even know the full extent of the problem."

"Why is that?" I was beginning to feel Ethan's frustration and concern.

"Sometimes women don't realize they're pregnant, and when they abort spontaneously, they think they're just having a heavy cycle. It happens more often than you might think. It's nature's way of getting rid of abnormal cells. I suspect that's the truth with whatever phenomenon is going on here. What we see is just the tip of the iceberg."

"And what is the count on the iceberg, my boy?"

"Enough to make the State Medical Examiner call the CDC and ask for an investigation. The difficult part is that neither of the local doctors seem to want to cooperate."

I couldn't control myself. "Well, Winston Wallace is an asshole, but what is the excuse Doc Baxter gave you?"

Ethan laughed again. "Don't tell anyone, but I couldn't agree with you more about Dr. Wallace. Ed Baxter is something else again. He's a sweet old guy, but he seems depressed and exhausted. I understand his wife died last year, and he had open heart surgery shortly thereafter. Maybe he's never really fully recovered. He's begged off several appointments we've made, and I understand that he's cut back on his patient load. He's not seeing any maternity patients at all now."

"I'm sorry to hear that." Mother smiled softly. "Ed delivered Paisley and Cassandra. He's a dear man. I haven't seen him since last Christmas when he had dinner with us."

"Jeez, pity the poor baby that has to see Winston's mug with his first breath."

"Paisley, that's very unkind."

"Don't worry much about that, Mrs. DeLeon. The way things are going there may not be any babies to pity."

CHAPTER THREE

Before my father died, he and my mother had enjoyed what many think of as the good life. Most of their indulgences were kept within the realm of genteel good taste; however, my mother was guilty of excess in one area: bed linens. She loved the luxurious feel of soft, silky sheets. Pretty lace coverlets, warm cashmere blankets, satin duvets, and down pillows were her downfall. I could sleep on a wooden floor, but I must admit, I love being the pampered recipient of the objects of her obsession.

The sheets on the four poster bed—the one I'd had since I was ten years old—were of the finest pima cotton in a lovely soft pink. Four plump down pillows graced the head of the bed, and a beautiful old Grandmother's Flower Garden quilt in shades of rose and green was folded across the bottom. The quilt just happened to have been made by my own grandmother from hundreds of pieces no bigger than a nickel. It was all the cover I needed at this time of the year. The big old house was up on a hill, and we always enjoyed a pleasant breeze from the direction of the lakes. At night I opened all three of the tall bay windows in my room so I could hear every note of the nighttime chorus of crickets and frogs.

I had fallen asleep listening to this symphony of nature shortly after ten. I was still snoozing soundly in my soft cocoon of luxurious pink comfort when Cassie banged loudly on my bedroom door at one o'clock in the morning. She flung it open without waiting for me to invite her inside.

"Mom! Wake up!"

She disappeared into the adjoining bath where I heard her blowing her nose. I struggled to disengage from the arms of Morpheus and make some sense out of the situation.

"Humpf, whatf, wah time is it?"

She came out of the bathroom swabbing her face with a handful of tissues. Her eyes and nose were red, making it obvious she had been crying.

"What in the world is wrong, Cassie? Is Gran all right?"

"Gran? Oh, I guess so."

She sat down hard on the side of my bed and bounced me into a further state of wakefulness.

"Mom, we are in terrible, terrible trouble. Ethan has been arrested."

She started crying again.

It was on the tip of my tongue to say that it was "he" who was in trouble not "we," but that would have been an insensitive and provocative remark. Besides, I couldn't imagine that Cassie was right. What in the world could our mild-mannered Ethan have done to get himself incarcerated?

Most of the arrests reported in the weekly paper were for driving under the influence. Rowan Springs was in a so-called dry county, but the local moonshine trade was a thriving business. I'd bought the white wine and Cointreau we served with dinner at a specialty shop in Nashville over a year ago. Ethan, I remembered distinctly, hardly touched either. Speeding was my next guess, but in that funny little car? Forty-five miles an hour would be too much to expect out of that ancient VW engine.

Whatever it was, I was sure his offense could not be very serious. Reassured by my own thoughts, I pushed myself up to a sitting position and plumped two pillows behind me.

Cassie was still crying. Her shoulders were shaking with deep heartfelt sobs. Feeling certain that this was just another episode of the perils of motherhood in the post-teen years, I patted her arm and suppressed a yawn.

"There, there, Cassie, dear," I sighed. "I'm sure we can straighten this out in the morning. I'll go talk to Chief Joiner and . . . "

She raised her head slowly. Her tear-filled eyes flashed sparks of indignation and outrage.

"Mom, this isn't just another teenage melodrama!"

She always had been able to read my mind. I closed my eyes. This was going to be one of those nights. The pillow was so soft and the sheets so inviting. Maybe if I kept my eyes closed she would go away.

"Ethan is in jail for rape and murder, and I don't know what to do!" she wailed.

I raised my head so fast I hit the lampshade. I had to make a lightning grab to keep lamp, bulb, and shade from falling to the floor.

"Oh, my God! Why didn't you tell me? Oh, crap! Does Mother know?"

Cassie looked at me with exasperation.

"Well, first of all, I have been trying to tell you for the last ten minutes. Secondly, all Gran knows is that we had a late-night phone call. I guess she wasn't too worried. She went back to sleep."

"Nonsense! Call her in here and tell her what's going on. She might work herself into a stroke imagining things. I'll throw on some jeans."

Five minutes later we were all sitting in the library drinking the hot coffee that Mother had brewed after the phone call. She didn't know the reason for the phone call, but she knew it might require caffeine, bless her heart.

"Let me call Andy Joiner now. I can find out in two minutes flat exactly what is going on and put an end to this dreadful speculation."

"Mother, it's one o'clock in the morning. I'm sure every soul in Rowan Springs, including Ethan, is asleep. Let's not make matters worse by waking Joiner and his whole family up. A peeved Chief of Police is not what we need right now."

Cassie jumped up and began to pace back and forth in front of the open French doors. A breeze which smelled suspiciously of rain began to blow softly into the room.

"Mom's right, Gran. But I do want you to call first thing in the morning. Seven sounds reasonable, don't you think so, Mom?"

Her face was white and strained under her long, dark hair, and her big brown eyes betrayed her fear. I was beginning to get worried about her.

"Cassie, come and sit down, honey. If you get all worked up and emotionally exhausted you will not be able to help Ethan one little bit. We need to keep calm and think clearly."

"You're right, Mom. I guess I'm overreacting. After all, it's probably some stupid mistake."

She plopped down on the sofa next to me. "He just sounded so tired and worried. That's what upset me."

"Dear, tell us exactly what happened," urged Mother softly.

"Ethan always calls to tell me good night and, well, other things," she blushed lightly under her summer tan. "Tonight he was late. I was a little worried, but not much. The phone rang about eleven-thirty, right, Gran?"

"Eleven thirty-three."

"Anyway," she continued, "it was Ethan calling from the police station. He said I was his 'one phone call.' I was pretty upset, but I didn't let him know."

"Excellent, my dear," approved Mother.

"Wonder why he didn't call the CDC, or somebody in Atlanta?"

"He doesn't want anyone in Atlanta to know, Mom. He made me promise not to tell. He gave me his computer password. I'm supposed to go to his apartment tomorrow and send an e-mail to his office so no one will suspect there is a problem."

"How very peculiar. I would have thought he would have been screaming for help from Uncle Sam. They probably have all sorts of legal eagles who help back up their people in the field. I'm sure Ethan isn't the first doctor from the CDC to ever get into trouble."

Cassie was busy playing with the hem of her gown. Finally she looked up at me, her eyes shining with unshed tears.

"That's just it, Mom. He's apparently been in trouble before." A tear escaped the corner of her right eye and slid down the smooth curve of her cheek.

"He's rather, well, he called it unconventional, in his approach to his work sometimes. He, uh, he has a police record."

"What kind of record?" I asked pointedly.

"Breaking and entering, receiving stolen property, that sort of thing."

"That sort of thing? My goodness, Cassie, we've been harboring a veritable Pepe La Moko!"

She looked at me tiredly, "Pepe La who?"

"Never mind. I can't believe that nice guy with the big warm smile is a hardened criminal!"

Cassie jumped up and stomped her bare foot with all the expertise of an angry toddler.

"He's not a criminal! Those were charges filed against him by a rogue drug company he was investigating two years ago."

"Oh, dear, drugs."

Cassie whirled around to face her grandmother.

"Don't you start, Gran! Oh, I should have known better than to count on you two for help. You never liked anyone I ever dated. But Ethan's different. I love him. I'll marry him even if he goes to prison. You'll see!"

She fled from the room leaving us staring at the empty space she had vacated.

"Paisley, what does one wear to a jailhouse wedding?"

"Stripes are definitely out," I answered sourly.

CHAPTER FOUR

None of us got much sack time that night. Cassie locked herself in her room and cried inconsolably. Mother and I agreed that we couldn't go back to sleep, so we took turns making coffee and dealing hands of honeymoon bridge. We weren't exactly taking things lightly, we just didn't know what else to do.

The sun pinkened the horizon at around five o'clock. I added two bowls of oatmeal and some buttered toast to the coffee tray when it was my turn for kitchen duty.

"Have you been stacking the deck, Mother?"

"Paisley! How could you even suggest such a thing? One miscreant in the family is enough, don't you think? I'm simply having a streak of good luck, that's all."

"Six hearts?"

"Fortune's smile."

The warm cereal made me sleepy despite the caffeine in the gallons of coffee I had consumed. Somewhere in the middle of another of Mother's outrageous bids I fell asleep.

"Mom! Gran! It's seven o'clock. Time to call Chief Joiner!"

Cassie had to shake me awake this time. I was practically comatose.

"Stop shaking your mother, Cassandra. Her eyes look like

they're getting a little loose. I'll call Andy Joiner."

I fell limply back on the sofa cushions. Paralysis had set in from my hairline down; I could hear what was going on, but I couldn't move. I never have been able to function very well without a good night's rest.

Mother went to the kitchen to make the call. That big sunny room was her personal domain, and she always felt as though she had more control over any situation from that vantage point. Cassie followed behind her like a lost puppy.

Speaking of which, Aggie had been abandoned by her mistress of late and had adopted me as her significant other. The puppy had spent the night curled up at my feet. She was licking my stockinged toes in an effort to arouse me enough to let her out for her morning walk.

There is nothing quite as uncomfortable as warm doggie spit going cold on your feet. After about ten minutes of her efforts, I pushed myself off the sofa with a mighty effort and staggered up to open the French doors.

The morning breeze refreshed me somewhat as it whisked away the mental cobwebs. I slipped loafers on over my wet socks and went out in the yard with the dog.

A late-night rain had soaked the ground, and the sidewalk was awash with earthworms in various states of decomposition. The few birds that had not yet gone south for the winter were out, chomping away with a vengeance on this unexpected slimy buffet.

Aggie hated getting her feet wet, which is probably the reason she knew to lick mine. She hurried through her morning ablutions and raced back to my side looking vastly relieved and more than ready to return to the warm, dry comfort of the house.

Mother and Cassie were filing back into the library. They both looked like they had lost their last friend.

"Looks like de news ain't so hot."

"Mom, please don't make fun. You always try to make light of the most serious things. Please don't this time."

I went over and gave her a hug. She tried to resist, but I persisted, and soon she was sobbing against my shoulder.

"That bad, huh?"

"It looks quite dreadful, dear. I couldn't get many details out of Andy, but from the little he said, Ethan seems to be in a lot of trouble. I left a message on Bruce Hawkins' answering machine. The good doctor will be needing a good lawyer."

"I still think we should call his office at the CDC. Surely there's something they can do."

Cassie rose up quickly and wiped her face on her sleeve.

"No!" she entreated, "I promised Ethan. No calls to Atlanta. I can't do anything but send the message he asked me to until I talk to him again."

She looked at me through a wash of tears.

"Mom, will you help me log on to his computer and send the e-mail? I know how, but I don't want to make any mistakes, and I'm still a little upset."

"Of course, Cassie. I'll go with you." I yawned hugely, "I'm in tip-top shape myself."

"Take a shower, Paisley. You'll feel better. I'll have some nice hot tea ready when you get dressed," offered Mother. "And you all had better go before Chief Joiner decides to visit Ethan's room and confiscate his belongings as evidence."

"Wow! I hadn't thought of that. You're right, Gran. Hurry up, Mom"

The shower helped and so did the Earl Grey with four teaspoons of sugar. If we were lucky, we'd be back home before I crashed from my sugar high.

I let Cassie drive Watson, my mean green Jeep Wagon. I'd bought it the year before, when we'd first gotten involved in what Mother called "capers." It had all the necessary equipment for what I had imagined I would be needing for sleuthing. So far, all we had used was the oversized cooler under the jump seat in the back.

Dr. Ethan McHenry had been in Rowan Springs for about six weeks. He and Cassie had met in the beginning of August at our annual "Bright Leaf Festival." Our town is in the middle of the most fertile tobacco growing country in the southern United States. We've celebrated our prosperity and good fortune every year since 1935 with a street festival, square dance, beauty pageant, and arts and crafts show.

This year an antismoking wag wrote a letter to the editor of the local paper suggesting that we add a phlegm spitting contest and a chest x-ray exhibition to the festivities. Even though I was amused, I had to agree. I'd given up cigarettes the minute I knew I was pregnant with Cassie. Nevertheless, we all dutifully attended each event and unashamedly enjoyed the ice-cold sparkling apple cider, tender delicious funnel cakes, and gloriously fat-filled, indigestible deep-fried corn dogs.

Cassie had met Ethan at the quilt exhibition. They struck up a conversation in front of a particularly beautiful, intricately quilted Log Cabin design. Ethan asked her to accompany him to the square dance at the high school, and she had invited him out to lunch the next day to meet her family. We had all liked him immediately—even Aggie. They had been seeing each other for at least some portion of every day since that first night.

I never dared to ask Cassie how intimate their relationship was because it was none of my business. I yearned to know, but I had always tried to respect her boundaries. She had never been so serious about a young man before. Cassie wasn't exactly fickle, but she did have very high standards and was usually bored with her gentlemen callers in a matter of days. She would probably have tired of Ethan had he not come to need her so desperately.

When he'd arrived in Rowan Springs, Ethan rented a garage apartment behind the home of two of my late grandmother's friends, the Parsons sisters. Miss Lolly and Miss Hannah were in their seventies. Their father had made a fortune in the 1920s selling lumber, and the sisters still lived in the big home Papa Parsons had built for the family in his heyday. Neither of them had ever married, although there were rumors that one of them had nurtured a secret obsession for a married man for decades.

The Parsons' house was covered with gingerbread millwork. Curlicues and arabesques dripped from every eave and soffit. The difficulty in later years was finding someone willing to paint all the doodads and what-nots. Gradually, the house deteriorated, and the sisters grew into suspicious old ladies who peered from behind frayed lace curtains as the rest of the world passed by.

I was really surprised that Ethan had been able to persuade them to rent him the apartment. They seldom went out anymore and rarely opened their doors to strangers. I finally decided that Doc Baxter had arranged it. He was one of the few people they saw. Doc still made house calls for some of his older patients, and he was especially fond of the old ladies. Their mother had been a good friend of his mother's. Ties of family and friends were strong in our little town, and people had long memories. That alone was reason to behave yourself and not do something "unforgettable."

Ethan's apartment was above the garage and consisted of two rooms originally intended as servant's quarters. The stairway to the entrance was discretely turned away from the main house so that neither master nor maid could observe the after-hours activities of the other. For this I was very grateful because I did not wish to be seen or questioned by anyone. Cassie apparently hadn't thought beyond the immediate necessity of meeting Ethan's request. I wanted to keep us from being implicated as accessories after the fact.

Cassie reached up under the eaves on the landing and retrieved the door key. The room inside was sparsely furnished. A wooden table had been placed in front of a large window in the corner. That was the sunniest spot in the whole place. The rest of the living room and the smaller adjoining bedroom, really only an alcove, was shrouded in shadows and gloom.

Cassie pulled me over towards the table by the window where some expensive computer equipment was neatly arranged. Most of the stuff was state of the art and very sleek and compact. The computer itself was a laptop like mine, but newer and with more memory. The printer was a dilly—small and portable, it looked more like a ladies black plastic purse. There was also a scanner and something very unusual on the floor next to the table—a paper shredder. I wondered if the sisters Parsons had rewired the place for all of Ethan's electronic goodies.

Cassie turned on the computer, and I sat down in a rickety old wooden chair next to her to observe as she tentatively pushed buttons.

"I think I've done it right. I wish I weren't so nervous."

She wiped her palms on her jeans and typed in Ethan's password. I didn't ask and she didn't tell me what it was. The screen flashed with a network logo, and then the letters "CDC" and a menu. Cassie read each selection carefully before she made her decision.

"Here we go."

She moved the mouse and pointed at one of the titles on the screen. "Infectious Diseases Branch of the NCEH."

Another menu popped up and she breathed a sigh of relief. "I'm in, Mom. Now I'll just type in his e-mail password and his user ID, and then I can send the message to his supervisor. Damn!"

"What, what?"

"I made a mistake . . . wait, there I backspaced . . . okay!"

Dr. Ethan David McHenry's mailbox opened up like a neon rose. There were at least thirty entries, but Cassie ignored everything except the messages from a Dr. Eloise Haywood.

I was surprised that his boss was a woman. I had assumed that like most government agencies, the CDC was an old boy's club. I can be sexist, too.

Cassie moused over to the most recent message from Dr. Haywood and clicked. A brief message flashed on the screen.

"Ethan, here's the info you requested. State's getting antsy. Try to have something concrete for us ASAP, but CYA. E."

"Now Mom, here's the part I'm not sure about. He said just 'reply.'

Where is . . . ?"

I squinted at the top of the screen and saw it as soon as she did.

"Aha!"

Another mousey click and the screen changed again. She got busy on the keyboard and typed in Ethan's message.

"Doing fine. Wish you were here. Hot on the trail. Let you know soonest. AC. E."

"That's it? That's the big message? That had to be sent this morning?"

"Please, Mom, don't freak on me. I have to exit the right way, or I'll mess up."

I stood up and stretched my weary limbs. I was worn out and fed up. "Freak? Freaking message, that's what," I huffed under my breath.

I glanced out of the window and saw one of the Misses Parsons peeking in Watson's windows. Just at that moment, she turned and caught me staring back at her. I gave her a goofy grin and waved back, then, impetuously, I grabbed all of the floppy discs I saw on the table and stuffed them into my big leather handbag.

"Quick, Cassie, unhook the modem and the laptop and put them in my bag. We've got company."

CHAPTER FIVE

I descended the narrow staircase with as much dignity as I could muster. The old woman was standing next to Watson, her tiny little foot tapping out staccato displeasure on the brick driveway.

"Miss Hannah?"

"Heavens, no! It's Lolly you're talking to. I'm Lolly Parsons. Who are you?"

I made a silent invocation to my grandmother's spirit and asked for help with this nosey old bag. The last thing in the world we needed was for her to call the police.

"I'm Paisley Sterling . . . John and Anna's first child."

"Paisley Sterling. I remember you. You used to tease my cat. I never did like you."

I tried to smile but my lips were dry and they stuck to my teeth. "Oh, I am sorry about that. Children can be a nuisance sometimes. I'm sure I was a holy terror. How is your cat now?"

"Dead."

"Oh."

Cassie came bouncing down the wooden stairs with my leather handbag slung over her shoulder. She looked like she didn't have a care in the world.

"Hi, Miss Lolly. My, don't you look pretty today. Have you been to that beauty shop again?"

She gave the little old woman a quick peck on the cheek.

Miss Lolly beamed from ear to ear as she gave her cap of tight white curls a proud pat. I watched in amazement as she deftly avoided my gaze and smiled fondly at my daughter who was no more Southern than a turnip, but had learned from observing her grandmother how to walk the walk and talk the talk.

"Cassandra, dear, how nice to see you. Won't you come in and have some tea? Hannah has made some of that orange walnut bread you like so much."

"I do wish I had time, but Mom and I . . . have you met my mother, Paisley DeLeon?"

Miss Lolly sniffed suspiciously, "I thought she said her name was Sterling."

They went on discussing me as if I were not standing there like a display room dummy.

"Sterling's her maiden name. My grandmother is Anna Howard and my Grandad was John Sterling. You remember them?"

"Why of course I do, child. They were fine people and so was your great-grandmother Howard. She was a good friend of mine when we were schoolgirls. And your great-grandfather was a fine figure of a man."

A faint blush covered her wrinkled old cheeks. "But I'm sorry to say," she went on, "your mother was nothing like any of them. Bad seed, she was. Used to torment my poor Mr. Whiskers."

She glared in my direction. I smiled until my cheeks hurt but Cassie laughed. Pretty soon they were both laughing. Miss Lolly hid some very bad teeth behind her skinny old hand as she tittered away at my expense.

I grabbed my leather handbag from Cassie, almost dropping it because of the unexpected weight of Ethan's electronic goodies, and headed for Watson. I heard Cassie wisely covering our tracks as I climbed in the driver's seat.

"Looks like Dr. McHenry is not at home. I'll be back later, and we'll both come in for some of that wonderful bread. Tell Miss Hannah not to eat it all."

She gave the old bag a gentle hug and hopped in beside me. I stomped childishly on the gas and the tires squealed as we took off.

"Whew! Looks like we got away with it. Head for home, Mom!"

"Humpf."

She started laughing again. "Mr. Whiskers! What did you do to her cat? It must have been something really awful for her to hold a grudge this long."

I chuckled then. It was good to see Cassie laugh, even if it was at my expense.

"I spray painted him from head to tail."

"Oh, my God, Mom. That *is* awful. The poor thing!"

"I know." Now I couldn't stop laughing.

"I probably shouldn't ask, but what color?"

"White. It was a black cat, and when it crossed in front of me one day I was sure I would have bad luck unless I did something. So I got some white spray paint and made a stripe down its back like a skunk. It seemed like a great idea at the time."

"How old were you?"

"Eight or nine."

"You definitely were the bad seed."

"I know, I know."

When we got home, we took the contraband from Ethan's apartment into the library and set it out on my father's big desk. I had to move my own laptop and the notes for Leonard's new book over to the library table to make room for all of Ethan's equipment.

"My goodness, Cassie, you brought the whole kit and caboodle!"

"Why not? I knew there would be no second chance."

Cassie carefully plugged everything into the corresponding receptacles and I spread the floppy discs out.

"Nothing is labeled. He just has them numbered," complained Cassie.

"Look closer. The numbers aren't sequential, and they have too many digits. I bet it's some kind of code. I bet he has the discs encrypted, too. Probably takes yet another password to read them."

"Why would he go to that much trouble?"

"Probably no trouble at all to him—just standard operating procedure."

"What makes you say that?"

"Think about it. Why would he leave all this out in the open where anybody could come across it if it were so easy to read?"

"Mom, you seem to forget that all this was locked up in his apartment. Aren't you being just a little melodramatic? After all, he's not Superspy."

"Okay, turn it on and see for yourself."

Cassie sat down and went through the motions again. This time I watched closely to see if I could catch Ethan's login password, but her fingers were too quick on the keyboard. She slipped one of the discs into the "A" drive and went to "File Manager." A big red box appeared across the screen with a message in black letters "Enter Password." Cassie typed in the password she had used to login. Another message flashed across the screen.

"You are locked out. Please contact your supervisor."

"Wow! Looks like you weren't kidding. How did you know, Mom?"

"Leonard told me."

"Hah!"

"Seriously. Our new book is all about industrial espionage. I had to read up. I learned a lot."

"I bet Leonard knows even more."

"Humpf."

We trudged into the kitchen where Mother was busy layering a lovely looking salad in a big glass bowl. Cassie sneaked a white mushroom cap and a hunk of Parmesan and went to the refrigerator for a drink.

"Perrier, Mom?"

"Sure."

"Gran?"

"No thanks, dear; but I'll take a glass of iced tea, if you don't mind."

I was amazed at Cassie's composure. Our little foray this morning seemed to have gotten rid of her anxiety, or a least gotten it under control. During lunch she regaled Mother with the story of Miss Lolly and my misadventures with her striped cat.

"Paisley! What a naughty child you were. It's funny, but I don't remember anything about that particular incident."

"That's because Granpa Howard hushed it up for me."

"You're kidding?"

"I think the old lady had a crush on him. Anyway, he made me fork over all my allowance. He pitched in the rest and together we bought her a dozen yellow roses. He said she would have misunderstood red ones."

"I should think so!" agreed Mother.

"Am I missing something here, or is this some old-fashioned thing?"

"You would do well to learn more about the language of flowers and love, my dear. Young people nowadays have no sense whatsoever of romance. It's all slam, bam, thank you, m'am!"

"Good grief, Mother. Not in front of the children."

Cassie went to her room after lunch to pick out a "visiting your boyfriend in jail where he is being held for a capitol offense" outfit.

I helped Mother with the dishes. When we were done, we both decided a nap was the only way we would live to see another day.

She went to her room and I headed back to the sofa in the library. Poor lonely little Aggie dusted my heels with her long white beard as she tagged along behind me.

We had just curled up on the big, red chintz-covered sofa when Cassie entered. She was dressed in a soft, full-skirted yellow dress with a tiny pink flower print. Her long hair was tied back with a matching pink ribbon. She looked sweet and innocent and lovely—not at all like a gangster's moll.

"Do you want me to go with you, sweetie?"

"No, Mom. I think I need to see Ethan alone."

"Oh, thank God. I'm exhausted."

"Sweet of you to offer, though. Maybe you can come with me tomorrow."

"Cassie, maybe he'll be out tomorrow. This whole thing is probably one whopper of a mistake. Come home with some good news, okay?"

"Sure thing, Mom. May I take Watson, for luck?"

"Of course. And please pay some attention to this canine ragmop when you get home. She's driving me crazy."

Aggie hopped up and traversed my prone body like a mountain goat. She lay down at my feet and started licking my toes, one at a time.

CHAPTER SIX

I thought I would fall asleep immediately, but my mind kept nagging my body awake. Through heavy-lidded eyes, I stared at the bright red, yellow, and orange leaves as they danced and swirled in the wind outside the French doors. Fall was definitely here. I could already see the squirrels' nests exposed to predators in the forks of the big old oak on the field side of the back fence.

Mother had a fierce ongoing battle with each and every squirrel on the farm. She called them fancy rats with delusions of grandeur. She vowed that they were responsible for everything from house fires to the high unemployment rate.

Last year she placed a wicked, evil-looking squirrel trap in the back yard. When a poor furry soul wandered inside Mother called one of the army of high school students who worked for her to come and carry the cage far away and bring it back empty. I secretly believed that the crafty kid would let the squirrel out before he left the driveway—insuring himself a future phone call and another five bucks.

Mother forgot to disarm the trap last May when we went to visit Cassie at Emory University. When we returned home we found a poor little dead squirrel huddled up on the bottom of the cage. It had obviously starved to death.

The trap disappeared the next day. I haven't seen it since. From the look of the size of the nests, we would be hearing lots of fancy deluded rats playing in the attic this winter. Mother was right about one thing, though. Squirrels carried diseases like all rodents. What was that word Horatio had told us about—vector?

Squirrels were vectors and so were prairie dogs. Why was that so important? I fell asleep in a mild state of curiosity. I dreamed I was running and running on a wire wheel in a big cage and getting nowhere.

I awoke fours hours later in a dark, chilly room with no furry little companion to keep my feet either wet or warm. I lay there puzzling for a moment, trying to get my bearings. Then I heard Aggie's welcome home bark. Cassie was back.

I stood and stretched, surprised to feel remarkably rested. And I was famished.

I headed toward the kitchen to let Cassie in and feed my face.

The back of the house was warm and bright with good smells coming from every corner of the kitchen. My mother's answer to everything is "when in doubt, cook!" I opened the oven a tad to peek and got smacked on the behind with a wooden spoon.

"Paisley Sterling, you'll fall my cake!"

I rubbed my smarting nether parts and opened the back door for Cassie. I knew better than to try and correct my mother's grammar.

Cassie slumped into the kitchen with a long and mournful mien and a worse disposition.

"Get out of the way you stupid dog!" Immediately contrite, she bent and lifted the fat, squirming puppy into her lap.

I sat down at the table across from Cassie and waited for her to open up.

"He's such an idiot!"

I knew better than to reply to that.

"He doesn't even try to defend himself. He just keeps saying, 'I didn't do it' over and over, but he won't explain anything. I just don't understand, Mom. He needs help, but he refuses to let me call Dr. Haywood, or anybody in Atlanta. What are we going to do?"

She turned her lovely tear-stained face to me. She must have cried all the way home.

"What about Bruce Hawkins? Mother, has he returned your call yet?"

Mother carried the unfrosted cake and a big bowl of icing over to the table and sat down.

"I talked to him about an hour ago. That's why I'm baking."

Cassie and I exclaimed in unison, "Uh-oh."

"Yes, I'm afraid the news is not so good. Bruce is representing the family of the victim, or victims, I should say. He cannot even recommend anyone else because it might be considered a conflict of interest. He said he was sorry because he'd met Ethan when he first came to town and liked him a lot."

Cassie's face got even longer and more morose looking. She was absently stroking Aggie's soft furry ears. I was a nervous wreck waiting for the first nip of those nasty little teeth. She never let any of us, including Cassie, pet her.

"Cassie, tell us exactly what the situation is—not what Ethan says, but what Joiner told you."

"That's just it," she cried. "I couldn't talk to Chief Joiner. They made me go in through the back of the jail. I never got to the front office, so I didn't get to see anyone else. The deputy said it was for my own safety. Something about the town being 'riled up'—whatever that means."

"So, we still don't know exactly what happened."

Mother cleared her throat and licked the icing-covered spatula. I was astounded. That was a first. She must really be upset.

"I spoke to Mavis," she said quietly.

"Ah, ha! Now we're getting somewhere."

Mavis was an erstwhile friend of Mother's. She had a police scanner and the biggest personal address book in town. Mavis knew everybody's business before they did. I should have suggested that Mother call her in the first place.

"Mavis heard the call over the police scanner when the young woman telephoned for help. I think her name is Hayes, Brittany or Brandy, one of those 1980s names. Anyway, she called 911 and said her father had been shot. Mavis heard the dispatcher order a police car to the Hayes' farm and then call Doc Baxter. When the police got there, the girl's father was lying out on the side of the road by his mailbox with a bullet through his head. The girl was found lying unconscious on the front porch."

I glanced at Cassie and watched her face grow paler as her back stiffed.

"When the doctor got there he revived young whats-her-name and put her in the ambulance. On the way to the hospital she accused Ethan of raping her. When they told her that her father was dead, she said Ethan must have done that, too."

"Impossible!" cried Cassie.

"Go on , Mother," I encouraged grimly.

"Chief Joiner himself went over to the Parsons' house and quietly arrested Ethan. He was in his apartment working on some papers. He claimed that he knew nothing about Mr. Hayes being killed, or the daughter's rape, but he couldn't explain some really bad scratches on his hand and arms."

"No, no," moaned Cassie.

"Mavis said they photographed his wounds and booked him. The judge has refused to set bond since it's a murder case."

Cassie jumped up, dumping the sleeping puppy in a furious snarling heap on the kitchen floor.

"Ethan is innocent! He could never do anything like that!"

"Listen to me, Cassandra! Your friend is in big trouble, but you can help him if you don't wallow in your own feelings. His little genius medical brain seems to have shut down for the moment, and we're going to have to do the thinking for him. So cool it and calm down."

She stared down at me for a moment, then sat down hard on the kitchen chair. Aggie jumped back up on her lap immediately.

"You're right. You're absolutely right." She tucked in her chin and grew three inches taller. I was proud of her. "Where do we start?"

Mother knew.

"Cake, anyone?"

CHAPTER SEVEN

After bracing ourselves with several cups of Queen Anne tea and a slice or two of Lady Baltimore cake, we took our full tummies back to the library—the gracious room that had provided the comfortable headquarters for our previous sleuthing. I loved the big brick fireplace, the soft jewel tones of the oriental rug, and the twin comfort of overstuffed sofas. The many photographs of family and friends lining the walls never failed to remind me of where I belonged in the grand scheme of things.

Fortified by the aforementioned ladies Baltimore and Queen Anne, we sat around Dad's desk with yellow legal pads in hand and waited for some monumental inspiration.

"This is ridiculous," protested Mother. "I don't even know what I'm supposed to be considering. Paisley, give us a starting point, dear. And don't ask for any more cake."

"Whatever do you mean?" I asked with feigned innocence.

"You have that look in your eye."

"Please, you two. Let's get serious," begged Cassie.

"Okay, okay. But Gran's right. We don't know diddley. For instance, when and where did Brandy, or Brittany meet Ethan? Was he really at the Hayes's place that night? And if not, how did he get those scratches? And, I think, most important of all, what is Ethan doing in Rowan Springs in the first place?"

"He told us the other night, Mom. He's trying to find out why so many unborn babies are dying,"

"Yeah, but is he really investigating the environment or the medical establishment?"

"Oh, I hadn't thought of that."

"Well, I think that's where we need to focus."

"I could call Ed Baxter."

"I don't think so, Mother, not just yet, anyway. I think we have a good starting place right here in this room."

"You mean Ethan's laptop?"

"Yes, Cassie, that's exactly what I do mean. If he won't talk to us, maybe his computer will."

"But that's so indiscreet, Paisley. It's like snooping in someone's closet. Dreadful manners."

Mother looked so prim and proper I almost laughed. "But isn't that just what we are? Snoops?"

"Gran, you can't argue with that. You're the one who loves this detective stuff." Cassie tapped her fingernail on the top of the closed computer case. "You are forgetting one thing though, Mom. We couldn't read that disc. How are we going to let the computer do the talking if we can't gain access?"

"I've been thinking about that. Remember the other night when Horatio was here? He was telling us about Ethan's work in Africa and his search for the host of the Ebola virus."

"Yes."

"Remember the word he used?"

"I do. Dear Horatio was quite informative. The word was 'vector.'"

"Well, Mother, I think that our young doctor is very intelligent, but not so creative. He probably uses words that are very common and familiar to him like 'vector' for encrypting all of his medical research. I imagine he is annoyed that he has to do it at all. Most doctors I know feel a little superior to the general public. And, excuse me for saying so Cassie, but Ethan is probably no different from the rest of the genus 'white-coatis superiorus.'"

"Most people, myself included, wouldn't understand any medical terminology at all. Why would he take it one step further and bother encrypting his work in the first place, dear?"

"As I explained to Cassie earlier, the government probably has rules for everyone across the board, from the Department of Defense to the CIA. I'm sure there are generic mandates to protect information."

"Okay, Mom, if you're so much smarter than Ethan, let's see you try."

"Not me—Leonard. If I'm going to waste the remaining little grey cells in my cerebrum on this, then Leonard and I get a story out of it. Deal?"

"Deal."

"Now, what's Ethan's password?"

"He changed it to 'Cassie' when we met."

"I rest my case."

I plugged away on Dr. McHenry's computer for three hours. Cassie fell asleep on the sofa, and Mother kept the teapot full of Queen Anne. I tried everything I could think of from "vector," to "Ebola," to "Kinshasa," to "Tarzan," with no luck.

And it took forever. Every time I tried a new word and got kicked out I had to log on again. To say it was frustrating was definitely an understatement.

"I could have sworn it would be 'vector.'"

"You had me convinced, dear. It was a good thought. Very creative and . . . "

"Stop it, Mother. You're just saying that to bug me. Bug! Bug! Maybe that's it."

And so it was.

When I got in, I yelled, "whoopee" loud enough to awaken Cassie. She inadvertently kicked Aggie, who nipped her hard on the foot.

"Ouch! Damn dog! Ouch! Did you really do it, Mom, uh, Leonard?"

"Look for yourself."

They both came to peer over my shoulder at the columns of medical data whizzing across the little screen of the laptop.

"Shouldn't we stop it, or print something, or something?" asked Cassie.

"Beat's the hell out'a me."

"Language, Paisley, dear."

"Sorry, Mother. But I don't know what all this means."

"Maybe I could ask 'white-coatis superiorus.'"

"Very funny, Cassie. No, I don't think we should let the good doctor know we have breached his security until we manage to save his butt."

"Paisley!"

"Oh, Mother, for heaven's sake."

"Exactly."

It was getting late in a long hard day. My afternoon nap had given me a false sense of energy. After the initial euphoria of finding my way into Ethan's computer wore off, so did my vim and vigor. I slumped over the desk and watched the bytes of information I did not understand speed past. My eyes watered with the strain of my efforts and the screen blurred in front of me.

"Sleep, I need sleep."

"I think we all do, dear."

"But, Mom, poor Ethan."

"Sorry, Cassie, I can't think anymore. I've shot my wad."

"Common and vulgar pronouncements not withstanding, Cassandra, think of your poor Mother for a change. You've had her up and going since one o'clock this morning. That's almost twenty-four hours. Let her go to bed, dear. She'll function much better in the morning."

They made me sound like a machine.

But Mother was right, as usual. Early the next morning I was back at the desk trying to puzzle out Ethan's discs.

Cassie brought me tea and toast, which she nervously devoured while watching me flip through the screens of data.

"Understand anything, yet?"

"Don't get crumbs on the keyboard!" I responded testily, "And I'm hungry. Where's my toast?"

"Gran will probably bring you some."

"I may have to go on strike if . . . "

"Anyone for some more toast and jam?"

Mother came in with a tray of lovely looking dishes of jam and butter and two racks of warm toast. She sat down on the sofa next to Cassie and they served themselves breakfast.

"And me?"

"Oh sorry, Paisley, dear. Here, have a slice."

She extended the plate of buttered toast but Aggie got there before me. With a beautifully executed leap that would have put the Flying Wallendas to shame, she took the toast from the plate and was out of the room before we could say a word.

"Never mind. I'll wait until lunch," I grumped.

"Umm, you want this last half of mine, Mom?" asked my gluttonous child with her mouth full.

"And lunch had better be good!"

CHAPTER EIGHT

Cassie left around ten to visit Ethan. Mother had some shopping to do. I hoped she was planning to buy something good for lunch. They left me and my loving canine companion to decipher the computer discs alone. We were not doing too well. I finally divided them into three piles, "difficult," "impossible," and "you've got to be kidding."

I had never taken any courses in statistics, but I'm sure that even if I had, I would have been just as lost trying to understand the endless columns and charts.

Ethan was an epidemiologist—a medical doctor who studied disease and its prevalence, and thereby, its prevention. I was a single mother, a former writer of children's books, who collaborated with a fictitious detective named Leonard Paisley on a series of mystery novels. The twain would never have met if it had not been for my lovely daughter. And that's what kept me going. I had to help Ethan to make Cassie happy.

When I finally came across Dr. Ethan McHenry's journal, I could hardly believe my good luck. The first entry was six weeks ago, the fifth of August. He had made an appointment to meet with the two medical doctors in town, Ed Baxter and Winston Wallace. Wallace had showed up, but Baxter had canceled with the excuse of not feeling well.

Ethan had been immediately put off by Wallace's attitude of self-importance and his disinterest in the problem at hand. Wallace made the firm assertion that the high fetal death rate was just a seasonal thing and of no real importance. He arrogantly insisted that the CDC would find that their statistics were off. They were simply exaggerating the situation, and as soon as they got their noses out of his business everything would return to normal. Ethan explained that he had been called in by the state epidemiologist. If he left, someone else would just take his place.

Wallace left their meeting in a huff.

There was another entry later that day: Ethan had traveled twenty miles to the Women's Free Clinic in Morgantown. Four young women from Rowan Springs had been there for consultations. Three of them had planned to have abortions but they had miscarried before they could return for the procedure.

I stopped reading for a moment and sat back in my father's big leather swivel chair. I don't know why, but I was somewhat surprised to learn that an abortion clinic, even under the guise of a free clinic for women, existed so close to Rowan Springs. This area was deep in the so-called "Bible Belt." I had assumed that abortion was a dirty word around here.

I had never really examined my feelings on the subject because I had never had a reason to do so. I took a moment to ruminate a bit before deciding that nobody should have the right to make that decision for me. I also discovered, somewhat to my surprise, that I would never be able to terminate a pregnancy of my own.

Neither Cassie nor Mother knew that I had lost a baby shortly after my husband Raphael had disappeared somewhere in the jungle between Columbia and San Romero. Rafe himself had not even known of our coming happy event—I had been saving it as a surprise for our anniversary party. The party was canceled when the host vanished due to unknown circumstances. I lost the baby a week later. Twelve years had passed, but I still felt the aching emptiness.

Mother came in with my requested luncheon tray a little after twelve. I told her about the three clinic patients as I moved over to the sofa to sit beside her. Between mouthfuls of shrimp salad and croissant, I asked her for her opinion on abortion.

"I'm sorry to say that after sixty-two years, I still haven't formulated a firm idea. In my day it was terribly illegal, you know, and carried a dreadful stigma. It's nice to see that young girls no longer have to risk their lives out of shame. But the awful truth is that there is no more shame. People feel free to do the worst things nowadays. Still, I think it's important that a woman have the right to choose."

She carried the luncheon tray back to the kitchen, shaking her head and mumbling to herself. I reached down and absentmindedly began to pat Aggie. She growled a warning, and I stopped immediately. Scary dog. She had me really well trained.

I went back to my perusal of Ethan's journal. He recorded that he had gotten Wallace to agree to let him have a list of his pregnant patients. He had also obtained the doctor's grudging permission to interview them—if they agreed. Ethan noted that he was afraid that Wallace would bias the women against talking to him. He felt compelled to hurry and get in contact with them as soon as possible.

Wallace introduced Ethan to his medical office manager, Poppy Hunnicutt. She gave him a list of the names and addresses of the six women.

I scanned through the rest of the journal entries very quickly and saw nothing that looked like a interview. Those must be on another disc.

Ethan had made no mention of Cassie or their relationship in his journal. He did mention "socializing with the locals" on several occasions "in order to get the pulse of the community." I was a bit put off by that remark and scanned impatiently to the last few entries. I stopped quickly and backed up a page when I saw Brittany Allison Hayes's name flash by. She was listed with three other girls, the young women who had gone to the clinic in Morgantown. The other girls had aborted spontaneously, but Brittany was still pregnant. Farmer Hayes had not been protecting an innocent virginal daughter.

I heard a car pull up in the long, circular, gravel drive and looked up to see Watson's bilious green nose. I hurried over to let Cassie in the library door and stumbled over Aggie doing her little welcoming pirouette. We all very nearly went down in a heap. Cassie collapsed on the sofa laughing while the puppy joyfully licked her face.

"Wow, you're in a good mood. Something must have happened. Is Ethan out of jail?"

"No, but he's out of his funk and that's almost as good as far as I'm concerned. He had me really scared when he just sat in the corner and wouldn't talk. It was eerie. Almost like he was catatonic or something."

"So you had a nice visit, dear."

Mother had seen Cassie drive up and came to join in the welcome.

"As nice a visit as you can have with your boyfriend when he is in jail accused of murder, Gran."

"No need to be sarcastic, dear."

"I'm sorry. Yes, we had a nice visit."

She turned to me, "Ethan wants to see you, Mom."

"Me? He won't talk to a lawyer but he wants to talk to me?"

"That's right. And soon. Can you go down there now? Chief Joiner said it would be okay."

"Are you going back with me?"

She looked a little disappointed, "No, he wants to see you alone."

So, alone I went. After Andy Joiner helped me park Watson in one of the narrow little spaces behind the building that served as the Rowan Springs City Hall and Fire Department and the Lakeland County Jail, he led me thorough a back door and down a long, narrow hallway to Ethan's cell. A deputy parked himself in a chair just out of sight and sat nervously waiting for me to scream for help.

Ethan stood up when I entered and helped Andy close the door behind me, then he politely offered me a seat on the opposite bunk to his. Both beds were clean and neat, with snowy white sheets and dark blue wool blankets.

The cell walls and floor had been recently painted, and no graffiti or foul odors could be seen or sniffed. I was impressed. I would have to register to vote, so I could back Andy in the next election.

Ethan looked a little tired and wan, but he was clean-shaven and neatly dressed in jeans and a starched blue chambray shirt with "Lakeland County Jail" stenciled over the breast pocket.

Even though he had requested my presence, I knew he must be humiliated for me to see him under these circumstances. And to make matters worse, like an idiot, I started laughing. For a horrible moment I thought he was going to cry. I hurried to explain while mentally kicking myself for being so insensitive.

"I used to have a shirt just like that, only I made it myself, I mean the jail part. I used an indelible magic marker and wrote 'Oregon State Penitentiary' on the front." I directed him with a twirl of my index finger. "Turn around."

"Yep! It was just like yours, with big numbers across the back. I wore it to embarrass Mother when she insisted that I go with her to her shindigs."

He sat back down on his bunk and smiled.

"And was she? Embarrassed, I mean? Somehow I doubt it."

Ethan was feeling a little better. He gave me another little smile.

"And you would win the Kewpie doll. I was the one who always ended up being embarrassed because I was such a rebellious little creep."

"Not like Cassie at all." He relaxed his long body against the wall.

I breathed a sigh of relief and took at least one foot out of my mouth.

"No. Cassie has been a lady since the day she was born. Just like her grandmother."

"Mrs. DeLeon, thanks for coming. I really appreciate it. I'm sorry for all the trouble I've caused you and your family."

"Goodness, Ethan, you haven't caused us any trouble. You're the one in trouble—or haven't you noticed?"

He gave that "aw shucks" grin again, and I could tell he was feeling more like his old self.

"I have to admit that I was badly thrown when they arrested me. I'm afraid it took me a while to come out of my depression. I've been in some tight spots before, but never something as low on the totem pole as this."

He stood up and walked over to the high little cell window. He was tall enough that he could see out.

"My mother will never understand." He turned back, his face grim again.

"She's like your mother, but without the kindness and sense of humor. To her, appearances and professional demeanor are everything. This will be the last straw in my checkered career. She'll wash her hands of me even if I do get off scot-free. And it's a given that she'll fire me."

"Fire you, what do you mean, fire you? Mothers can't stop loving their sons."

"You don't understand. My mother is my boss at CDC."

"Dr. Eloise Haywood is your mother?"

He seemed genuinely surprised that I knew her name.

"Eh, I went with Cassie to send the e-mail to your office."

I thought quickly for a moment and decided to tell him everything.

"We also brought your computer back to the farm for safekeeping," I whispered.

He sat down hard on his bunk. The springs made a loud and musical protest against his weight. I held my breath for his reaction.

"Wow! Thank you, Mrs. DeLeon! At least she can't accuse me of being careless with confidential information. Thanks to you and Cassie."

He got that goofy lovelorn look on his face.

"I bet it was her idea, huh?"

"Yes, Ethan," I lied.

The deputy yelled a terse warning for us to stop whispering. "Look, Ethan, Chief Joiner won't let me stay in here much longer. We'd better get on with it. Why did you ask to see me?"

He cleared his throat, and the Romeo look vanished.

"Cassie told me when we first met about your work, I mean your detective work—writing the books and all. I was hoping you would help me out. Maybe you can find out what really happened."

He had turned a peculiar shade of red.

"I want to ask you and Leonard Paisley to get me out of this mess."

CHAPTER NINE

The afternoon was beautiful—sunny and warm—with a soft breeze from the south which lifted my hair and kissed my cheeks. High above, little fluffy white clouds scooted across an intense cerulean sky like naughty chicks scurrying home to mama. It was perfect weather, and there were no bars between me and the great outdoors. One hour in a jail cell was more than enough for me. I had left feeling infinitely sorry for Ethan.

Too unsettled to go home just yet, I decided to walk around and sort out my feelings. Ethan's request that I help him was not unexpected. I was already trying to help to some extent. But now that he was really counting on me to solve his problems, I wasn't sure I was up to it.

I tried to explain to him that I was not really a detective—just a writer who seemed to get in the middle of murderous muddles and had to figure her way out. I could not guarantee any results at all. But like others before him, he simply ignored what he called my modesty. He'd brightened like a hundred-watt bulb when I said I would do the best I could.

Damn! Another muddle. Leonard had better put on his thinking cap for this one. It was a dilly.

Rowan Springs had two main streets—one went north and the

other south. When they met at the courthouse square, they divided and went east and west as well. It had been a very nifty plan when the town was founded over a hundred years ago. Amazingly enough, it still worked today—with the addition of one or two traffic lights and a four-way stop sign here and there.

The jail, firehouse, and City Hall were on the north side of the square. The pharmacies and clothing stores were on the south side. A barber shop, a beauty shop, and one Tai Chi studio were on the west.

When I was a little girl, I used to shop for groceries with my grandmother at the A&P on the east side of the square. Rowan Springs was still a little country town back then. Farmers brought their wagons to town filled with fresh produce and live chickens and sold them off the tailgate. My grandmother always bought a nice fat hen for Sunday dinner. I usually made a pet of it before we got home and cried all night after she swung it by the neck until the body popped off and went flapping across the backyard. Somehow the violent demise of my new feathered friend never stopped me from devouring the juicy meat off the crispy fried pulley bone after church the next day.

The hitching racks were long gone and so were the grocery stores. They had moved out to the mini-mall on the road to the lakes where there was more parking space.

Once abandoned, the high-ceilinged old stores had been turned into offices for lawyers and accountants. Bruce Hawkins, Mother's lawyer, had been the only one in town to rebel against having an office on "Lawyer's Row." Instead he had turned the old Capitol Theater into a wonderful art deco homage to the movies he used to love and made his offices there.

I walked around the square lost in reflection and memories. My mind was a hundred years in the past as I admired the wonderful old carvings on the fronts of the buildings.

I did not see the crowd gathering outside of the jail until I rounded the corner of the courthouse. Andy Joiner was standing on the steps in front of his office trying to disperse what appeared to be the beginnings of an unruly demonstration.

I crossed the street and stood behind an obese, middle-aged woman with stringy grey hair. She was waving a homemade placard with the word "feend" misspelled in bright orange letters. I watched in morbid fascination as the flabby fat under her arms swayed grotesquely with her every movement. She noticed me watching her and turned around.

"You got daughters?"

She thrust the placard under my nose and waved it dangerously close to my brand new Ralph Lauren sunglasses.

"That crazy doctor inside the jail is killing our babies. You'd better join us and make your voice heard. We don't want his kind 'round here—even in jail. He's a monster!"

"How can he hurt you or your daughters if he's in jail?"

"He's a monster, I told you. Has them supernatural powers. Puts spells on people. Makes them do things they don't want to do. That's how he got poor little Brittany Hayes pregnant. Now she's carrying that devil's child." She ran over to another newcomer to the scene where I heard her repeating the same vicious spiel.

I hurried back to Watson and took the back road out of town.

Mother and Cassie were out in the backyard raking leaves where Aggie was busy rolling around madly in the biggest pile. I shucked my linen jacket, grabbed a rake, and went to join them.

"How's Ethan, dear? Holding up well, I hope?"

"Yes, Mother, and he said to tell you 'hello.'"

"How nice. I must send him some blackberry cobbler with the next one of you who goes back to town."

Cassie dragged her pile of leaves behind her to add to Mother's cache.

"What did Ethan want to see you about?"

Cassie looked like a beautiful wood nymph. Her hair was loose and blowing in the wind, with one bright orange leaf caught in the long, dark strands.

I bucked up my flagging spirits and forced a smile.

"He wants me and Leonard—and you two, of course—to find out who killed Hayes and raped his daughter—and get him out of jail."

"Oh, is that all." She discovered the leaf and tugged at the stem to free it. "Didn't he send me a message?"

I left the three of them raking, or in the case of Aggie, unraking leaves and headed back to my desk in the library. I could hear Cassie laughing at the antics of the puppy and considered for a moment going back to join them, but no matter how beautiful the afternoon, the truth was, I hated raking leaves. And relaxing on the patio watching them work would earn me no kudos. Besides, Cassie needed the distraction, and I needed her to quit crying herself to sleep. I hoped she would be too tired tonight to waste time on that nonsense.

And I had forgotten to tell them the choice bit of news I had learned: Brittany Hayes had claimed she was pregnant with Ethan's baby when she had been a patient at the Morgantown abortion clinic, long before he'd even arrived on the scene. She had probably cried rape to explain her pregnancy to her family, but why had she put the blame on Ethan? Since I was not positive of all my facts, I decided to keep the information to myself for a while.

From my vantage point behind the big desk in the library, I could watch Cassie and Mother as they crisscrossed over the back yard. After a while, Cassie went down to the carriage house and brought up the John Deere tractor with the wagon attached to the back. Cassie drove the tractor around to each big pile of leaves in turn and stopped while Mother scooped up the debris and loaded it in the wagon. After only a half turn around the yard the wagon was full. Mother climbed in back and hitched a ride down to the dry pond bed where we built our bonfires. They stopped, emptied the wagonload of leaves, and started all over again, with Aggie running round and round the moving tractor and barking maniacally the whole time. I decided the puppy would sleep well tonight also. It looked like I'd be the only night crawler. I was restless and could not get back to work for the life of me.

I shivered and realized that the room had grown a little chilly. My father had grown tired of emptying out ashes and installed some wonderful gas logs in the big open fireplace the year before he died. I pushed the magic plunger and a big beautiful fire appeared.

It was the first fire of the season. Usually we all gathered together for such an occasion, but everybody else was already having too much fun. I had to enjoy something.

I sat on the wide brick hearth for a few moment to warm my rear end, then took up my position behind the desk again. Ethan's computer was still on, and the screen saver—which I had not seen before—slowly moved across the monitor. Big red letters on a hideous purple background repeated over and over again, "ABORTION BUG."

I shivered again, but not from the cold. For the first time, I realized that there was something really malevolent going on here—something that I did not have a clue about. It was some "thing" that even Ethan did not really understand, yet feared nonetheless. He had managed to transfer that uneasiness to me this afternoon. He had never spoken the words, but I knew he was afraid that I might find what he had been looking for when he came to town. He knew that I would not be prepared. I had never been in a cave in Kinshasa. I would not know a vector if it bit me. And it just might.

CHAPTER TEN

I fanned the floppy discs out on the desk in front of me and wondered why they were called by that name. They were anything but floppy. There were ten of them in all. I wished I had made a list of the ones I had already scanned. I had been in such a hurry when I had finally figured out Ethan's encrypted password that I had just looked at them helter-skelter. Now I had no idea which ones I had reviewed and which I had not. I would have to start all over again.

I needed to get organized. The computer screen was too small for my organization chart. I needed something larger. I remembered tucking a large piece of cardboard under the bed, thinking I would need it someday. Smart lady. I needed it now.

What I did not know was that someone had let Aggie back inside the house. She was cooling her tummy and taking a nap under my bed. I got the cardboard but I also got a nasty nip from our furry little cobra. Damn dog!

I was in the bathroom putting on some antibiotic ointment and a Band-Aid when the police caravan pulled up in the driveway. Two Lakeland County police cars pulled in first and went on around the circle. Another cruiser followed a large unmarked Toyota van with dark tinted windows.

My heart leapt with joy. They were letting Ethan go! But then I saw Chief Joiner open the van door and help him out.

Ethan was handcuffed and shackled. He had to bend over to accommodate the chains. I realized with a sinking heart that he looked exactly like the old man in the storybook.

Cassie was on the tractor, but when she saw Ethan she hopped off and went running to him. When Joiner stopped her before they could embrace, I heard her angry retort without really under-standing the words.

Two deputies got out of the first car and stationed themselves at Ethan's side. Cassie stood meekly in front of him with a crooked little attempt for a smile on her face. It was a sad, pitiful scene and mercifully, over in less than three minutes. I didn't even have time to open the window so I could hear what was going on. Joiner helped Ethan back into the van and they all disappeared around the drive in a cloud of gravel dust.

Cassie stood like a statue until Mother tried to put her arms around her, then she shook off the embrace and ran toward the lane and the back field. Aggie had awakened when the cars pulled out of the drive and was now barking furiously as she saw her mistress running off to play without her. She slipped out when I opened the French doors to join Mother and went barreling down the lane in pursuit of Cassie. I found myself hoping a fox would eat her up.

The tractor engine was still running. Mother climbed up in the seat to drive it back down to the carriage house, and I hopped on the back of the wagon and rode down with her.

Honeysuckle vines with their dainty white flowers vied for space with wild berries on the back fence. I reached out and grabbed a couple of blossoms as we drove past. I pulled out the stamens and sipped the tiny drop of incredibly sweet honeysuckle nectar. Too bad there wasn't enough to bottle. Or maybe it was a good thing. Anything that delicious would be overwhelming in large amounts.

We drove down past the dry pond bed and back up to the

carriage house. The trees along the lane still had enough foliage to prevent me from seeing Cassie; besides, she was probably halfway to the big pond by now. I wasn't worried for her safety. There were no bogeymen in the woods.

Mother parked the tractor three times before she got it just exactly where she wanted it. When she finally turned off the engine, the silence made my ears ring.

"Wow, I thought you would never stop. What's the matter? Is there a prize for the farm with the best-parked John Deere?"

When she did not answer, I hopped out of the wagon and went forward to the tractor where she remained on the seat.

"What is it, Mother? Are you all right?"

Her face was grim and tight and her eyes were bright with tears.

"They are taking Cassie's young man to Teddyville to the state penitentiary. Andy Joiner was kind enough to let him come and say goodbye."

I was shocked. The prison in Teddyville had the reputation of being a dreadful place. It was almost a hundred years old. Built of huge limestone rocks, it sat high on a hill in the middle of a narrow peninsula that reached down into the Cumberland River. The area was flooded when the TVA dams were built fifty years ago, and the powers that be in the state penal system had decided that it would make a perfect home for the most incorrigible prisoners. The guards reportedly had carte blanche to discipline the men as they chose. There had been more than one charge of brutality made since I had returned to this area a year ago. Why in the world had they sent a man who had not even been tried for his crimes to that awful place?

I helped Mother down from the tractor, and we walked back up to the house as she filled me in with the reason.

"Andy says that a very nasty crowd gathered in town this afternoon in front of the jail. He was afraid he couldn't guarantee Ethan's safety here in Rowan Springs. That's why they moved him."

She stopped and looked at me, her eyes shimmering.

"Cassandra is devastated. What are we going to do, Paisley?"

A big yellow butterfly danced in front of my face and flew away. Rafe had always believed that butterflies brought bad luck. I could never bring myself to think that anything so beautiful could be a harbinger of misfortune, but it wasn't too late to change my mind.

I squeezed Mother's hand and pulled her toward the patio. The sun was hovering over the horizon, but it was still warmer outside than in the chilly house.

"It's almost time to turn on the furnace."

"I guess so," she answered distractedly.

"Look Mother, if Joiner took Ethan to Teddyville, it was the right thing to do, I trust him implicitly. He's a good man. I'm sure Ethan will be all right. I didn't mention it before, but I saw the mob when I was in town. There were some ugly threats being bandied about. Ethan's better off in Teddyville, believe me."

"I suppose you're right, dear." She smiled at me. "You usually are."

I grinned back. "Yeah, except when I'm too cheeky, or too smart-alecky, or too full of piss and vinegar."

"Paisley!"

"Or cursing," I added.

The sun sank slowly, leaving the sky awash with a gold and crimson hue. Mother looked look ten years younger in the rosy glow. I hoped I did, too. I was going to need some youthful energy to get us out of this mess.

"I'm starving! What gastronomic delight have you planned for dinner tonight?"

"The truth is . . . let's go out. My treat."

"What about Cassie?"

"Oh, you are so right. We can't leave her."

She looked to the heavens for some inspiration.

"I think I have some flounder in the freezer."

"Ugh! Frozen fish. Think of something else."

We had finally given up and gone in the kitchen to peruse the cupboard when we heard Aggie barking. I went out to the porch and unhooked the screen door for Cassie as she wiped her sneakers on the doormat.

"Boy! The lane is muddy. I'd better take off my shoes, Mom. Gran will get mad if I get mud on the kitchen floor. She won't feed me for fussin,' and I'm about to die of hunger. What's for dinner?"

She pushed past me and my open mouth before I could remind her that the puppy's feet were probably muddier than hers. I expected her to return with a face swollen with tears. I thought she might barricade herself in her bedroom for a week—tear her hair and wear sackcloth and ashes. She never ceased to amaze me.

Mother managed to put together a wonderful Welsh Rarebit, something Cassie had never eaten and I remembered only from my childhood. Cassie ate every bite and licked her plate. I watched in amusement as Mother tried her best not to reprimand her grand-daughter. Cassie finally burst out laughing.

"Gran, I can't believe it. I thought you would have a cow. You really are getting tolerant in your old age."

"Humpf."

I could stand the suspense no longer.

"Okay, Cassie, I give up. How come you're not locked in your room crying like a baby?"

"You said it, Mom, 'like a baby.' Well, I'm not a baby any more. If Ethan is to get out of this mess, he needs our help. I can't let him down."

She put her hand over mine. "You aren't going to either, are you, Mom?"

"No darling, of course not." I smiled and leaned over to kiss her on the forehead. "I'll do my best."

"Leonard, too?"

"You can always count on Leonard."

CHAPTER ELEVEN

Mother dismissed my piece of cardboard, calling it "puny," and brought out a big white poster board instead. It was just the ticket. She also found a couple of black and some colored magic markers. Since she printed more legibly than either Cassie or I, we elected her to make our little organization chart.

She divided the chart into columns: one for each floppy disc, with spaces for the files underneath. There was still plenty of room to add notes and comments. We were in business.

Cassie brought us a big pot of tea and some chocolate biscuits. She and Mother sat in front of the fire munching while I worked on the computer and Aggie lay comatose at their feet. Not even the possibility of falling cookie crumbs could rouse the exhausted puppy after her afternoon romp in the woods.

The disc I chose first had the lowest sequence of numbers written on the label. I had no idea what they meant and probably never would, but I had to start somewhere.

Disc number one turned out to be Ethan's log book. The file manager only read that one location on the disc. The last entry had been the day of his arrest. It was a big file, and I had only just begun to read it, but it would have to wait until later.

"Oh, Mom, by the way, Ethan said to tell you, 'look for the lambs.'"

"What the hell does that mean?"

"What lambs, dear? Paisley, language, please."

"I don't know, Gran. He couldn't explain with the Gestapo listening to our every word."

"Okay! Mother, for what it's worth, that's our first clue. Write it on the top of the poster in quotations."

"I thought the abortion clinic in Morgantown was our first clue."

"What abortion clinic? I thought this was about miscarriages and stillbirths, not about stupid people murdering babies."

"Is that really how you feel, Cassie?"

I don't know why I was surprised at her attitude. After all, she had been brought up Catholic, like Rafe's family.

"I certainly do! I cannot imagine anyone in their right mind having an abortion for any reason. Not even to save the mother's life. The baby comes first."

I saw Mother pulling herself up to give her little lecture. I tried to head it off at the pass. The last thing we needed tonight was an argument about abortion rights.

"I found the medical dictionary on the bookshelf today. Apparently the term 'abortion' is applied to fetal loss depending on the number of weeks from conception. Up until twenty weeks a fetus is 'aborted' either naturally or through intervention. After that it is 'stillborn,'" I added weakly.

Nobody was paying me any attention at all. Mother was sitting upright on the edge of her seat and just itching to sermonize. Cassie, however, was not yet ready to give up her soapbox.

"Too many females of my generation think of abortion as just another means of birth control. It's not birth control at all. It's murder due to lack of self-control."

"You certainly make a good point with that, dear, but don't you think . . . "

"Murder plain and simple," interrupted my darling daughter.

"Have you ever seen a little fetus, Gran? It has tiny little hands and . . . "

"Cassie."

". . . feet. What, Mom?"

" Mother, you too. Let's cool it, okay? If the Supreme Court has trouble with this decision, how in the world can you two hope to change each other's minds? It's way too emotional a subject for us right now, and it won't help Ethan at all. Let's put our energy into helping him."

"Certainly, dear. You're right as usual."

She smiled sweetly—too sweetly, and continued, "Cassandra, you could learn a few things from your elders."

I tried again, "Mother, could you please get us some more tea? The pot's gone cold."

"Never mind, Mom! You can't cut her off that easily. I'll get the tea so my 'elder' won't wear herself out."

"Cassie, that's enough!"

"Well, I never! No tea for me, Miss Cassandra. I'm going to bed. You know how we old people like our sleep. Good night, Paisley!"

They stormed out side by side and almost got stuck in the doorway. I started laughing, and they turned in unison to glare at me in fury. I laughed even harder and woke up the puppy. She raised her head sleepily and glared at me too, then, dragging her furry little tail tiredly behind her, she followed her mistress to bed.

And so I was left alone again to do the sleuthing. I wondered if Holmes ever had this much trouble with Watson and had just kept the knowledge of the domestic discord to himself.

I sighed and slipped the second disc into the computer. Once again I saw the columns and columns of numbers and formulas. This time I looked more closely and suddenly realized that they were laboratory results. The long numbers at the top of each column probably represented a patient. Each one had a red cell count and a white cell count. I recognized kidney and liver function studies, but there were some others I could not understand. The library in town would probably have a book on how to interpret medical tests. I could send Cassie down tomorrow—that is, if she would speak to me.

The third disc was more of the same, and so was the fourth, but the fifth held a little surprise. I found Ethan's "lambs."

Dr. McHenry had apparently visited the medical library at the CDC before he left Atlanta. He had included excerpts from several toxicology manuals and journals in his notes. They were in a file entitled "possible causes." It was not even written in caps. He obviously felt the information was of little significance.

There were three entries from environmental journals with cases of abortions in hazardous work environments—two in paint factories and one in a plant that manufactured plastics. They contained words that I could not even guess the meanings of and more columns and figures similar to the ones on the other discs.

It was not until then that I realized Ethan was planning to write a paper on the abortion cases here in Lakeland County. The laboratory results would make no sense to anyone but other professionals in his field.

I got up immediately and put the discs with the lab data in an olivewood music box on the library shelf. They would be safe there. I would be horrified if anything—a vicious puppy with sharp little teeth, for instance—happened to all of Ethan's hard work.

The next article was from a dental journal. It addressed the suspicion that dental assistants had a higher rate of fetal loss than other health care workers, but there was no definite conclusion made. We only had two dentists in town, and both of them had several young women working in their offices. I imagined that Mother would know their names. I could find out if any of them had lost a baby recently.

The most interesting entries were from a book on poisonous plants. Ethan had made several notes about crop plants with a high nitrate content, which was known to cause abortion in cattle and sheep. And there was a really gross entry on fescue seed used for lawns and gardens which contained "nematode galls." I had no idea what they were, but I decided to tell Mother we should pour concrete on the backyard posthaste. Yuck, nematodes! Not to mention galls.

Goldenrod was the culprit in an article about abortion in cattle in Virginia. I made a note of that because goldenrod was our state flower, although I personally thought of it as a weed.

Another of Ethan's entries was also close to home. I wondered if he realized that this part of the state was called the Pennyrile because of the abundant growth of the pennyroyal plant. That little jewel was noted to have been used by the American Indians as an abortifacient. The article added that it was a volatile oil, a colorless liquid that evaporated quickly at room temperature. Apparently enough to cause abortion would be lethal to the mother. Just breathing a little bit could cause seizures and coma.

Nematodes and seizures. I was getting nauseous.

Finally, there was the article about the lambs. This was what Ethan had told me to look for, and I read it with anticipation. Here again was a poisonous plant, *Veratrum californicum*, otherwise known as the skunk cabbage. It caused congenital malformations when fed to pregnant ewes during the second and third week after conception. The resulting "monkey-faced" lambs were usually aborted. Those that were carried to term always died shortly after birth, since their facial deformities prevented them from breathing and eating. The upper jaw and nose were poorly developed, and the eyes were usually joined into one big cycloptic organ. They were normal otherwise. Ha, I thought, how normal can a cycloptic "monkey-faced" lamb be? But this plant grew in the high mountain valleys of the Pacific coast and the Rocky Mountains, nowhere near us.

There was another *Veratrum viride* which grew in open woods and pastures throughout North America. This plant, Indian poke, had been used as an insecticide in the eighteenth and nineteenth centuries. Its toxicity was unpredictable. It had fallen into disuse until the 1950s, when an alkaloid it contained was found to have hypotensive properties. It was now used in some antihypertensive drugs such as Veratramine.

What part of this was supposed to mean something to me, or Leonard?

I went to bed and dreamed of lambs who ate bananas and climbed trees. It was a funny dream. I smiled in my sleep until I saw their big single eyes staring at me from behind the tropical leaves.

CHAPTER TWELVE

When I awoke the next morning, I found Cassie and Aggie in bed with me. I must have slept very soundly because I had no idea when they had crawled under my covers.

Aggie was whining to go out for her morning walk, so I slipped on my beloved old Cole-Haan moccasins, opened the French doors, and stepped outside.

The air was balmy, almost springlike, but the sky was a dirty pewter grey. And there was the slightly metallic smell of rain on the light breeze blowing from the south.

Aggie took her own sweet time. She puttered around endlessly under my grandmother Howard's big crepe myrtle and sniffed daintily at the tiny little wild violets my grandmother Sterling had planted at the edge of the driveway fifty years ago. I got impatient. I started to call her, but the wind picked up suddenly, lifting the thick soft fur on the dog's back until it stood straight up like a ruff. She raised her ears and eyebrows in a comical parody of alarm and scampered back to my side.

I looked to the south and saw big blackish-green thunder clouds boiling over the horizon. We were in for quite a storm if the wind kept blowing in this direction.

I stepped back inside and Aggie hurriedly squeezed in between my ankles. She hated thunderstorms and was a fairly good little barometer. I decided to batten down the hatches.

I unplugged Ethan's computer and mine, too. And just to make sure that Cassie would not try to turn it on during the bad weather, I stuck Ethan's in the big drawer of my father's desk. No sense taking any chances with government property. Thanks to Leonard's success I had plenty of tax dollars at work

Cassie was already up and dressed. She was cavorting with Mother in the kitchen, their feud over abortion rights apparently forgotten, as they danced and harmonized on "Dream a Little Dream With Me."

I sat down at the table and drank a glass of orange juice while I watched them frolic around the big kitchen looking for all the world like Fred and Ginger—or Ginger and Ginger.

When they finished, I clapped, Aggie barked, and they bowed. Quite a pleasant way to begin the day. Then I had to go and spoil it.

"Tut, tut, it looks like rain."

"The weatherman says 'no,' dear."

"Aggie says 'yes.'"

They turned to look at me.

"Oh! I'd better close the windows in my bedroom. How about yours, Cassie dear?"

"I'll get them, Gran. And I'll move Watson into the garage."

"Paisley, can you unplug the television and the microwave?"

"Sure thing."

I turned and winked at Aggie. "Wow, you've got some reputation, dog."

Aggie's prediction was correct. The storm was a dilly.

In Manhattan, I never noticed big electrical storms. It had just rained and gotten everything dirty and wet and nasty. Here on the farm, the force of nature could truly be seen in all its awesome power. Lightening flashed and thunder roared, to put it mildly. In the country, it was easy to understand why primitive man cowered in his cave and wondered what he had done to bring the wrath of the gods down on his poor head.

We three gathered in front of the big bay windows in the living room to watch as the fury of the storm play out before us. At times the old logs in the walls shook and the floor trembled. It was awesome.

Aggie perched miserably on the back of the sofa behind Cass with her head tucked between her paws. She yelped at a particularly loud clap of thunder and dove under the sofa as the lights went out.

"Damn!"

"Language, dear."

"Oh, Mother, for God's sake."

"Now is certainly not the time to blaspheme, Mom."

I got up to look for the flashlights muttering something about how you could take the girl out of Catholic school, but not the Catholic out of the schoolgirl, or some such nonsense.

I crossed the hallway and was opening the door to my bedroom when I glanced out the front door. I was amazed to see a car backing rapidly out of our driveway.

"What the hell?"

"Paisley!"

I felt the wind coming from the open doors in the library just as Aggie crawled out from under the sofa and started barking.

"Oh, terrific! You're a great watchdog after the fact!"

Sure enough, someone had broken into the library. In a flash of lightning, I saw pieces of broken glass from the French doors. It was almost as dark as early evening outside, but I could still see wet footprints on the carpet. And my laptop was missing.

"Damn and hell and piss!"

"Paisley! You really must do something about your filthy mouth. Oh, my!"

"Yes! Oh my! And, oh, dearie me," I responded sarcastically.

"Some piece of crap . . . Oh, excuse me, Mother. Some terribly misguided soul has invaded our happy home and made off with my very expensive computer. And, oh by the way, our intruder has also stolen the only copy of my new book in existence."

I glared at her in my anger as I continued, "My goodness, how very inconvenient." I raised my voice, "And damned pissing!"

I flopped down on the sofa in disgust, then jumped back up again in alarm as I remembered Ethan's discs. But they were still safely tucked away in the music box. Thank heaven I had stuck the other discs in the box when I had put his computer in the drawer. I wish I had been as careful with Leonard's latest adventure. My agent and best friend, Pamela, was going to have to be very understanding about the delay in finishing the first draft of my manuscript. I would have to start all over again.

Mother was picking up the larger pieces of glass. I knelt down to help her.

"I'm sorry about my language, Mother. I just can't believe someone would have the nerve to commit a burglary in broad daylight."

"It's hardly light outside, Paisley. This storm is wonderful cover for a thief."

Cassie finally came to see what was going on.

"What did I miss? I had to clean up after Aggie peed on the floor. Poor little thing was so scared."

"We've been robbed, dear. Someone broke in and stole your mother's computer."

"Mother's? Are you sure it wasn't Ethan's? I bet it was Ethan's they were after! That proves he's innocent!"

"Either that or he has an accomplice with big, wet, muddy feet," I said angrily.

"My, my, yes indeed. It does look like our burglar could have wiped his shoes before breaking in. I'll have to have the carpet cleaned."

"See, Mom. We just have to find a computer nerd with big feet and no manners and he's our villain!"

The storm washed the sky clean. When the thunder could only be heard in the distance, there was nothing but fleecy white clouds in the bluest of blues overhead. I looked at the clock and had a hard time believing it was not yet noon.

I vacuumed the rest of the glass from the library carpet and taped a piece of cardboard over the hole in the door. Carpet cleaner had removed most of the muddy footprints and everything looked pretty good again.

We had decided not to call the police and report the robbery. By now, Joiner would have figured out that Ethan's computer was missing. And I was also sure that Miss Lolly would have been more than eager to tell him about my visit the morning after Ethan's arrest. If he came to investigate the theft of my laptop, Andy just might have some questions about Ethan's and I did not want to answer any questions—not just yet, anyway.

After lunch I sat in the kitchen moodily adding up the cost of a new computer. With no police report there would be no insurance payment. To make matters worse, I could not remember how many chapters of Leonard's tome I had completed. All in all, I was fairly depressed. The last person in the world I wanted to see was Mother's weird friend Mavis Madden.

"Hello, hello, hello. Anyone at home? Did the wild wind take you and your little doggie to Kansas?" the woman cackled quite convincingly.

I let the old witch inside.

"Good morning, Mrs. Madden."

"Paisley, darling, you look positively ghoulish. How much weight have you lost, dear? Skin and bones, skin and bones."

Mavis fluttered and flapped like an old hen. She had a little black hat on with a bright red flower sticking out of the crown. The flower and her jowls waggled back and forth as she babbled on without stopping.

"Nice to see you, too, Mrs. Madden," I interrupted. "Have a seat. I'll get Mother."

As I escaped, I heard her voice going on behind me as though I had never left the room. I found Mother and informed her of the visitor. I had to push her towards the kitchen.

"Damn."

"Mother! Language, please."

"Oh, dear. Now you have me saying those dreadful things, too."

"Me? How about Mavis? Doesn't she get some credit for being a totally unpleasant and irritating old bag?"

"Come with me, Paisley. Please? I don't think I can stand her on my own."

She looked pleadingly at me. She was absolutely no good at trying to appear helpless and pitiful. Some day I would have to tell her.

"Okay. But just so long as she doesn't start asking me questions about my marriage."

Mother nodded in agreement.

"I swear I'll leave the room the minute she mentions Rafe, or South America, or even the word 'jungle.'"

"Done."

"Or 'guacamole' or 'burrito' or . . . "

"Enough, Paisley, dear. You've made your point."

"Or 'husband's gone missing and don't know where to find him, humm, Paisley?'"

We marched back to the kitchen like good little soldiers. Mavis was still talking as though she had a room full of people as an audience.

" . . . and so I said to Agnes Wallace, I saw your husband in Morgantown at that new restaurant with a woman young enough to be his daughter. They were sitting so close together you couldn't see light shine between 'em. And her a bottle blond, too. Agnes, I said, you're a saint to put up with that man. Anybody else would have more pride than to let a worm like that crawl in their bed at night."

"Mavis, dear, would you like some tea?"

"No, thanks. I just had lemonade at Agnes Wallace's. That was before the storm. It was hot this morning."

She looked out of the window accusingly. I was sure I heard Mother Nature's knees knocking together in alarm. Mavis was not one to be inconvenienced by anything—not even the elements.

She droned on about the misery in the life of poor Mrs. Wallace, misery that she had been only too happy to point out to the poor woman.

Mavis and I agreed on one point. I had always considered Winston Wallace to be one of Rowan Springs' lower forms of animal life. How he managed to hold on to his medical practice, I would never know.

"And now Ed Baxter has thrown in the towel just because a few of his patients miscarry. And since most of them have no business having any more brats, I look on it as a blessing."

My ears perked up. "What do you mean, Mavis?"

She looked startled for a moment. I hardly ever spoke to her. She warmed up immediately to her new audience.

"Well, you must be aware that Barbara Malls has two deaf and dumb kids already. And her husband just lost his job at the mill. He had no call to get her in the family way again. What with no money coming in, and her trying to school those poor little dummies at home. Good riddance, I say. And the same for Susan Arnold. She had that mongoloid baby two years ago, and Edgar Baxter told her the new one had the same problem. But she and Herb wanted it just the same. Imagine! And them being already in their late forties. Who's gonna take care of those poor little retards when their parents die, I ask you? Me and you! The taxpayers—that's who!"

Mavis seemed to have forgotten that she was at least sixty-seven and would no doubt have gone to her own little coven in the sky long before Susan and Herb Arnold made their "little retard" an orphan.

"Our taxes will be taking care of them just like our taxes are taking care of all those babies in Paradise Trailer Park. And speaking of trailer trash, Patsy Floyd has five little snot-nosed brats from at least four different men. Good thing she dropped the sixth before its time, I say!"

I watched little drops of spittle dry in the corners of her mouth as Mavis Madden continued spewing forth the vilest venom. She was quite a sight. Makeup had caked in the wrinkles on her cheeks and forehead, and bright magenta lipstick fanned out in the thin lines around her mouth like tiny varicose veins. Her mean little eyes were dark with muddy colored irises and yellowish sclera. She frightened me. Mavis had long ago passed the point of being just a meddling old gossip. She was evil. I would have nightmares again tonight.

Mother had zoned out completely, and I was so amazed by the quality of Mavis's meanness that neither of us had noticed when Aggie came in the kitchen. She had been quietly chewing away on the handle of Mavis's big black leather purse for some time. When the puppy burped, we all looked down.

Mavis jumped up and screamed. Her upper arms and bust wobbled and heaved with her agitation. She looked like a pink Jell-O mountain in clothes.

"Look what she's done! Look what your rotten little beast has done!"

She yanked the soggy, wet strap out of Aggie's mouth. And before I could warn her, she landed a smack solidly on the puppy's rump. Aggie whirled around and leapt at Mavis like a streak of fuzzy white lightning. She sank her teeth into Mavis's thick, purple-veined ankle with all of her might.

Mavis's scream was deafening in the enclosed kitchen.

"Ow! She's killing me! Get her off! Get her off!"

Mother and I watched, paralyzed, as Mavis ran around the kitchen dragging Aggie behind her like a furry little mop. With one tremendous effort, she finally managed to shake the puppy loose, grab her purse by the one remaining strap, and run out of the house like the hounds of hell were after her.

CHAPTER THIRTEEN

Mother and I looked at each other in horror. We both knew that Mavis was on her broomstick flying to the home of her next hapless victim with a marvelous, brand-new story to tell. Poor Agnes Wallace and her marital woes would have to take a back seat to the tale of the vicious beast that Anna Howard Sterling had turned loose on Mavis Madden. Aggie might even make the headlines in the weekly paper.

Cassie peeked in the kitchen to make sure our visitor was gone so she could raid the fridge. When Mother informed her of the events of the last hour Cassie's response was, "Good doggie."

Aggie hopped up into her lap and allowed herself to be patted for the moment. She seemed aware that she had done something momentous.

"The good doggie might end up in doggie jail if Mavis has her way. Then you'll have two pen pals."

I realized almost—almost—but not quickly enough, how mean my little joke might sound to her.

"Oh, Cassie, I'm sorry! What an idiot I am!"

Her pretty mouth wilted at the corners while her eyes filled up with gargantuan tears. Cassie had never been one to "cry small." No tiny little hiccoughy gasps for her. Giant sobs were her forte, and once she started she would have to cry herself out.

I jumped up and put my arms around her.

"Please forgive me for being so stupid and insensitive."

For a moment I thought she was going to shrug off my embrace, but she hugged me back, wiped her eyes and nose on a napkin, and surprised me once again.

"You're right, I would have two pen pals, but only one of them is guilty."

She sniffed loudly and patted me on the shoulder.

"I forgive you, Mom. But please, try to think before you speak next time."

I sat back down, once again amazed at the emotional evolution of my daughter. I wondered briefly if I could take any credit for this growing level of maturity, but I knew better. Cassie was just on the way to becoming a fantastic young woman. At least I could be proud even if I could not take credit.

She buttered a cold biscuit and poured on some honey.

"Gran, do you really think Mavis could cause trouble for Aggie?"

"She'll try, but I think everyone she tells the story to will be so amused, secretly of course, that no one will take her seriously. Aggie can go on being Aggie. I quite enjoyed it myself. And you are right, 'Good doggie!'"

"How in the world did that mean old witch get to be a friend of yours, Mother?"

"She was in my Sunday School class last year."

"Yoff go' ta' be kidding!"

"Cassie, darling, don't talk with your mouth full. You might choke, and Mavis's husband would have to come out here."

"Why on earth?"

"He drives the ambulance. That's why she knows so much about everybody's business. It's also the reason everyone is so reluctant to put her in her place."

"So that guy who drives around blowing that siren at the

drop of a hat is Mavis's true love? He seems so much younger than she is."

"He is—ten years, maybe fifteen. And he is a bit simple,"

"And he drives the ambulance? Come on Gran, really, is this the craziest little town on earth or what? Ethan calls it 'quaint and unique.'"

"Are you sure he wasn't referring to me?"

"No Gran, he thinks you are the most elegant and wonderful person he's ever met. He would love it if you were his mother."

"And what am I, chopped liver?"

"You, Mom? He does think you're eccentric. But you're an artist, so it's okay."

"What a relief."

"He did say he hoped you won't wear jeans to our wedding."

"I was thinking maybe the hot pink satin ones with the rhine-stones."

Cassie polished off two more biscuits while we mused over Mavis and the nasty stories she spread. But then an idea flitted through my brain, and I excused myself to return to my little atelier to pursue it.

I got down the olivewood music box and retrieved one of Ethan's discs, then pulled Ethan's laptop out of the desk drawer, turned it on, and opened the file. Sure enough there was the list of patients under the care of Edgar Baxter. Susan Arnold and Barbara Malls were on the list. So was Patsy of the trailer park.

I sat back in Dad's big chair and wondered what these women had in common besides being pregnant. The obvious answer was they all had the same doctor. And that's when I decided to do a little breaking and entering. After all, Leonard would not think twice about it. B&E was right up his alley.

I went back to the kitchen to share my plans. Cassie loved the idea and went immediately to her room in search of a burglary fashion statement. Something in black, she said. Mother, however, was appalled. I argued with her.

"If Doc Baxter hadn't closed up shop and refused to cooperate with Ethan, I wouldn't have to break in to see his files."

"So, Paisley, let me see if I understand your motives. You feel compelled to break into the office of one of my oldest and dearest friends because he had the audacity to quit his medical practice. Because he got old and tired and heartbroken over the fact that he couldn't save enough lives?"

"Well, of course it sounds bad if you put it that way."

I decided to take a nap in order to fortify my body for the coming nocturnal activities. Aggie is always on the lookout for someone to curl up with. She readily followed me to the library sofa, where I pulled a soft, handmade afghan over us, and we were soon snoring away in unison.

Cassie came in twenty minutes later to seek my opinion on her "stealing out in the dark of night" ensemble. She had to shake me awake. Aggie growled at the interruption of her slumber and took a quick nip at my bare toe in protest.

"Ow! For heaven's sake, what is it, Cassie?"

"My outfit, what do you think? Is this scarf too much? I thought it would come in handy if we had to tie someone up."

She posed and twirled in her black leather jeans and black cashmere turtleneck. I decided not to bite her head off. After all, just a short time ago, I had been mentally praising her maturity. In less than an hour she had digressed from nineteen going on twenty to fifteen again.

"Ummpf." I tried to hide my face in the soft down sofa cushion.

"What, Mom?"

She pulled the cushion away. I rose up, and the dog took another impatient nip out of my foot.

"My God! Is one little nap too much to ask? After all I've done for you? Eighteen hours of labor, six months of breast feeding, four years of college—all I'm asking is a tiny little one hour nap!"

"Oh, Mom, come off it. You don't do the maternal guilt shtick very well."

She grabbed the poker and held it menacingly as she posed in front of the fireplace.

"So how's it look?"

I gave up. I pulled myself up to a sitting position and decided on a little revenge.

"The sweater's fine, but the pants look a little tight in the rear. Have you gained weight?"

The poker clanked loudly as she thrust it back in the holder. Cassie was out of the room like a shot. She would be occupied for at least two hours trying on all of her clothes to see if her slim and perfect figure had changed a even centimeter. I snuggled back down. Aggie sighed and nestled against me. We slept.

I woke up a couple of hours later when Mother came in to make a grand announcement. She would drive the getaway car and serve as our lookout. She looked terrific. She and Cassie had collaborated on their choice of wardrobes. I was going out on a caper with Coco Chanel and Twiggy.

I was starving, but figured a nervous stomach full of food would not be a good thing. "Can we stop at the Dairy Queen on the way home and have a burger?"

"Of course, Paisley, dear. That way if someone sees us leaving the scene of the crime and calls the police with our descriptions we will be easy to find. They'll just look for three women dressed in black who are wolfing down hamburgers and french fries in a post-burglary eating frenzy."

"Maybe Gran is right, Mom. We should get in, out, and back as quickly as we can. Of course," she mused, "we could get the burgers to go before we break in the office and then eat them later."

"Cold hamburgers, dear?"

"Enough with the hamburgers! It was a dumb idea. Forget it. Let's go."

"You always get so testy, dear. Whenever we get involved in anything that is just the least bit . . . "

"Mother, can we please go? We're wasting time analyzing my nervous reaction to illegal activities."

"Well, you should work on it, dear. Look at me. I'm cool as a cucumber, and so is Cassandra. Maybe some meditation exercises. I have a new book you could . . . "

"Mother, if you don't get your elegant little butt out of the door and into Watson in the next two minutes you can't go. I'll leave you here to worry all alone. We'll just see how cool, calm, and collected you are then."

"No need to threaten me, Paisley, my girl. It's so unbecoming."

If she could have run in her high-heeled, black suede, thigh-high, Donna Karan boots she would have. Instead she walked as fast as she could to the car and climbed in with all the grace and decorum she could muster. My mother, dressed to the nines, taking me to commit a felony. I loved it!

CHAPTER FOURTEEN

Mother drove so slowly into town that we became an positive road hazard.

"Well, so much for keeping a low profile! That's the second time we've gotten flicked off, and three people have blown their horns at us on Main Street. Way to go, Coco!"

"Paisley Sterling DeLeon! The Bible promises a long and happy life to those who respect and honor their parents. I hope you're prepared for the worst!"

"And just what does the Bible say about parents who drive the getaway car for their children while they are committing a crime?"

"Mom! Gran! You all are just a little bit too nervous. Maybe we should call this off for now and do it another time. I'm sure anything we can find tonight we can find tomorrow night, or next week for that matter."

"Mother, park over there under those trees, and let's relax for a moment. Cassie is right. We've got way too much adrenaline going on here."

Mother pulled the Jeep wagon over to the curb and parked under the cover of three very large cedar trees. The limbs hung down almost to the ground, forming a protective canopy over the dark green car body. We had found the perfect hiding place, which was about the only thing we had done right so far.

"Hey, Gran, this is terrific. Way to go!"

Our vantage point was at the end of a side street just one block from the courthouse square. The object of our interest was straight ahead across the narrow, one-lane alley which served as both service drive and back entrance for the stores that lined Main Street.

Doctor Edgar Baxter still occupied the same office space he had when I was a little girl. He shared the old two-story building with the town's oldest pharmacy. I remembered going through a Dutch door in the doctor's office to sit behind the counter while the pharmacist mixed up whatever potion had been prescribed. Then he or his assistant would hold a lollipop out in front of me, so I would swallow the nasty-tasting concoction without a fuss. After a particularly bad bout of whooping cough in my fourth year, I developed a hatred of lollipops and the pharmacist.

Needless to say, Dr. Baxter's office did not hold many pleasant memories for me. The one good thing was that I did remember every inch of the place. I knew right where his desk and his files were. This would be a piece of cake.

We sat in silence and watched as the owners of the Main Street stores turned off their lights and locked up to go home for dinner and a good night's sleep.

I found myself yawning in the toasty warmth of the car just thinking about it. I stretched my shoulders and neck and casually looked out of the back window. I was horrified to see the red glow from the brake lights extending like a beacon from our hidey hole!

"Mother," I whispered harshly, "do you have your foot on the brake?"

"Oh, my goodness!"

She took her foot off the pedal and we lurched forward into a large overhanging evergreen bough. The heavy limb slapped forcefully against the wide glass windscreen and snapped off one of the windshield wipers. It went flying into the air and fell in the middle of the street with a loud metallic tinkle.

"Turn off the engine now!" I hissed, "Damn! We might as well send up a flare just in case some poor idiot hasn't noticed us!"

"That's it! I'm leaving. I'll walk home. You two can fend for yourselves. I'm just not cut out for a life of crime. Paisley, you're obviously much better at this than I, you do it."

She pulled the keys out of the ignition and threw them in the back seat. I turned around to try to locate them in the dark and saw a car approaching. I grabbed her by the scruff of the neck, or rather, by the collar of her Calvin Klein black leather jacket just in time to prevent her from opening the car door.

"Duck down! Somebody's coming."

Cassie and I dove for the floor at the same time and banged each other on the head so hard we saw stars.

"Ow! My God, Mom, I always knew you were hardheaded," she whispered. "I think I'm bleeding."

I struggled to clear the ringing in my ears, "Don't be a goose. That's just something wet down here on the carpet."

I felt around with my hand on the floorboard.

"Yuck! Wet and sticky. Remind me to get the car cleaned this weekend."

"Sure thing. If we're still at liberty."

"Are they gone, Mother?"

I dared a peek up over the seat.

"You mean, is he gone?'"

"He who?"

"Horatio, that's who!"

I could hear the anger in her voice.

"Did he see us?"

"I certainly hope not! How could I ever explain this utter nonsense to him?"

"What in the world is Mr. Horatio Raleigh doing out at this time of night?"

"Maybe he's two-timing you, Gran."

"Don't be foolish, Cassandra. You know we don't have that kind of relationship."

"Maybe you don't, but he does."

"He probably has a stiff to prepare for a funeral tomorrow."

"Don't be vulgar, Paisley."

Cassie and I sat back up in the seat and looked around cautiously. All the stores were now closed. The only sounds we heard were the katydids and the crickets singing in the yards of the big houses that still bordered the edge of the business district of Rowan Springs.

"It's now or never," I whispered. "You still with us, Mother? Or are you going to fink out again?"

She sighed dramatically, "I'm here, aren't I? Just please do it quickly."

"Okay. Here's what we do. Mother, you open the front door and push down on the little button so the overhead light won't turn on. Cassie will sneak out of her door, and I'll get out on this side. We'll cross over the street up by the alley and go in through the back entrance. That is, if this lock-picking set I bought at the Spy Factory works."

I patted my pocket where I had hidden the nifty little set a locksmith friend had told me about for one of Leonard's heists.

"I understand, Paisley. Good luck, and please be careful. It would be a shame to tarnish the Sterling family name with a police record."

"You should have thought of that earlier. Go, Cassie!"

We opened the doors as quietly as we could and slid out of the car. Cassie pulled her turtleneck up over the lower part of her face so that only her eyes could be seen in the dark. I hunched my shoulders down and pulled the collar of my black denim jacket up. It was the best I could do.

We scurried across the street and hid for a moment behind a big holly bush at the corner of the dentist's office.

"Ow!"

"What?"

"Prickles."

I crouched down as low as I could and ran across to the alley. Two large garbage cans next to Doc Baxter's back entrance afforded the perfect hiding place while I tried my hand at picking the lock.

Five minutes later I was cursing and sweating like a long-shoreman.

"Damn! It wasn't this hard when Jimmy did it."

"Let me try, Mom."

"Did you go with me to the Spy Factory? Did you see how it was done? Do you even know Jimmy? I think not!"

"Let me try while you rest a minute."

I let Cass take the lock-picking tools and slumped down on the cold, hard cement of the doorstep, wiping the sweat out of my eyes. My hands were trembling and my heart was pounding.

"I want my money back, that's what I want. Forty dollars for nothing but three broken nails, a skinned knuckle, and . . . "

"And an open door! Come on, Mom, we don't have all night."

Unpleasant childhood memories of the measles, mumps, and chicken pox came back in a rush as the medicinal smell of alcohol and ether filled the darkness.

"Doc Baxter's private office is in the back, down that hallway." I stepped in front of her. "Here, follow me, and pull your sweater back down off your face or you'll sweat to death."

We made our way cautiously down the hallway past four examination rooms, two on each side. The old-fashioned leather examining tables were now covered with white disposable paper. I remembered crisp white sheets which I had held onto for dear life while I wailed in terrified misery as my sore throat or aching ears were probed and poked.

There was a small dispensary on the left at the end of the hall, its shelves crammed with boxes of pharmaceutical samples, cotton balls, and gauze bandages of all sizes. Large bottles of different-colored liquids balanced precariously on a shelf sway-backed with age. I wondered how long it would be before it all came tumbling down. After only three weeks unattended, the office already looked abandoned and forlorn.

Edgar Baxter had started his professional life in this office when he was a young doctor straight out of medical school. His wife, Julia, had been his nurse and receptionist for the first few years until they had "made it," then Julia quit working and started trying to have babies. She never succeeded. Bored and bitter, she finally found solace in alcohol and the drug samples she took from the office. She'd died almost eighteen months ago of chronic liver disease. And though no one ever acknowledged it out of respect for Doc Baxter, she had been an alcoholic, plain and simple.

CHAPTER FIFTEEN

The private office Edgar Baxter had occupied for over four decades was much neater than I had expected. It was situated in a large interior room with no windows to distract him. There were two doors: the door from the hallway and another one which opened to a bathroom. The bathroom had another door as well, that opened into the dark pharmacy. The facilities were apparently shared.

Each of us had brought little penlights, but I now turned on the larger flashlight I had tucked into the back of my jeans and upended it on the desk as we looked around the room.

One wall was occupied by floor-to-ceiling shelves of medical books and journals. I checked some of the dates. Most of them were current issues. Apparently the doc kept up with the latest professional news.

All of the drawers of his big old oak desk were unlocked and opened easily but neither of us could find anything of interest—just pens and paper clips and other office supplies.

Baxter had no computer. Old-fashioned oak file cabinets no doubt held the information I was seeking. I took the list of patients I had printed from Ethan's computer out of my pocket and went to pull the charts.

"Hey Mom," whispered Cassie, "look at this!"

How many times had I heard my daughter say that during the last twenty years?

"Don't bother me now, Cassie. We can't stay here forever," I replied in an irritable whisper.

"Okay then, if you don't want to examine a large cardboard filing box labeled 'Obstetrical Patients 1997-2000.'"

"You're kidding!"

"Shsssss!"

"Wonder what this is doing here?"

"I don't know. I just found it tucked under the desk. It looks like he was planning to move it somewhere."

"Terrific! Let's just take the whole box home."

"But, Mom, he's bound to come back looking for it. What'll we do then?"

"Look, Cassie, we can't possibly review all the charts under these conditions."

"You're right there, Sherlock. You're sweating like a pig, and I'm about to die in this wool sweater. It's like a greenhouse in here. You'd think they would have turned off the furnace to save money when they closed the office."

"Probably can't. These old buildings only have one common furnace, and the pharmacy is still open for business."

"So what's your plan, Mom?"

My throat ached from the forced whispering and I was dying for a cold drink.

"Let's take this file box home and go over it at our leisure—meaning tonight and tomorrow. We can bring it back tomorrow night and no one will be the wiser."

"We hope!"

"We hope."

"Okay, I'm with you. You grab that end. I've got this one."

Cass hefted her end of the box. It was heavier than it looked. She staggered and accidentally backed into a small table in the corner.

There was a loud crash and the sudden smell of something pungent and medicinal.

"Damn! What in the world is that?"

I held my nose against the odor as I bent down to pick up the broken bottle. The wet label was already smeared and barely legible.

"All I can tell is it's 'highly flammable.'"

"Great!"

Cass set the box down and opened the door to the bathroom.

"There are some paper towels in here. We can clean it up and toss the bottle. Maybe the doctor will forget it was ever here by the time he comes back."

"What's that!"

Our voices had grown increasingly louder. I dropped mine back to an urgent whisper as I turned my flashlight off and peeked out of the crack in the door to the hallway. Down by the entrance, another light was bobbing along with someone's measured tread. We only had a few moments before they reached us. I closed the door as quietly as I could.

"Quick! Grab the box and let's get out of here."

"How?"

There was panic in her voice.

"Through the bathroom. The pharmacy is on the other side. We can get outside from there. Hurry!"

We each lifted the heavy file box and lugged it into the bathroom. I closed that door and turned the inside lock hoping the locked door would buy us some extra time.

Cass braced her end of the box on her hip as she opened the other door into the pharmacy. The street lights shone in brightly through the big front windows. We no longer needed our flashlights. As a matter of fact, if anyone had peered in from the street they could have seen us huffing and puffing as we dragged the heavy box across the back of the store to the side exit.

"Do you think they have an alarm system?"

"There's only one way to find out." I told her. "Open the door and get ready to run."

Cass bit her lip and opened the door. Nothing happened.

"Thank God! Now let's go!"

Cass opened the door wider and peeked out.

"Gran's gone!"

"Don't be silly. You just can't see Watson under those trees."

I awkwardly maneuvered my side of the box around to the door and looked out to the empty street.

"Mother's gone!"

"Duh!"

"My God, what'll we do?" My mouth was dry as a bone and my breath rattled in my throat like a pair of dice.

"Well, we could walk out of here totin' this one ton box. It's only four miles or so to the farm," Cassie hissed. "I'm sure no one will notice us, including whoever that is in the doctor's office."

"Twit!"

"Okay, then tell me 'O great writer of mysteries,' what would The Honorable Leonard Paisley do?"

My heart leapt with joy and relief as I saw Watson speeding down the side street with my beloved mother behind the wheel.

"He would hitch a ride with Mata Hari! Let's go!"

Mother careened to the curb and slammed on the brakes. We dashed out and opened the back door—overhead light be damned! Cassie pulled and I pushed the heavy box into the back seat, and we piled in on top of it. I started to shout something dramatic like "Fly like the wind!" but Mother needed no encouragement. She was down the block, around the courthouse, and halfway home before I caught enough of my breath to admonish her.

"Where have you been? You had us scared half to death!"

"I had a nature call," she sniffed. "I had to run home for a moment."

"You had to pee! And you left us swinging in the wind for that?"

"Don't be common, Paisley. What was I supposed to do? I don't have a car commode like Queen Elizabeth, and I really had to go. Maybe we should invest in . . . "

I sank down on the cardboard box. The top folded in under my weight, but I was exhausted and way past caring. I let her prattle on about the advisability of our purchasing a port-a-potty for Watson until we reached the safety and comfort of home sweet home.

Cass and I carried the box to the library and dropped it in front of the fireplace with weary relief. Mother hurried to the kitchen to try and appease our anger at being abandoned by fixing us a celebratory feast.

I was in the middle of my second roast beef and horseradish on a sourdough bun when I heard the siren.

"Is that the fire alarm?"

"Yes, dear. It's still mounted on the top of the fire station. They only use it when there's a really big fire and they need to call out the volunteer firemen."

"Too bad Mavis is still so angry, Mother. You could phone and find out what's going on."

"I imagine it will be quite some time before Mavis speaks to me again. Amy from our Sunday School class called this afternoon to tell me Mavis was sitting propped up on the sofa with her leg bandaged to the hip. She has that poor simple husband of hers running around fetching ice cream and bonbons and magazines. Mavis is quite the actress."

I was still curious about the fire. "Who else has a police radio?"

"Forget about calling anyone, Mom. In case you hadn't noticed, it's twenty past three."

I yawned hugely, "No wonder I'm so sleepy. Those files will have to wait until tomorrow. After all, 'tomorrow is another day.'"

"I've heard that before. If I weren't so sleepy, I might remember where."

"You poor culturally deprived little child. What did the sisters at the Escuela San Romero teach you? Remind me to take your not-so-classical literary education in hand some day."

Mother had slipped off her high-heeled boots, and looked petite and fragile in her stocking feet. I was beginning to feel guilty about my outburst in the car.

"I'm sorry I got angry, Mother. I was just acting out of fear. You really had us scared there for a moment."

She waved her hand distractedly. "Forget about it."

"Then is something else the matter?"

She looked at me with the lovely brown eyes that Cass had inherited. "It's just that sometimes I think perhaps we get carried away and do things we shouldn't."

"Like break into your doctor's office and steal his files?"

"Exactly."

"Point well taken. Let's go to bed."

"Goodnight, dear."

She leaned over and gave me a quick peck on the cheek. "In case you haven't noticed, your daughter has fallen asleep on her plate."

CHAPTER SIXTEEN

I felt a sense of *deja vu* when I got up the next morning and looked out of the bathroom window. Chief Andy Joiner was here again. He was leaning his big, rumpled, bear's body against his police cruiser and talking to Mother. This time I opened the window just a tad so I could hear their conversation.

" . . . started in the Doc's office and spread to the drug store. It looks like arson, but we can't be sure until all the tests are back from the lab in Nashville."

Joiner ran his big hands thorough his thinning hair.

"Whoever did it broke into the office through the service entrance. We don't know if anything was taken. Doc Baxter says he never kept any money there. And what equipment he had was too old to be worth much. Nobody seems to have any idea who would want to torch the place, or why. The building is not worth much by today's standards but the insurance won't begin to replace it. Doc Baxter seemed almost relieved when I told him, like the fire kinda set him free. He's tired. I don't think those of us who've known him for so long realized just how tired he got taking care of us for all these years. I hope he goes away and gets some rest. Maybe he can sit on a beach somewhere and do nothing for a while."

Joiner paused. That had been a long speech for him. He seemed very ill at ease and more than a little embarrassed. When he continued, I realized that he had been talking to avoid getting to the unpleasant reason for his early morning visit.

"I came out this morning, Miz Sterling, because last night someone saw a vehicle leaving the scene of the fire. They said it looked something like that Jeep Cherokee of your daughter's. It was that same weird green color, too. And one of the firemen found this in the middle of the street."

He reached in his car and pulled out the windshield wiper that had snapped off Watson last night.

"Damn!' I whispered under my breath. We were dead ducks for sure.

Joiner was showing the wiper blade to Mother.

"I'm afraid I'm gonna have to ask you to let me take a look at your vehicle. That is, if you don't mind, M'am."

I picked up my comb with trembling fingers and tried to smooth the night's sleep out of my hair. No use going out to 'fess up looking like a total wreck. I wondered what to wear to jail. It should be something comfortable, something that would not show wrinkles or dirt too easily. Mother would know just what to choose. I looked back outside and watched as she carefully examined the incriminating piece of metal.

"It certainly looks like a windshield wiper," she agreed. "But how can you tell what car it came from? They all look alike to me."

He held it out arm's length so he could find what he was looking for.

"See there, the name . . . 'Jeep' . . . those tiny little letters."

Apparently Chief Joiner was getting very farsighted.

"Oh," she responded carefully.

"Like I said, Miz Sterling," he insisted, "I need to see your wagon."

"Well, I'm sorry, Andy, but my granddaughter has gone out in it this morning. When she gets back I'll surely call you." Her smile was tight and brittle.

He looked everywhere but at her face. I almost felt sorry for him.

"It's not that easy. I'm gonna have to stay here till she gets back, just in case."

"Just in case what, Andy?" she asked pointedly.

"Well, you know."

"Are you suggesting that my daughter had anything to do with that unfortunate business downtown last night?"

He rocked back and forth from one big-booted foot to the other, thrusting his hands roughly in his pockets, probably to keep from chewing on his fingernails.

"Look, Miz Sterling . . . "

"And one could infer from your conversation," she continued unrelentingly, "that you think we might be so bold and impertinent as to try to circumvent justice."

Joiner looked heavenward as if begging God to open a hole in the ground so he could fall in and disappear. He looked miserable.

About that time I heard the sound of a car engine. Cass was coming around the circular driveway towards the house.

I mentally reviewed my options for an incarceration wardrobe again while I watched my mother turn a particularly interesting shade of green, somewhere between celadon and mint.

Joiner turned toward Cass as she drove up the gravel driveway. She slowed down as she neared the two of them. With the engine still running, she called out, "Hi Gran! Hi Chief Joiner! Tell Mom I forgot her hair spray. I'll be back in a few minutes. You want something from the grocery?"

Mother looked like she was going to vomit but she gamely held up her end of the conversation.

"Yes, dear, get some celery."

Cass laughed gaily. She hated celery and we all knew it. I imagine that she knew Mother could think of nothing else because her attention was on not one, but two, bright and shiny windshield wipers. They were sitting exactly where they should be on Watson's front windscreen.

Cass pulled on around the driveway and headed back towards town. Andy Joiner and Mother stood for a moment and watched her leave. Then Mother turned to face him, flashing a brilliant smile.

"Well, Andy, give Connie my love. We'd really like to have you all out for dinner sometime soon. Tell her to give me a call and we'll arrange things just between us girls."

Andy smiled back. He looked almost as relieved as Mother did.

"Sure thing Miz Sterling. We'd like that. Constance thinks the world of you. And she loved Paisley's last book."

He hopped in his cruiser with the agility of a man half his age and no cares in the world. He even waved as he drove off.

I turned away from the window to realize that I had been holding my breath for what seemed like ten minutes. My head was spinning and little black stars sparkled in front of my eyes. I sank slowly to the cold tile floor because my knees were too weak to hold me up. I was still there when Mother came bursting into the bathroom.

"How did she do it? How did that blessed child manage to pull that off?"

She smiled gaily into the mirror as she ran my comb through the sides of her always flawless hairdo.

"My, your father would have been proud of her today, and her's too, no doubt."

"No doubt," I answered sourly.

Rafe was always one for outsmarting the authorities.

Cass did not return until after I had showered, dressed, and had two cups of really strong tea with lots of little raw sugar cubes. I was beginning to feel more like myself when she came bouncing into the kitchen, all smiles and good humor.

"Whatcha think, huh? Am I not the best, the greatest, just the cat's meow?"

"You've been listening to too much Glenn Miller, but 'yes' to all of the above, my sweet. Now tell us how you managed to pull it off."

She pulled out a kitchen chair and plopped down.

"Pull it off is exactly what I did."

She turned to Mother. "Sorry Gran, but you'll have to replace one of the windshield wipers on your Continental."

"What?"

Mother loved her car. It was white with red leather seats. She cut quite a sporty figure behind the wheel.

"Well, you see, after I passed out on the table last night I couldn't really get back to sleep once I went to bed. I guess I got overstimulated. Like you used to say I did when I played too hard, Mom. Anyway, I started thinking about our little adventure, and I remembered the wiper popping off in the street. As far as I know, it's the only piece of evidence we left behind. I decided to go back early this morning and retrieve it so nobody could trace it to us. But then I thought, what if somebody sees that Watson is minus a wiper and guesses what happened? I went down to the garage and tried to unhook Gran's. I finally had to break it off," she added apologetically. "And I superglued it onto Watson. Then I went to town and saw . . . Mom, it's all burned down. The doctor's office, the drug store . . . it's just a smoldering mess of rubble. And it stinks. I guess from all those chemicals."

She grabbed both of my hands. "Do you think I started the fire? Remember, when I knocked over that bottle of flammable what-ever-it-was?"

"I don't know, Cassie. I honestly don't know."

A horrible thought occurred to me. "Oh, my God, what if that other person was burned in the fire?"

"Oh, Mom, I didn't think of that!" Cassie's white face mirrored what my own must have looked like.

"Take it easy, you two, and calm down. Andy told me that no bodies were found in the building. What's more, the fire started not in Edgar's private office, but in the dispensary."

"Thank God!"

Cass sank back down in the seat and poured herself a cup of tea with shaking hands.

"Yes, thank God that we are only burglars and not arsonists or murderers. But do you realize that now we have a file box full of charts and nowhere to return them?"

"Can't we just take them to Edgar, dear?"

"Oh, yeah, and say what? 'Hi Doc, here's the files we stole out of your office the night it burned down. Sorry we couldn't sneak them back in like we had planned, but, oh well!'"

"Hmm, I see what you mean. That does pose somewhat of a problem."

"Well, Mom, just look at it this way. At least we have all the time in the world to check them out now."

She stuffed some more buttered toast in her mouth, her worries about being a murderer apparently forgotten.

"And if we find something," I mused, "how can we introduce that 'something' as evidence to clear Ethan's name when we purloined the files in the first place? We'll be incriminating ourselves."

"I'll go to prison to save Ethan," declared Cass.

"Not me."

"Mom!"

"Who'd feed Aggie?"

We took a vote after our late breakfast and decided three to nothing to take the rest of the day off. Besides, we had to go to Morgantown and get a new wiper blade. Cass was a little reluctant at first because she was counting the days that Ethan had been behind bars. They added up to a grand total of four by now. She had called Teddyville three times each day to inquire about him but had never been allowed to talk to him personally. His hearing had been postponed another week, so he would have to stay there at least ten more days no matter what we did. I convinced her we had to cover ourselves first so we could continue to try and help him.

We left for Morgantown.

My college friend, Bubba, who had sold me Watson, was only too happy to slip me a new windshield wiper under the table. Getting it on the car was another problem. I knew Bubba would never tell the police we had been there, but I was concerned about the rest of his employees, so we drove to an isolated picnic spot near the lake. We had to tug and scrape and pull and push because Cassandra had used extra heavy-duty superglue, but finally, with the help of some really smelly fingernail polish remover, we got the wiper from the Lincoln off of Watson. Attaching the new one was a piece of cake. Now no one would ever be the wiser. Except we had to go buy another wiper blade for the Continental.

By the time we had accomplished all of our CYA "Cover Your Ass" errands it was nearly four o'clock, and we were famished. When Mother suggested that we eat at Sallie's, we readily agreed. We had not been there since last year, and I, for one, could manage a tender, juicy, two-inch-thick pork chop at least once every twelve months.

The servers were still wearing silly *Gone with the Wind* dresses with paper flowers in their hair, but the food was good, and the homemade flowerpot bread was fresh and hot.

It had been a while since we had been out, and after last night, we needed to relax. My batter-fried mozzarella sticks were the best yet. Cassie moaned passionately over her Hot Brown with Mornay sauce, while Mother delicately devoured a large dinner salad. The meal was great, and the company couldn't be improved upon. It wasn't until I was licking the last drop of burnt caramel sauce off my dessert spoon that I heard the commotion.

A rowdy customer in the back dining room was apparently

causing the staff some real problems. Twice, I observed the manager hurrying past with a worried look on his face. A few minutes later two strong-looking young busboys quietly ushered the problem customer outside. Mother and I clearly saw Dr. Winston Wallace being firmly escorted out the back door. He was accompanied by a blonde who definitely was no lady, and just as definitely not his wife.

CHAPTER SEVENTEEN

We drove home through the natural forest that was the land bridge between the two lakes. I lowered the windows so we could enjoy the sweet fragrance of the wild honeysuckle. The air was warm and almost balmy with a soft, gentle breeze blowing from the direction of the lake. We got an occasional glimpse of the shore through the screen of pine and cedar. The still, dark water was calm, and its surface mirrored the big white moon above. It was a beautiful romantic night that was definitely meant for two.

Cass was very subdued. I surmised correctly that she was missing Ethan.

"Don't fret, Munchkin, he'll be free soon."

"I hope so, Mom. I really hope so."

"Cassandra dear, your Ethan is a very intelligent and resourceful young man. I'm positive he will weather this little difficulty with no ill effects whatsoever."

"Gran, if you say 'someday you'll look back on this and laugh,' I swear I'll pitch you out of the car."

"Why, I would never say anything so trite. I might, however, express that same sentiment in a more unique and creative way. It is true, you know, dear."

"I don't think so, Gran. It may have been true for you and Mom.

I know both of you have been through some really tough times. You and Grandad had a terrible war to endure. Mom and Dad protected me during a wild South American revolution. But I'm afraid I'm not made of the same stern stuff as you two." Her voice broke. "I don't think I can keep my chin up much longer."

I thought about stopping the car and consoling her, but Mother had other ideas.

"What utter nonsense! I can hardly believe my ears. You, my dear child, are full of . . . what does your mother say? Crap!"

"Gran!"

"Mother!"

"Well, I mean it, Cassandra. Don't you know that being afraid and full of doubt doesn't mean you're not courageous? Courage is going on with your life no matter how frightened and doubtful you are. You have shown some real backbone these last few days. You have been clearheaded and quick-witted enough to take care of details the rest of us overlooked. I congratulate you for that."

"Thanks, Gran. I guess sometimes I just feel like small potatoes around you and Mom."

"Wow, am I dreaming?"

"No, Mom. I really admire you both. And I appreciate the way you all have handled this business with Ethan. Neither of you has ever once suggested that he could be guilty, and you've both taken tremendous chances trying to help him. I don't know anyone else who has such a terrific family. I am a very lucky girl."

I was speechless. I had just received the maternal equivalent of the Oscar, the Tony, and the Pulitzer. My first thought was of Rafe. How proud he would have been of his little girl; he had loved her so very much. I suddenly wished for him with all of my heart and soul. I didn't allow myself to do that very often. It served no purpose and only made me sad. I bit my lip and struggled against the tears that threatened. After all, I was made of sterner stuff. My daughter told me so.

Mother said she was exhausted and went to bed as soon as we got home. I think she was as touched as I had been by her granddaughter's speech and simply wanted to savor it in solitude.

Cass and I grabbed some iced tea and headed for the library. We had work to do.

We pushed the heavy cardboard file box around until it was under the bright light of the floor lamp. Just like it said on the top, it contained the files on obstetrical patients for the last three-and-a-half years. Yesterday, I had found a notation on one of Ethan's logs that the average birth rate for Rowan Springs was seven to ten births a month. It was clear that Doc Baxter had more than his share of the patients. There were at least three hundred manila folders in the box. I pulled one out at random and began to read.

"Well, we need a medical dictionary, that's for sure. And maybe a Sanskrit translator."

"How so?" asked Cassie.

"Take a peek at the handwriting of our esteemed medical practitioner."

"Hmm, Sister Maria Mercedes would definitely give him a D- in penmanship."

"I always thought that ridiculous scratching on prescriptions was some sort of code that only the pharmacist could decipher. Looks like it goes farther than that."

"It must be something they teach in medical school."

"Yeah, 'Obfuscation 101.'"

"Obfus-what?"

"It means 'I can't remember how to spell pancreas, but if I write like this, no one will ever be the wiser.'"

"How in the world are we going to be able to find something in these charts that will clear Ethan if we can't even read them?"

I sighed. I didn't have an answer for her.

We divided the first year of charts in two, and each of us took a pile to one of the sofas to read. Cassandra was asleep within five minutes. The folders slid off her lap and onto the carpeted floor like a deck of cards. I smiled and got up to cover her with the afghan. After all, she had been up since early this morning saving our butts. I kissed her softly on the forehead and sat back down.

I read through ten charts before I started to get the hang of things. Each folder held an average of three forms. The first page was an assessment of the patient on her first visit to the doctor. It recorded her name, address, and all the rest of her demographic information. Her medical and family history and a physical exam report were also on this front sheet. The next two pages were a log of sorts, which listed the dates of all prenatal visits and the results of the doctor's findings. There was a space on the bottom of the last page for the outcome of the pregnancy. Certain other things were noted there as well, such as whether or not the patient wanted a Caesarian section at delivery or a tubal ligation afterwards. On one chart, there was a notation that the pregnancy was a result of rape. Another stated that the mother wanted to give the baby up for adoption.

I began to feel like a slimy, sleazy, Peeping Tom. This information was private and very confidential. I decided that we had no business pawing through the most intimate details of other people's lives. We would have to find another way to help Ethan.

Cassie moaned and shifted position in her sleep. Aggie trotted over from her resting place by the door and hopped up on her stomach.

"Uhpff!"

"Sorry, honey, I should have stopped her, but I was getting ready to wake you up anyway. It's time to go to bed."

"But what about all this?" she questioned sleepily as she waved a tired hand at the folders on the floor.

"I'll tell you about it tomorrow. You've had a long day. Go to bed."

"Okay, Mom. I love you."

I got up and gave her a big hug.

"I love you, too. You're the most wonderful daughter anyone ever had. Thanks again for what you said on the way home from Sallie's."

"Umm."

She gave me a crooked smile and stumbled off to her bedroom with her fussy little dog bringing up the rear.

I opened the French doors and sat back on the sofa to enjoy the soothing night music of the crickets and katydids. It had been a year since someone had crept into this very room bent on my untimely demise, and I was just now becoming comfortable with open doors in my own home.

Mother had assured Cassie that Ethan would come out of this business unscathed. I wasn't so certain. I had experienced the posttraumatic effects of life-threatening situations. I had suffered nightmares for years after we left San Romero. The worst one, which I shared with no one, was that Cassandra had disappeared along with my husband. I had awakened from that little nocturnal epic drenched in sweat and crying like a baby.

No matter how brave Ethan pretended to be to impress my daughter, I was sure he had bad dreams about that terrible disease-filled cave in Africa. We were all frail and vulnerable inside no matter how tall and strong we appeared on the outside, and Dr. Ethan McHenry was no exception.

A strange sound echoed in the dark recesses of the backyard, and the katydids immediately paused in their raucous chorus. I jumped up and hurriedly closed and locked the doors. A quick dew of perspiration coated my upper lip like a little wet mustache, and my heart played a game of leapfrog between my ribs. I went to my room reciting a short, quiet litany of prayers for the safety of those I loved. I ended my spiritual conversation with a plea for dreamless sleep, put on my nightgown, and crawled into bed.

CHAPTER EIGHTEEN

The next morning we held a war council at the breakfast table. Cassie didn't share my squeamish concerns about invading the privacy of the women whose charts we had stolen. Mother, however, agreed with me.

"Paisley's right, darling. I have felt all along that we shouldn't have taken that route to help Ethan. Nothing good can come from a negative act. We need to keep everything we do open and above-board."

"Now you're talking about Karma, Gran. I thought you pished and tushed my so-called heathen beliefs."

"I don't know anything about your Karma, dear," huffed Mother. "I do know there are plenty of biblical commandments to tell us what we should and should not do."

Cassie opened her mouth to continue the argument, but I interrupted.

"What did Moses say about a regular visit to the doctor?"

"What? Not again, Paisley!"

It took me thirty minutes to convince my mother to make an appointment with Dr. Winston Wallace.

When she finally did call, the receptionist was efficient and polite and promised to work Mother into Wallace's morning schedule. I suspected the doctor wasn't as busy as his staff tried to make us believe. He wasn't exactly being discrete about his girlfriend, and Rowan Springs was a typical small Southern town. The people here might enjoy the notion of quiet romantic liaison, but they would disapprove of a flagrant "in your face" affair. I would be surprised if his appointment book did not reflect their disapproval.

We drove to town in Mother's Lincoln. One thing we had all agreed on was that Watson had better stay out of sight and out of mind for a while. On the way, we had a heated discussion about the purpose of our visit. I wanted to check the layout of Wallace's office in case we needed to make a midnight visit to his digs. I also wanted to see how he handled himself after last night's little debacle at Sallie's. Maybe we would get lucky and see if his lady friend was an employee. Mother disagreed with our going altogether. She particularly objected to our suggestions about what her chief complaint should be.

"Cassandra, I think it's very disrespectful of you to suggest that your grandmother has pinworms."

"I didn't say you had them, Gran. I just said you could complain of itching around your . . . "

"Please, my dear, that's quite enough! This really won't do. Paisley, turn the car around. I cannot imagine how I allowed myself to be talked into this. Paisley, I said turn around!"

I pulled over to the curb and parked. "Look, Mother, unless you want Wallace pawing over your virginal . . . " I turned and glared at Cass, "granddaughter, you will have to be the patient. You're the only one who can keep him occupied while we snoop around. After all, you're the lady with the marvelous gift of gab. I might just slug him, and Cassie, well, Cassie is out of the question."

She pulled down the visor and checked on her beautifully coifed hair and perfectly made-up face.

"All right, I'll do it. But I'll decide what my ailment is. No more suggestions from the vestal virgin. Agreed?"

"Absolutely," I assured her.

"Cassandra?"

"Of course, Gran, just as you wish," she said, smiling wickedly at me in the rear view mirror. "Now about this 'virgin' thing . . . "

"Cass, that's quite enough."

Winston Wallace's clinic was in a modern office building on the edge of town. There was a lot of cedar and smoked glass, but very little actual design to the place. The structure looked like something between a New Age cathedral and a Japanese sushi restaurant.

There was one beat-up old farm truck in the patient's parking lot. Behind the building, I could see an older model BMW, a new Mazda sports coupe, and a Ford Taurus which had seen better days.

At first we had trouble finding the front entrance in the expanse of smoked glass and cedar shake. We had to walk across a "garden" of varicolored pebbles and slate stepping stones to reach the door. On each side of the entrance was a wide empty hole lined with heavy black plastic. I puzzled over what the holes were for until I saw the dried-out water lilies and the rotting dead fish at the bottom.

"Ugh, nasty!"

I had to agree with my daughter.

The reception room was a pleasant surprise. The smoked glass let in enough light to give a mellow look to the severely modern furniture, and large ceramic pots of well-tended plants graced every corner. The floors were Mexican tile with a judicious scattering of hand-woven rugs here and there, and several large paintings on the walls, mostly with a Southwestern motif, added just enough color. I wondered who was responsible for the décor—Wallace, his wife, his mistress, or his decorator.

Mother walked slowly up to the receptionist's desk. She looked for all the world like a little kid being forced to go to the dentist.

"I'm Mrs. John Sterling. I called earlier for an appointment."

A handsome middle-aged woman with a fresh clean face and salt-and-pepper hair appeared at the window.

"Hello, Mrs. Sterling, I'm Poppy Hunnicutt. I'm really pleased to meet you. My brother played football at the high school when your husband was coach."

Mother's face blazed in embarrassment. She hadn't counted on having to misrepresent herself to someone she knew. But like the true Southern lady she was, she held her head high and pushed on.

"Why, of course, Poppy. I remember Hank very well. He was a charming boy. We were so sorry to hear . . . "

Poppy's smile covered an old hurt as she interrupted, "Yes, well, we all were." She noticed me and Cassie for the first time. "Are these your daughters?"

Mother smiled at the compliment. "This is my daughter Paisley and my granddaughter Cassandra. They're staying with me for a while."

"Nice to meet you both," said Poppy with that smile again. It made her seem too good to be true. I was reminded of Willy Shakespeare's ". . .smile, and smile and be a villain."

"Now what is your complaint, Mrs. Sterling? Why are you seeing the doctor today?"

Cassie and I crowded up behind Mother. Neither of us wanted to miss this. But she was too smart for us.

"May I fill out one of those little questionnaires?" She pointed to a clipboard with some printed forms attached to it that was hanging from the desk. "I'm sure that will apprise the doctor of my problem."

"Why, of course. Here's a pencil. Just bring it back to me when you're finished. The doctor will be with you shortly."

Cassie and I looked at each other.

"Damn," she whispered. "Mom, go sit beside her and see if you can read what she writes. I'm dying to know."

But Mother chose a seat in the corner, well away from the rest of us. There was nothing we could do but sit opposite each other on the big squishy Italian leather sofas and read old magazines. I was halfway through the March issue of "*SKI!*" when Poppy opened the door and asked Mother to follow her. Cassie and I stayed in our seats and waited for a full five minutes. When Poppy didn't return to the front desk, I got up and casually made my way over to the door. I pushed it open to see long, carpeted corridor opening to four examining rooms. There was another door at the end marked with the unisex symbols for men and women, obviously a bathroom. That gave me an idea of what my excuse would be if I got caught. I motioned for Cassie to stay seated and then slipped through the door.

I slunk down the hall like a good little sleuth, pressing my ear against each door and listening as I passed by. Mother was in the second room on the left. I heard her arguing with Poppy about the necessity of removing her clothing and smiled at the exchange. I knew Mother would hold her own.

There had been one other car in the patient's parking lot and no one in the waiting room. Somewhere there had to be another patient. Sure enough, just as I reached the last door on the right I heard the knob turn and saw the door opening. I darted back to the next empty room. I had barely made it inside when Dr. Winston Wallace stepped out into the hallway. I peered through a crack in the door and watched as the doctor helped an old man on crutches hobble back to the waiting room.

"Mr. Jackson, you have to stay off that knee if you want it to heal. No more farming for at least two weeks. You had a nasty cut and a worse infection. The pills I gave you will help, but you can help yourself more by just resting for a while with your leg up."

"But Doc, I got nobody to help me and it's hayin' time. I gotta mow before it rains."

"Look, Jackson, I can't be responsible if you don't take my advice. If you don't like what I have to say, then find yourself another doctor. But be sure and pay his bills faster than you pay mine."

"Aw, Doc, I don't mean nothing against you. I'm just up again' it."

The door closed on them, and I couldn't hear the rest of their conversation. I started to leave my hiding place when Wallace opened the waiting room door and called out.

"Betty Lou! Can you please come up to the front?"

The floozy from last night stuck her blonde, overly permed head out of the bathroom.

"Whatcha want me for?"

"Poppy is with a patient, and Mr. Jackson needs to make another appointment."

"Sooorry! It's my lunchtime."

She left the bathroom and walked slowly toward Wallace. Her hips swayed with the rocking motion of a small boat in high seas. Her white uniform was very short, very tight, and cut very low in the front. Instead of white stockings and thick-soled occupational shoes she had on black high-heeled sandals with stockings to match.

"Please, Betty Lou, can't you help our patient first?"

"Soooory."

She spoke the word very slowly with an excruciatingly unpleasant accent.

"This morning you distinctly said that I was to leave and return from my lunch exactly on time. Now didn't you say that?"

"Well, yes I did." Wallace hurried down the hall and met Betty Lou almost in front of the room in which I was hiding.

"Dearest," he whispered, "please try and cooperate a little. You know daddy will make it up to you."

"Weeell . . . " She pouted perfectly drawn bright red lips.

"I'm sorry I spoke so sharply about your timecard, but three hours for lunch yesterday was a bit much, don't you think?"

"If I stay and help out, I'll be late again today, and you'll be mad."

She snaked her ankle around his leg and rubbed her inner thigh against his hip.

"No, darling, I promise. If you help out now you can stay an extra half . . . "

"Ummm?"

She poked him in the chest with a long red fingernail.

"Okay, you can stay another hour." His breath was coming in huffs and puffs like an old steam engine.

She broke away from him and straightened her short skirt over her hips. "Okay, I'll give the old geezer an appointment. But you tell that bitch not to get all bent out of shape if I mess up her precious appointment book. She thinks she owns the place. She's always making nasty cracks when you're not around. I hate being treated like trash, sweetie," she whined. "When are you gonna get rid of Poppy like you promised?"

"Now's not the time to discuss . . . "

Betty Lou was suddenly furious.

"You always want something when you want it! I never have what I want when I want it! When is it time for Betty Lou? Never! That's when. Take care of your stupid old patient yourself! I'm going to lunch. And just maybe," she added slyly, "I'll take the rest of the afternoon off. I don't feel so good. I got a headache coming on, and I think maybe it's gonna last all week, if you get my drift!"

"But, baby!"

She pushed past him and out the door into the front waiting room. He started to follow and then turned and hurried back to the room I was in. I backed hastily away from the door. Wallace turned the knob and started to push it open. The farmer saved me.

"Doc? When do you want me to come back? I gotta get going. The missus is waitin' down to the catalog store for me to pick her up. She'll be madder than a wet hen."

"I'm sorry, Mr. Jackson. Listen, Miss Hunnicutt will call you tomorrow and set up another appointment, okay?"

"Thanks, and I promise I'll try and rest some this afternoon."

"Wonderful, just wonderful."

During their exchange I looked frantically around for some-place to hide. The room was bare except for the examining table, a chair, a sink, and a dirty clothes hamper. The hamper was my only option. I quietly moved the chair next to the hamper, climbed up in the seat and then stepped down inside what was really a large cloth bag on a frame. I pulled a dirty towel up over my head and held my breath.

One second later, the door opened and I heard Wallace step inside. He pulled the chair back across the room. I heard the paper on the examining table crinkle and tear as he climbed up. There was another sound, like a bottle uncorking, and then a gurgle. The idiot was drinking on the job! More paper tore as he climbed down and cleaned off the table. And then he was gone.

I climbed carefully out of the hamper, sat in the chair, and looked up. The ceiling was made of a suspended tile system. One of the tiles directly over the examining table was slightly askew. I gently lifted the roll of paper off the table so I wouldn't have to step on it and climbed up. I was nearly as tall as Wallace, so reaching the ceiling was no problem. I lifted the tile and set it aside. The ledge at the top of the cinder block wall was full of bottles. There were several different kinds of wine and at least two bottles of Scotch, but mostly there were lots of bottles, full and empty, of vodka. There were also several boxes from phar-maceutical companies, each one spilling over with drug samples. I reached out and grabbed the nearest one. Percodan. I had read enough to know that Percodan was very addictive and certainly not something a doctor or anyone else should be slugging back with alcohol. He had to be pretty deep into his addiction to still be standing after that little cocktail.

Poor Wallace. Poor patients! I thought perhaps I had found the reason for all the miscarriages. Even if Mother refused to come this time, Cassie and I would have to make a little return visit to Wallace's office at midnight. Invasion of privacy, or not, I needed to look at the records of his pregnant patients. I only hoped his handwriting was better than Doc Baxter's. Somehow, I doubted it.

CHAPTER NINETEEN

Mother was righteously pissed. Not only had Wallace had the bad taste to inquire about her bowel habits, but he had also committed the unpardonable sin of asking her age. She had finally asked him if he had been raised in a barn, which was her ultimate insult, and stormed out when he looked merely befuddled.

"Well, I never! I cannot imagine what so-called medical school awarded that foolish young man a degree. Did you see a diploma anywhere in the office, Paisley?

"Well, I really didn't . . . "

"It certainly wasn't Vanderbilt, of that I am positive. And it couldn't have been Emory. You know how hard it was for our Cassandra to get into Emory. And she was at the top of her class."

"Not exactly, Gran. I know you like to brag but . . . "

"Well, the likes of that young man would never make it at any prestigious university. The only place he would be truly welcome is in some village desperate for an idiot."

"Like Rowan Springs," I laughed.

"Wow, Gran, you're really mad. I don't think I've ever seen you so mad."

"And do you know? I think I smelled something funny on his breath."

"If you only knew," I said softly.

"What, dear?"

"Nothing, Mother. Thanks for going, even if it was a dead end."

Might as well start derailing her train of thought as soon as possible.

"And was it, dear? A dead end, I mean?"

"Mother, I can safely say that we never have to speak to Winston Wallace again. How much did he charge you, by the way?"

She opened her purse and pulled out the charge sheet.

"Miss Hunnicutt said she would file my insurance. It doesn't look like there's any specific amount mentioned here."

She put on her little half glasses and looked closer.

"Why, I didn't have a blood test, or a urine culture. That's a mistake. I'll have to call when I get home. Remind me Paisley, please."

"That is odd. Of course I'll remind you. I wonder if he's running a little insurance scam on the side. Oh, well, at least he gave you that food supplement."

"On the contrary, dear. This little tin of powder with impossible claims to better health cost me sixty dollars"

"What? My God, that's highway robbery."

"Not if it actually improves my stamina, my sex drive, my memory, and my waistline. Or if it also makes my hair thick and shiny and helps me grow liver cells."

"Gran, does that can really say all that?"

"No, dear. But Miss Hunnicutt said all that when she asked for the sixty dollars. She said my insurance wouldn't pay for it, but the doctor wanted me to have it anyway. All of his *senior* patients use it." She sighed. "I don't quite think I have ever left a doctor's office feeling so depressed."

"I'm really sorry, Mother. I'll pay you back for the magic powder. Maybe we can feed it to Aggie. If it's all that great, it might do something for her disposition. Can I buy you an ice cream? That's what you used to do for me when I had to go to the doctor when I was little."

She managed to pull such a pitiful face I almost laughed. My mother was the antithesis of the poor helpless senior citizen. She looked radiant and really quite young in her smart, pale grey linen suit. Her silver-white hair and dark brown eyes were accentuated by the light tan she had acquired on the tennis court that summer. The Sterling family pearls encircled her still taut and slender neck, and my father's small but perfect diamond stickpin sparkled in her lapel. She had been, and still was, a beauty. Winston Wallace had made a serious mistake. My chic little mother never forgave an enemy, and Dr. Wallace could now count himself among that fabled legion. I decided to keep the knowledge of his dirty little habit to myself. She had enough ammunition, no need to start a full-scale war. She would do quite nicely with what she had already.

When we got home, Cassie took Aggie for a walk. I hung up my jacket and joined them down in the orchard. Aggie was busy chasing a grasshopper, and Cass was leaning back against a cherry tree, looking very pensive indeed.

"A penny for your thoughts."

"I always believed that was such a stupid thing to say, even when I was a child. Besides, you know what I'm thinking. Ethan's been in jail for five days now, that's almost a week."

"Yes, dear, I know." I tried not to laugh. She would never have forgiven me. But I was in a good mood. We might just be a few hours away from solving part of Ethan's problem. I had high hopes that the puzzle would soon fall into place.

"I think I might have some good news for you, Cass."

She turned away from examining some dried amber-colored sap on the cherry tree trunk.

"What news?" She frowned at me. "And don't try to make something up. I can tell, you know."

"Of course, and I wouldn't dare. Don't think for a moment, Cassie, that I don't know how important this is to you. And Ethan is a fine young man. We will all do our very best to help him."

"I know, Mom. I'm sorry."

She smiled at me as a big fat tear rolled slowly down her perfect cheek. She sniffed and wiped her nose on her sleeve. Someday I would have to reprimand her for that, but not now.

"Okay, what's your good news?"

I told her about Wallace's ceiling stash and his conversation with Betty Lou. I finished with, "I really don't know for sure, but I have a hunch that we just might find what we're looking for if we sneak back there tonight."

"My God, Mom. You're really suggesting another midnight outing with The Three Stooges?"

"Well, the truth is, I was thinking about keeping the number down to two. Since your grandmother had an attack of conscience after our last little escapade, I was actually considering keeping this between us chickens."

"How can we possibly do that? You know how she is. We can't do anything without her finding out."

"That's fine with me—after the fact. If we come home with the information I think we're going to find in Wallace's files, I'll tell her all about it myself."

"Oh, Mom, I don't know. Last time got pretty hairy. I'm not sure I can . . . oh, what the hell! Sure! How do we do it?"

I had been mulling over that very problem for the last hour and I thought I had come up with a solution.

The first part of our plan worked famously. Cassandra announced at dinner that she was going to spend the night with a girlfriend in Morgantown. She asked permission to borrow Watson for the evening. I kept quiet because I knew Mother would not.

"Oh dear, do you really think we should take him out of hiding so soon?"

"I have no other way, unless . . . but I'm sure you wouldn't want me to use your Lincoln, Gran. Would you?"

"Why of course, my dear. You're an excellent driver. Just promise me you'll not go to any of those drive-in food places and eat in my car. You know how I hate the smell of onions and grease."

Cassie laughed. "I know how you love the smell of leather!"

"Don't be cheeky, dear. I am, after all, the gift horse."

"Yes, Gran, and thank you."

My daughter, my partner in crime, stood up and kissed her grandmother on the cheek. She was as cool as a cucumber.

"I'd better go and get a few things together, for the overnight, I mean."

Mother turned to me.

"What about you, Paisley? Do you have any plans for tonight or shall we have a nice game of gin rummy?"

I yawned hugely.

"Actually, Mother, I was thinking about going to bed a little early. But," I hastened to add when her eyes widened in surprise, "we can play a few hands if you like."

"Lovely! If you don't mind cleaning up here, I'll go find the cards and set up the game table in the library."

"Terrific. Be there in a minute."

Now was the time for the second phase of Operation Wallace. Cassie was supposed to pack my dark jeans, black sweater, and tennis shoes in her overnight bag. When she came through the kitchen to leave out the back door, I would slip the flashlight and some plastic bags into her duffle.

"Have you seen the flashlight, Paisley, dear?"

Mother came back into the kitchen and rummaged through the utility closet.

"Oh, here it is. The cards fell back behind the sofa and I can't see without a light. I do hope Aggie hasn't found them first and chewed them up. I'd better hurry. See you in a minute, dear."

And just like that, she was gone with the most essential part of my gear.

"Drat!"

I opened the closet and looked for a second flashlight. There were at least five more, but I could tell by the weight of each as I picked them up that they had no batteries.

"Mom! I'm ready! I've got the plastic bags. Give me the light."

I grabbed the nearest empty flashlight and ran to the kitchen "dump everything in" drawer. Sure enough, there was a lovely box of batteries.

"Here, take this. We'll put the batteries in later."

"When should I come back to pick you up?"

"Shhhush! You know she has a bionic car. She can hear across a football field."

"Sorry," she whispered. "When should I be at the bottom of the driveway?"

"I think about twelve midnight. What are you going to do until then?"

"There's a movie on I want to see. I'll be at the theater."

"For five hours?"

"It's a Mel Gibson. I'll see it twice."

"Gotcha!"

CHAPTER TWENTY

Mother and I played cutthroat gin rummy until I dozed off and slumped over on the sofa. She shook me awake at about ten minutes after twelve.

"Oh, my gosh! I'm late!"

"Late for what, dear?"

"Er, why bed, of course."

I yawned and stood up to stretch.

"Let's go to sleep, Mother."

"I think I'll stay here awhile and read. I'm not really sleepy. Goodnight, dear."

"Goodnight," I answered dispiritedly.

It was almost impossible to sneak out of the house with her still awake and sitting in the library. I couldn't leave through the French doors as I had planned, and she would hear if I left out the front or the back door. I went to my room and sat on the bed to think. Cassie had been waiting for me at the bottom of the drive for fifteen minutes now. I hoped she wouldn't lose her cool. I hoped I didn't lose mine.

There was nothing else to do but open the window and go out that way. The only problem was that we would have to get back in the house the same way, and it was a good six foot drop.

I considered changing out of my favorite linen pantsuit but I was already late. Besides, Cassie had my jeans and sweater in the car. I could put them on in the back seat while she drove out to Wallace's sushi cathedral.

I opened the window as quietly as I could and slipped the hooks of the screen up. We still had the old fashioned kind that hung from the top. I got a wooden coat hanger, again, one of the old fashioned kind, and wedged the screen open so I wouldn't snag my clothes on a ragged piece of wire. I climbed onto the windowsill and prepared to jump.

"Arrfff!"

I had completely forgotten Aggie! She must have followed me to bed since Cassie wasn't here. Now I would either have to take her or find something to occupy her while I escaped. I climbed back down from my perch and looked around the room. Suddenly I remembered my treasure trove of gourmet jelly beans. I kept them hidden in the back of my walnut chest for special occasions and truly rotten days when I couldn't get Rafe out of my mind, or when Cass was away and I was lonely. They would have to do. I opened the jar and poured out a handful. I grabbed a licorice, a root beer, and a cinnamon before she could lick them and piled the rest on the floor. Poor thing. I almost felt sorry for her. She would probably have a tummy ache tomorrow.

I climbed back up in the window while the dog was busy gobbling down the candy. She didn't give me a second look as I dropped down over the windowsill to the soft ground below. The coat hanger lifted out easily and allowed the screen to slide gently back into the frame.

I was free! I felt the same joy I had experienced when I was a child and my sister Velvet and I sneaked out of the house on summer nights to climb up on the sun-warmed roof. I would have to do this more often. I practically skipped around the side of the house and past the wing where the library was. I could see Mother reading on the sofa. As I watched, she got up and went to the French doors to look out at the night sky. She had turned some of the lights off in the room and would be able to see me clearly if I went down the driveway.

Again, I had no other options. I would have to go down the steep bank in front of the house. I walked out to the edge of the front yard and squeezed through the border of ornamental evergreens. I tried very hard not to think of the creepy crawlers that might decide to hitchhike in my hair and stepped carefully through to the other side. The first step was the hardest. There was nothing there. The bank was steeper than I remembered, and I went tumbling head over heels down the incline. I rolled all the way to the bottom before I came to an abrupt halt in the ditch next to the road. I sat up too quickly and had to wait for a moment until my head stopped spinning. I moved my arms and legs gingerly, but to my surprise, I discovered that I was completely unhurt. The soft, leafy undergrowth on the bank had kept me from serious injury. I got up, brushed myself off, and climbed up to the road. Cassie was parked just where she promised she would be. When I tapped on the window to get her attention, she jumped so high she banged her head on the roof. I was still trying to control my laughter when she finally got the window down.

"Mom! Where have you been?"

"Don't ask, just open the back door and let me in so we can scram. I hope nobody has seen you waiting here. They might call Mother to tell her someone's trying to steal her car and can't get it out of the driveway."

"Don't worry. Only one car went by and I don't think it was anyone we know."

I relaxed against the soft leather seat and took a deep breath. Miraculously, my lovely linen suit seemed to have survived my adventure unscathed.

"Where's the duffle bag? I want to change clothes."

"Oh, my gosh! Your clothes!"

"Don't tell me you forgot!"

"Oh, Mom, I'm sorry! I was thinking that somehow Gran might look in my bag. I got sidetracked and ran around putting in a nightie and stuff that would look normal if I were really spending the night away from home. It slipped my mind that you needed your jeans."

"And sweater and tennies!" I answered crossly.

"I said I was sorry. No need to be a fussbudget."

I held my tongue. It was an argument that could have lasted until dawn. I asked a question instead.

"Where do you think we should park the car? It's a little conspicuous."

"This morning when I was waiting for you and Gran, I noticed a delivery entrance. Maybe we could park in there and pull up as close to the building as possible. Unless somebody comes in the back parking lot, and I doubt that at this time of night, we won't be seen.

"Great! Good thinking, Cassie."

Then I remembered something else I had forgotten.

"Damn! The lock-picking set."

"It's in the bag."

"Thank you, God."

"How about, 'thank you, Cass'?"

"You, too. But you forgot my jeans."

"I thought we declared a moratorium on that subject. There's the driveway. What a weird design for a building. It almost looks like a bad dream."

I had to agree with her. In the moonlight, it looked even more peculiar. The smoked glass reflected white celestial orbs in every window and the stepping stones became big, round, black jellyfish in a sea of pebbles. The place gave me the creeps. Cass snaked the Lincoln into the single lane of the delivery entrance and turned off the engine.

"Here we are again, Mata Hari and Wonder Woman."

"More like Abbott and Costello. Where's the lock-picking kit and the flashlight?"

"Here. I put the batteries in while I was waiting for you."

She handed the flashlight back to me.

"You hold it for me while I pick the lock."

"Cassie, that's my job."

"Who did it last time? And in record time, I must say."

"Okay. But let's hurry. I don't think we'll be disturbed at this time of night, but who knows where we'll have to look to find what we want. It could take us a few hours."

We got out of the car as quickly as we could to minimize the time the interior light would be on. I had to figure out someday how to disengage that little sucker so it wouldn't be a problem on occasions like this. Maybe Leonard could find out for me.

The bright moonlight was all the light Cass needed to pick the lock. I had to admit she had a natural talent as a burglar. In less than two minutes flat we were inside.

We decided to keep the lights off. There was way too much glass in the front. Any passerby would be sure to see if even the smallest light were on. We didn't need the police investigating, and besides, Mother would never forgive us if we got caught and embarrassed her.

"I guess we don't need to whisper, but somehow I can't help it."

"I know what you mean."

I stopped in front of the room I had hidden in that morning.

"This is the room with Wallace's goodies in the ceiling. But I think we should leave that for last. Let's go for the records of his pregnant patients first. I hope we can find out that he did something to make them abort. At the very least we can get him for malpractice. Then they'll have to re-examine Ethan's part in this whole business."

We found the records with only the light of the moon from the skylights overhead. They were in a little room behind the reception desk. There were four filing cabinets with three drawers each. I was right—this could take a while. We closed the door to the hall and turned on the flashlight.

"Mom, do you remember the names of any of the patients from Ethan's log?"

"That's another thing I forgot."

I slapped myself in the forehead. Leonard would be disgusted with me. He would never forget anything that elementary.

"No, damn it, but I do think I'll recognize them if I see them. You hold the flashlight and I'll thumb through the files."

We spent the next two hours bent uncomfortably over the file drawers in the cramped little room and found only two patients for our trouble. My back was killing me and my eyes were blurring.

"The flashlight is getting dim," observed Cass.

"I thought it was my eyes."

"No. It's the flashlight. But I don't understand. I just put in two new batteries."

"Was the battery package open?"

"Yes, but no batteries were missing."

"Then that's it."

"What?"

"Mother probably took two brand new ones out and put two used ones back in the package. That's her idea of saving energy."

"Well, hell! What'll we do now?"

"I say we put these files back. I can't see anything out of order. These women had nothing more serious than hay fever. The drugs and liquor are positive evidence of Wallace's malpractice. Let's go for his ceiling stash while we still have some battery light. We can grab a bottle of vodka and some of those drug samples. That's enough to show Chief Joiner."

"Okay, Mom. I'm with you."

We quickly replaced the files and found our way back down the hall to the examining room with the magic ceiling.

Cassie carefully climbed up on the table while I held the waning flashlight. Two seconds later everything went black. I laid the flashlight down on the table and steadied her legs.

"Damn and double damn! Hold still, Cassie. Don't fall."

"I'm fine, Mom. Here, I've got some matches in my pocket."

"You're not smoking again, are you?"

"For heavens sake, is this the time to go into that?"

"You'd better not be. Cigarettes will ruin your health."

"And all this stress from committing burglaries won't?"

"Just light the match before you lose your balance in the dark and fall like a dummy. I'll tell you which ceiling tile to lift up."

Cassie lit the match and held it up to the ceiling. She was standing a little farther from the wall than I had been this morning. I stood there puzzled for a moment as I tried to decided which tile I had moved. Just as I remembered which one it was, the heat from the match set off the sprinkler system. Suddenly we were drenched with a cold, stinging shower of water. Cassie screamed and stepped backwards on the examining table. Her foot rolled over on the useless flashlight, and she came tumbling down on top of me in a heap of whirling arms and legs. We were wallowing on the flooded floor trying to untangle ourselves when the bright overhead lights came on and Winston Wallace stepped into the room, pointing a vicious-looking shotgun at our wet little heads.

CHAPTER TWENTY-ONE

I was soaked. My hair was plastered to my face in little corkscrew auburn curls, and every time I tried to get up, my shoes slid wildly on the wet floor. I finally gave up and sat back against the wall with my legs straight out in front of me. After a second thought, I held my hands up.

As suddenly as the water came on, it went off. The silence was complete except for the drip of the water from the table, the chair, me, and Cassie.

Wallace's head and face were wet too. Water dripped off his chin as he leaned over and peered intently at us.

"What the hell!" he shouted. "You're . . . why, you are Anna Sterling's daughter! And that's your . . . .! Please tell me what in the hell is going on here. You have about two seconds before I call the police."

He pushed me hard on the shoulder with the barrel of the shotgun when I tried once more to get up. "No! Just sit right there. Don't move a muscle."

Cassie was shivering next to me.

"Mom, I'm freezing!" she whispered.

My maternal instincts overcame the shock and fear of being so rudely discovered.

"Go ahead and shoot me if you must, but I'm getting up and so is my daughter. And you are going to find us some dry clothes. This air conditioning will give us both pneumonia, and I'll have to sue your sorry ass."

"Just sit right there, lady! I hardly think you are in any position to be giving me orders."

He flipped open his cellular phone and started to dial 911.

"Go right ahead. Chief Joiner will be very interested in that illegal stash of controlled substances you have hidden in the ceiling. As a matter of fact, you'll just be saving me some trouble."

He slumped back against the doorway like someone had slugged him in the stomach. His face turned an unhealthy pasty white where the fake suntan makeup had washed off. I had finally succeeded in letting the hot air out of this pompous little ass. Somehow it didn't feel as good as I had imagined it would.

"Come, Cassandra, help me up. My shoes keep slipping."

I struggled up, and with her strong-armed assistance, regained my footing. I looked down in horror at my beautiful linen suit. It was ruined! I had pared my wardrobe down to a few beloved and very basic essentials since I no longer had to dress like a fashion plate every day. This outfit had been a favorite. I could feel it shrinking as I breathed.

"Damn! Come on, Wallace. This is all you fault. Get me one of those silly little white coats you wear, or something—anything. Cassie needs one, too."

I took the shotgun out of his slack hands and put it very carefully on the examining table.

"We won't be needing this."

I pushed him out the door and down the hallway. He stopped at the entrance to the record room. There was another little alcove off to the side that I had not noticed before. He pointed to a closet and then sat heavily on a chair in the corner. Cassie opened the door and found several stacks of green scrub suits on the shelf. She grabbed the first one she saw and sprinted around the corner to change. I leaned back against a filing cabinet and waited until she was finished. She reappeared quickly, and in spite of the disaster our evening had turned into, I had to laugh aloud. The pants and sleeves were way too short for her long limbs. She looked like an adolescent jolly green giant after a growth spurt.

"Now it's your turn. Let's see how terrific you look in these things."

She thrust another set of scrubs at me. I followed her lead and went around the corner to strip off my wet clothes. I hung my beautiful suit over the back of a plastic chair and straightened it out as best I could. Maybe Mother would be able to wear it. It would mostly likely shrink down to her size by the time it dried. I sighed deeply and slipped on the dry clothes. I had the scrub suit Cass needed. I had to roll up the long legs of the pants so I could walk without tripping. I slipped off my soggy shoes and went back to the closet to hunt for some socks. I could hear Cassie talking to Wallace around the corner. She was herding him into the break room demanding something hot to drink. I hurried to join them. I could use a cup of something hot, too.

Wallace was sitting in a chair staring at Cassie with red-rimmed eyes. She moved about the tiny kitchen humming as she prepared three cups of instant chicken noodle soup and brewed a pot of fresh coffee.

"Wow! This little fridge is loaded. Look, Mom, fresh homemade cinnamon buns. And no raisins! Hooray!"

My daughter, the burglar, made us a tasty little post-midnight snack which two out of three of us enjoyed immensely.

"I always say, there's nothing like a little breaking and entering to work up an appetite."

Wallace looked at me in astonishment.

"You can laugh and make fun of this . . . this criminal activity? And dragging your own daughter along? What kind of people are you?"

"Well, for one thing, we're not drug addicts or alcoholics. And *we're* not committing insurance fraud. And for a fine old-fashioned third, neither are we guilty of unethical medical conduct, or malpractice, or the murder of little babies."

"Murder!"

He stood up on shaky legs and pointed a long thin finger at me.

"How dare you accuse me of murder!"

His legs gave way and he fell back down in the chair, spilling the cup of soup down the front of his suit.

"Now see what you've done. Cassie, please hand me some paper towels. We'll have to sponge off this model citizen before we call the police and let them decide who's guilty and who's innocent."

"No, please."

Wallace held his head in his long bony hands. They were not the strong, capable hands of a natural born healer. I remembered his frustration and impatience with the injured farmer. What forces had been applied to this weak little man to make him become something he was obviously so unsuited to be?

"Maybe you can tell us why we shouldn't call the police," I urged softly. "Let's start with the pharmacological piggy bank in your ceiling."

For the next fifteen minutes we sat through Wallace's self-pitying, tearful performance entitled *An Attempt to Justify My Sins*. He blamed his parents, his teachers, his mistress, and God Almighty. The only person he left out was his wife. I found that curious.

"What about your wife, Agnes? Does she not understand you, either?"

He jumped up and pounded on the table.

"Leave her out of this! She had nothing to do with anything. Agnes is a saint, I tell you. I love her! She is the only thing in my life that's not dirty and perverted." He slumped back down in the chair. "It's not her fault I married her for her money."

He dropped his head in his hands and started crying. He looked like he would be occupied for a while.

Cassie pulled me out in the hallway and closed the door behind her.

"Oh, Mom. Isn't that sweet?" she whispered.

"Yeah, well . . . "

"It's so romantic."

"Sorry, Cassie, but I see nothing *romantic* about a man so greedy that he marries for money."

"No, not that part, the love part."

"He certainly has an odd way of expressing his affection. Getting stoned on vodka and Percodan, and screwing a cheap blond. That's the kind of man I'd want coming home to me each night, yes sirree."

"But, Mom, he does love her."

"Ah, yes, love."

I ran my fingers through the jungle of my hair. I was tired, and I knew I sounded cynical.

"Cassie, love is something you don't fool around with. You don't bestow it lightly, and when you accept it from someone else, you cherish it for the rest of your life. I'm not sure how much honest-to-goodness love an incomplete person like Wallace has to give, or how much he can really appreciate in return."

Her beautiful young face shone with innocent disbelief. Cassie had already been indoctrinated by David O. Selznick, Andrew Lloyd Weber, and Jane Austen. She devoutly and naively believed that love conquers all. I was just a bitter old broad who was spittin' in the wind.

CHAPTER TWENTY-TWO

I could have used another cup of coffee, but from the loud sobbing sounds coming from the break room I could tell that Wallace was not over his crying jag.

"You think we should go home?" asked my daughter.

"Hell, no! After all this trouble? I'm not leaving here without some answers."

"What was the name of that girl Ethan's supposed to have raped?"

"What a clever child you are, Cassandra! Her name is Brittany Hayes. Let's see if she has ever been a patient of Dr. Strangelove."

I sneaked a quick peek in the coffee room. Wallace was still holding his pity party. We had time to peruse his files.

We found the chart on the Hayes girl right away. It was fairly thick. She had been a patient of Wallace's since he had opened his practice six years ago. Her mother brought her in for painful menstrual cramps. At first the girl had refused to let him examine her but finally relented. Wallace stated very clearly in the chart that the girl was not a virgin. Furthermore, he suspected that she had been the victim of sexual abuse. Upon questioning, the mother broke down and admitted that she thought her husband was molesting the girl but was afraid to do anything about it. He wanted to go to the authorities, but she refused. He had to let them go home. Had to let the girl return to the den of the predator.

I was beginning to feel somewhat better about Winston Wallace. At least when he first started his practice he had some sense of right and wrong. I wondered what had happened to him in the meantime.

Brittany was a stranger to the office until one day three years later when she came in by herself with a deep laceration at the "vermilion border," which I finally realized meant lip, and a severe contusion to the right cheek. She tearfully confessed to Wallace that her stepfather had been abusing her off and on since she was ten. Since her mother's death the year before, he had been after her almost continuously. She was fifteen years old, three months pregnant, and infected with gonorrhea.

"Oh my, God, Mom. How sad. The poor thing. I feel like such a heel. I've been hating her all this time for implicating Ethan, and she's a victim herself."

"Don't get one thing confused with the other. There's no doubt that she's a victim of abuse, but Brittany's no longer a little girl, Cassie. She's a grown woman—just a year younger than you are. You'd think she'd know better."

"You're not suggesting that Ethan really did murder her father?" croaked Cassie.

"Of course not! I'm saying that she is a young woman who has made some poor choices with her life. I'm not forgetting that she's had some very bad luck, but so have a lot of other people. That doesn't excuse her falsely accusing Ethan of rape and murder."

"Mrs. DeLeon," Winston Wallace protested from the open doorway, "what are you doing in my confidential files?"

Romeo had joined us. I straightened up too quickly and had to fight to overcome a wave of dizziness. I was getting really tired.

"Cassie, can you make us some fresh coffee? We need to have a little chat with Romeo, here."

CHAPTER TWENTY-THREE

Cassandra made the coffee extra strong. After a cup loaded with sugar and cream, I had a resurgence of energy.

"Dr. Wallace," I began, "it's late, and I'm afraid good manners and tact are not my forte at the best of times, so I'll jump right in with both feet. I believe you are to blame for the rash of miscarriages occurring here in Rowan Springs in the last few weeks."

I might as well have slapped him.

He whispered hoarsely, "It's not true. I may have done many things, but I have never hurt one of my patients." He repeated emphatically, "Not ever!"

"How can you be so sure? You must have been drunk or stoned at least half of the time."

"I admit my addiction has caused me to act somewhat indiscreetly, but I assure you I am not responsible for any loss of life."

He looked like he was going to cry again.

"Can we act a little grown up here, or do I need to call Andy Joiner to mediate?"

"No, please, ask whatever you wish. I'll answer to the best of my knowledge."

"How many of your patients have had unexplained miscarriages?"

He didn't hesitate at all.

"Three, and those were just in the last two weeks. I thought it strange myself. Under other circumstances, I would have welcomed the CDC's investigation. I would have worked with Dr. McHenry as an interested colleague. But you must understand, I couldn't place myself, or my practice, under scrutiny. I had just begun to realize how serious my, er, problem was."

He looked even more sheepish.

"That's when I decided to end it all."

"I was wondering what the shotgun was for," said Cassie.

"Let's get back to the point." I interrupted. "If you didn't do anything to cause these abortions—then, who did?"

"I tried to discuss the problem with Edgar Baxter. Dr. McHenry told me Edgar had canceled appointments with him. Well, he put me off as well."

I looked at him with a raised eyebrow.

"No, I'm not trying to put the blame on Baxter, but an overwhelming number of the young women were his patients. And my three had been his patients until he closed his practice. Two of those young women had even had amniocentesis procedures performed. The genetic tests on those babies were absolutely normal. You may not know it, Mrs. DeLeon, but the fetus is very well protected by the mother's body. There's little short of certain viruses or severe trauma that can harm a healthy fetus."

"What viruses?"

Cassie had been listening quietly until now, but she had a big stake in this part of the conversation.

"Toxoplasmosis, brucellosis, and certain other viruses that cattle and some

domestic animals carry."

"Ethan said that had been ruled out."

Wallace looked surprised. "Really? Then I haven't a clue what's going on. My patients were healthy, normal young women. Not one had ever been really ill before. Their pregnancies were progressing nicely, and then suddenly two of them miscarried. The last one lost her baby three days ago."

"You said, 'really ill.' Did any of them have a minor problem that maybe you might have overlooked?"

Wallace didn't take offense at my question. His scientific mind had been addressed. He was just as curious as we were.

"Two of them had never been sick a day in their lives except for seasonal allergies. The other one had been thrown from a horse when she was fifteen. There was some question of a damaged pelvic ligament, but that would not have been a problem until much later, when she was in her sixth or seventh month. I'm just as puzzled as Dr. McHenry is, I assure you."

"Speaking of Dr. McHenry, do you know why he might have gone out to the Hayes' farm?"

"Brittany Hayes was the young lady who was thrown by the horse."

"Is that how she lost her first baby?"

"Really, I do protest you're going through my files. Those are confidential and private. You have no business . . . "

"Yeah, yeah," I interrupted. "Look, Wallace, a man's life and reputation is at stake. I'm sure that's something you can understand. If you don't, you'd better start thinking about it. Help us help him, and we'll help you."

I was getting tired. That sounded stupid even to me.

He sighed and rubbed his eyes.

"Brittany did lose her stepfather's baby when she fell from her horse," he admitted. "I believed at the time, and still do, that she fell on purpose. She risked her life by taking matters into her own hands. I treated her sexually transmitted disease, but she refused to let me tell anyone about her pregnancy."

"She was a minor! How could you keep silent? Isn't there some agency that helps children in trouble like that?"

Wallace shook his head sadly. "Unfortunately, we don't have any mechanism in place in Rowan Springs to handle problems like Brittany's. Her stepfather had sole custody of her. He probably would have sued me if I had suggested he was abusing his daughter. She was too afraid to confront him, and I'm ashamed to admit, so was I."

Cassie had another pertinent question.

"Is Mr. Hayes the father of Brittany's baby—the one she is carrying now, I mean?"

"I have no idea. She has become a rather hardened young woman. She refused to tell me who the father was. I guess she knew she couldn't count on me. I'm afraid I've let down a lot more people than my wife."

"I guess you were wrong, Mom. We're back at first base. After all this, we haven't found out anything to help clear Ethan."

"I can tell you something." Wallace braced his shoulders and attempted to simulate a stiff upper lip. "I cannot accept that Dr. McHenry murdered Hayes. I saw the man's body when they brought him into the emergency room. There is no doubt in my mind that Hayes fell on his own gun. His death was an accident."

CHAPTER TWENTY-FOUR

"Are you sure? breathed Cassie.

"Quite sure! As a matter of fact, he was the inspiration for my own demise. I was coming here tonight to get rid of my little piggy bank, as you called it, and then I would have had an accident like the one he had."

"Why did they arrest Ethan if it was an accident?" asked Cassie.

"The girl implicated him. She said he killed her stepfather. I hesitated to speak up. My, er, problem has made me pretty much a coward. I was sure the truth would come out sooner or later."

Cassie was furious. "How dare you! You let an innocent man go to jail. You're a coward—a selfish, spineless, miserable coward!"

She fled from the room. I considered running after her but I was so tired. Someone had to stay rational and calm. I elected me.

"Okay, so you didn't speak up for Ethan. Did anyone else examine Hayes— someone who might have come to the same conclusion you did?"

"Maybe. Edgar Baxter rode in the ambulance with the girl and her father. I was at the hospital when they arrived, and Baxter went in the ER with the girl. I pronounced Hayes and sent him to the morgue."

He looked at me hopefully. "I haven't signed the death certificate yet. At least I can make amends by making it an accidental death. Will that make your daughter happy?"

I decided to take a wild shot at him. "Let's make my mother happy. When did you start scamming Medicare and the private insurance companies?"

He jumped to his feet and did a pretty good imitation of a six year-old having a temper tantrum.

"Never! Never! I've done a lot of things, but not that!"

"What about the sixty dollar food supplement and sex potion for senior citizens?"

I was sure of my ground here and he knew it. He stopped his little dance and sat down.

"Poppy, Poppy Hunnicutt. She tells patients that I want them to have BioCal. I have nothing to do with it. She takes the money in cash. I've never seen one dime of it."

This man's moral sensibility astounded me, unless . . .

"What's she got on you Winston?"

"Her, her brother," he stammered. "The football player. He was in an accident. I passed him on my way home from the country club. I had a few drinks under my belt, but the boy was bleeding profusely, so I administered first aid at the scene. He seemed to be stable when I got in the ambulance. On the way to the hospital he went sour. He was dead before we arrived. His spleen was ruptured. There was massive internal bleeding. There was nothing I could have done, but Poppy smelled the liquor on my breath in the hospital parking lot. She said she would tell if things didn't go her way from then on. I thought all she wanted was a little extra income from the nutritional supplement. I guess it's gone farther than that."

He started crying again.

I'd had enough. I went in search of my daughter and found her sitting outside on the steps.

"We'd better skedaddle. The sun's about to come up. We've still got to sneak back in the house, or at least, I do. You can come driving in later this morning whenever you . . . "

Cassie turned towards me. I recognized the look on her face. I had seen it once before when she'd asked me if there really was a Santa Claus. I sat down next to her on the hard concrete and took her arm.

"Yes, Virginia, there really is . . . "

"Oh, Mom, don't make fun. This is serious."

"Can't 'serious' wait until we've had some sleep?"

"You always told me the Mom Shop was open any time."

"You're right," I grumbled. "Shoot."

"That's exactly what I'd like to do, shoot Dr. Wallace. How could he have made such a mess of things? For everybody! You were right to be disgusted. He is so self-indulgent that I want to smack him. And he uses love as an excuse for everything."

She watched intently as the sun began to edge up over the horizon.

"It's made me wonder if I really love Ethan as much as I thought I did."

"Oh, ho! That's the problem."

"I like him, I really do. He's funny and smart and dedicated. I admire him tremendously. And I have to admit that I love being adored by him. I feel like a goddess bestowing favors. It gives me a sense of power. According to you, that's not what love is all about."

I was silent for a moment or two. My brain was fuzzy and thinking was almost physically painful.

"Mother used to tell me that I would know when Mr. Right came along. That sounds like a fairy tale in this day and age. Everyone is so self-indulgent nowadays. Their credo is 'if it feels good, do it.' People are cohabiting at the drop of a hat with men, women, and barnyard animals."

"Mom!"

"It's true, darling, and you know it. But there are still some decent souls coming down the pike. I think your Ethan is one of them. He may be your Mr. Right, but he could also be just a tad early. There's no shame in not being ready yet, Cassie. If he loves you enough he will wait. If he doesn't, then you don't need him in the first place. I'm glad you're hesitating. I think you're still too young. When you do tie the knot, you'll be married a very long time. You can afford to start a little late. Besides, I'm not ready to be a grandma yet. And imagine what it would do to your grandmother to have to add a 'great.'"

Cassie chuckled. We both gave a simultaneous "Wow!" as the sun popped up over the tree line and another beautiful day was born.

Cass turned and gave me a quick hug.

"Thanks, Mom. You can take your shingle down now."

"Let's go home."

CHAPTER TWENTY-FIVE

I sent Cassie to retrieve Mother's flashlight while I went to fetch our clothes. Winston was crying again. I slipped down the hallway like a ghost and was out the door before he knew it. If he wanted to say anything more to me it was too late. My name and number were in the phone book. Wallace had a quarter. He could call.

Cass was already in the driver's seat. She backed the Lincoln out of the delivery entrance and was waiting with the door open. I chucked our clothes in the back seat and off we went.

"I'm exhausted, Mom. Do I have to wait until later to come home? Can't I just come in now? We're going to have to tell Gran where we've been sooner or later."

"You're right. It might as well be sooner. Besides, I don't think I'm quite up to climbing back in the house. And I need a bath. I must be allergic to the soap they washed these scrubs in."

Cass turned and sneaked a peek at me.

"My goodness, Mom! Your face is all broken out! You look like you have the measles. What's wrong with you?"

I turned down the mirror flap on the visor and looked at my face. Sure enough, I had a major rash. My whole face was covered with little red bumps.

"What in the world?"

I was starting to itch like mad. The skin on my arms and hands was popping out in the same red rash.

"This is just great! All I need is some kind of plague now that all the doctors in this town have gone strange."

As we pulled in the driveway I happened to glance over at the side of the hill where I had taken a tumble last night. In the early morning light it was easy to identify the soft, leafy undergrowth which had cushioned me from injury. On my bumpy way to the bottom I had rolled over and over in a thick, hearty patch of poison ivy.

Cassie parked the car down behind the carriage house, and we retrieved our clothes from the heap in the back seat. I shook my head again over the ruin of my favorite outfit.

"Damn! I really loved this pantsuit. Now look at it."

"Look at your birthday suit is more like it. You really need to do something about that rash."

"I know, I know."

We walked slowly back up to the house in the early morning sun. A hazy blanket of moisture hovered over the tall grass in the fields. Dew twinkled like diamonds in spider webs in the corners of the back porch eaves. It was a perfect day. I was sorry that I would spend most of it asleep in bed, but I was so tired I could hardly pick up my feet.

"Mom, do you smell that?"

I stopped and leaned against her shoulder as I took an experimental sniff.

"Bacon?"

"Yes! And coffee and . . . Wow, I'm starving!"

She took off so quickly I almost fell down. I stumbled after her and made it to the porch door just as it slammed in my face. I had to stand there for a moment until I was able to summon the energy required to push it open.

Cassie was already seated at the kitchen table with a knife in one hand and a fork in the other. Mother was spooning hot buttered grits onto her plate, which was already loaded with creamy scrambled eggs and crispy bacon. There was another plate on the table. It was at my accustomed place and held only a solitary bran muffin and a banana. I was going to be punished for sneaking out. I sighed and slid into my seat, forcing a smile.

"Good morning, Mother. Thanks for the breakfast. We are very hungry."

"Well, my girl, you have some explaining . . . "

She turned and got a good look at me.

"My God! Paisley, what has happened to you?"

Mother leaned over and gave me a closer inspection.

"Poison ivy! Oh, you poor child!" She sat down hard in her chair, forgetting her anger. "Where in the world have you two been? I've been worried sick all night."

"I'm really sorry, Mother. I honestly thought you wouldn't know that we were gone."

"I didn't until Agatha started throwing up jelly beans all over the house."

"Aggie's sick?"

Cassie crammed the last piece of bacon in her mouth and jumped up from the table. She dumped her plate in the sink and ran water over the rest of her grits and eggs before I could stop her. My stomach gave a protesting grumble as I settled for a bite of bran muffin.

"I'll trade you the tale of our adventures for a decent breakfast."

"You're a middle-aged woman, Paisley. You should be thinking about your health. The most I can offer you is a poached egg."

"Well, in that case, I think I'll just go on up to bed."

I pushed my chair back and started to get up.

"Of course, since you are going to be very ill with that much poison ivy in your system I suppose it wouldn't hurt—just this once."

"Two eggs, scrambled, and some of that lovely bacon. And please pass the butter. This muffin wouldn't be half bad with some jam. Have you got any more?"

An hour later I was full to the scuppers and sitting in a soothing oatmeal bath. When I fell asleep and almost slid under the water, Mother finally gave me permission to get out and pat myself dry. The rash was worse on my lower legs and feet than it was on my upper body, but my face was swollen, and my right eye was almost closed.

"We're going to have to take you to someone, Paisley. I guess you don't want me to call Dr. Wallace after all the things you told me. I think there's an allergy specialist in Morgantown. I'll call and see if I can get you an appointment for this afternoon."

I looked at her pleadingly. I just wanted to sleep. The last thing I needed was another car trip.

"Sorry, dear, but this is a really bad rash. I wouldn't be surprised if you started to run a temperature.

"Okay, whatever you say."

She pulled back the covers of the bed I had been yearning to climb in for so many hours.

"Oh dear!"

We stood there and stared at the big splotch of doggie vomit staining my lovely pink sheets. Little pieces of red, green, and blue jelly beans were a predominant ingredient in the mess.

"Oh, Mother, it's my fault. I gave them to her. I'll clean this up."

"No, dear, you're exhausted. You go curl up in my bed. I'll wash your sheets later."

Bless her heart. I took her up on her offer and slept until three in the afternoon.

The allergy specialist in Morgantown was very nice. His waiting room was full of snuffling, sneezing, and coughing patients, but he saw me right away. I was an emergency, he said, an allergic crisis. I did have a fever, and my head was swimming. He gave me a shot of something that brought me back down to earth. That's when the itching started. I got another shot for the discomfort and some lovely cool lotion as well. I was out of the office in less than twenty minutes and slept all the way home.

The next morning, Cassie tapped lightly on my door and brought me a poached egg and some tea and toast. The middle-aged woman's breakfast. She sat with me while I ate.

"This is the sixth day in jail for Ethan, Mom. And we still haven't learned anything that will help him."

"That's not really true, Cassie. We know that he is not the father of Brittany Hayes's baby since she was pregnant before he came to town."

"Big wow," she answered sourly. "That doesn't prove he didn't rape her."

"You forgot that Wallace told us he didn't kill Hayes, either. When he signs the death certificate and declares it an accidental death, the murder charge will be dropped."

"Will that be the end of it?"

"I don't honestly know, Cassie."

"I wish I could just talk to him. It's so unfair."

"I agree with you. But Ethan himself has some culpability in this. If he had gotten a lawyer or even accepted one appointed by the court, then maybe he would have been treated differently. This vow of silence is ridiculous. I'm sure his mother is wondering what's going on. It's been almost a week since she's heard from him."

"Maybe we should send another e-mail."

I poured myself the last of the hot tea from the little brown pot while I thought about it.

"No, I am not manufacturing news," I said decisively. "Ethan wants things his way, and we have no choice but to go along with it. And think about this situation very carefully, Cassie. Ethan is a maverick. Are you going to like being married to a guy who never follows the rules?"

Wrong question at the wrong time. Her pretty face crumpled up like a used paper towel. She ran out of my room and slammed the door behind her before Aggie could follow. The puppy and I stared at the closed door for a full minute. Then Aggie started whining. I sighed and got out of my cozy little nest to release her.

Now that I was up, there was no reason not to get dressed. I was pleased to note that the rash had receded on my hands and arms. My legs and feet were much better, too. I showered quickly and applied the last of the lotion to the last of the rash. My face was fairly clear of offending red spots. At least one doctor around here knew his business. I had to take my hat off to the allergist.

Mother was in the kitchen making lunch. A very pretty pasta salad sat in a big bowl covered with plastic wrap. I started to peel off the wrap and sneak out a black olive but she stopped me.

"Get your dirty paws off of that!"

It wasn't as bad as it sounded. We've all been saying that since Velvet was two.

Instead of blowing out the candles she had stuck her entire face in her birthday cake and eaten it from the inside out. Grandpa Howard had hastened to rescue the cake and little blond blue-eyed Velvet had stopped him with that same pronouncement. He had sat down on the floor laughing. It was a story he never tired of telling. Velvet's saying had become part of our family lore.

"Mabel is a little under the weather. I thought I would help them out with some lunch."

"How about my lunch?"

"You just ate breakfast, Paisley."

"Her kids aren't going to like pasta salad. I'll make them some peanut butter and jelly."

"Yes, and I suppose you'll eat one for every two you fix for the children."

"Que sera, sera."

CHAPTER TWENTY-SIX

Mabel and her husband Apollo lived a short distance down the road from us, which put them fairly far out in the country. Their double-wide trailer was nestled in a hollow on five acres of beautiful green lawn surrounded by miles of white picket fence. They also owned fifty acres across the road where Apollo grew tobacco and kept ponies for his children. Besides growing tobacco, he sometimes worked three jobs at once to keep his family fed and clothed in the manner he felt they should become accustomed to. He had already helped three older children through state university and was busy preparing the road for the next three. Apollo had my vote for Father of the Year.

When we neared the house, there was silence instead of the usual noisy gathering of children and animals. Apollo appeared at the door and ushered us quietly into the spotless living room. He was a little bantam rooster of a man no taller than Mother and a lot shorter than Cassie. On a normal day he was so enthusiastic and energetic that he seemed bigger. Today he was dwarfed by worries.

He made a grave and graceful speech of welcome once we were all inside.

"Miz Sterling you don't know how much I appreciates your coming. We thank you kindly for the food and the company."

"Apollo, you know we would have come sooner if you had just let us know Mabel was not feeling well. When did she become ill?"

"That's just it. You know how that ole woman of mine is. She's so ornery she hardly tells a body anything. I just found out myself last night. I had to practically squeeze it out of her. Maybe she'll tell you more. Would you talk to her, please? You, too, Miz Paisley, if you don't mind."

"Of course, Apollo," said Mother as she patted his shoulder reassuringly. "Why don't you and Cassandra feed the children some of those peanut butter and jelly sandwiches?" She winked. "They're a specialty of Paisley's. And there's some pasta salad and roast beef in those other containers. Better set them in the refrigerator."

I followed Mother back to the master bedroom at the rear of the double-wide where Mabel lay huddled in the middle of the bed. A meticulously stitched and very beautiful double wedding ring quilt was pulled up almost over her head. When she heard us coming and tried to sit up, the cover slipped back and revealed her pale, strained features.

"Mabel! What's the matter?" gasped Mother.

"Miz Sterling, praise the Lord, and thank you for coming."

She grasped Mother's hand tightly with her own.

"I didn't want to scare Apollo, but I think I'm gonna lose this baby."

She broke down, crying softly.

"Nonsense, Mabel! We won't let that happen. Come, Paisley. Help me get her up. We're going to take her to the hospital right now."

"I can't do that, Miz Sterling. You know how stubborn that ole man of mine is. He won't accept any help from the county, and we just don't have hospital money right now. He hasn't sold the tobacco yet. We were countin' on that money coming in before the baby came."

"Mabel, I don't want you to worry another minute about money.

That's what friends are for. Paisley, hand me her houserobe and those slippers."

"He won't take your money, either, Miz Sterling. You know as well as I do how he is."

She suddenly doubled over in pain.

I could tell that Mother was searching desperately for an argument to convince her friend. Apparently she had a sudden inspiration.

"Apollo will build my new porch addition this winter. I'm just advancing him some of the money for costs."

Mabel smiled in relief. "Yes, he'll be more than happy to build that new porch. I'll see to it."

Her face wrinkled in pain again.

I wondered if maybe we shouldn't call the ambulance. Then I remembered Mavis and her weird husband. We could get her to the emergency room just as quickly as that awful woman's husband.

"Mother, slip her other arm in that robe and help me get her on her feet."

Mabel was very weak. She spoke quietly to her husband and children for a moment and then leaned heavily on my arm. We practically had to carry her to the car. Apollo stood at the door and watched as he held the frightened children close to him. He looked so pitiful I almost cried. Cassandra couldn't stand it. She ran back to the door and spoke urgently to him. He came running out to the car and hopped in back.

"Yore sweet chile says she's gonna stay with my kids so I can go with Mabel. I'm mighty grateful, Miz Paisley. And to you too, Miz Sterling. I'll build you one hell of a porch."

"Language, Apollo," remonstrated his wife weakly before she fainted.

The emergency room of the Lakeland County Hospital was fairly well up to date for a town as small as Rowan Springs. The county commissioners had learned early on that the hospital had to be well equipped because of the proximity of our town to the lakes.

The summer boaters were always having accidents, and the tourists were notorious for drinking and driving while on holiday.

Because of the absence of our two local physicians, the emergency room was manned by a circulating roster of doctors from neighboring counties. Mabel was very lucky. The physician on call was an Ob-Gyn from Morgantown. He examined her quickly and wasted no time in starting her on an intravenous drip. He explained to Apollo that it contained something to stop the uterine contractions that were causing her early labor, and plasma to replace some of the blood she had lost.

By the time she was stable and asleep in a room on the second floor, Mabel's husband was exhausted and ready to go back home to his little ones. He had been assured by the doctor that Mabel would sleep though the night without any further danger to her or their unborn child. He could do no more here, and his babies needed him. I asked Mother to take him home and pick up Cassie. I wanted to stay with Mabel.

"Paisley, dear, please don't get into trouble."

"Why, Mother, whatever do you mean?"

"Ask Leonard, he knows."

After they left, I wandered down to the hospital cafeteria. My stomach was telling me it was way past supper time. Sure enough, the cafeteria food line had closed, but a kindly kitchen worker took pity on my hunger and prepared a thick ham and cheese sandwich for me. She also gave me a cup of lovely hot tea. I sat at a corner table in the kitchen and ate as the cafeteria workers cleaned and closed down for the evening.

I begged one more cup of hot tea and snagged four little packets of sugar to take with me. The stairs were just around the corner, so I took them back up to the lobby. Just as I opened the stairwell door, I heard the public announcement system. The very pleasant voice apprised visitors that it was time to leave and sternly gave them ten minutes to comply.

I let the door close in front of me and leaned back against the wall trying to figure out what to do. Something had made me decide to stay with Mabel, and I was bound and determined to do so even if I had to break a few rules. Her floor was the next one up. I couldn't remember her room number, but it was at the end of the hall. The question was, which end? I decided to cross that bridge when I came to it. The thing to do now was to stay out of sight until things had gotten quiet. The basement floor was the best place to remain unseen. People seldom take the stairs up. With the cafeteria closed, there would be no reason to go down them either. I retraced my steps and found that there was a sub-basement. The corner of the landing below was well out of sight from the stairwell. It was a perfect hiding place. Using my shoes as a broom, I swept out the corner and took up residence. My tea had gone a little tepid but I savored the sweetness and the flavor. In five minutes it was gone and I was bored.

I counted the stairs going up and the ones going down. I counted ceiling tiles and the squares in the vinyl floor. By the time I had finished counting everything, the sounds from the cafeteria had ceased and the elevator was no longer going down to the basement level. I crept back up to the lobby and opened the door just a tad. The receptionist was gone and the lights were dim. I was willing to bet that the front doors were locked. At one time or another I had seen a sign that directed all after-hours traffic to the emergency entrance.

It was ten o'clock. The next shift of nurses was due to change at eleven, a little tidbit I had learned from Cassie the summer she had been a volunteer candy striper at a hospital in Manhattan. I could sneak into Mabel's room now. I just had to make sure I was out of sight at eleven and then again at the next change of shift at seven in the morning. After that, I could go back down the stairs to the cafeteria, have my breakfast, and mingle with the incoming visitors, with no one being the wiser.

Everything was going fine until I got almost to the landing on Mabel's floor. I heard the door to the stairwell above open and froze.

"What else do you want besides coffee, Annie?"

There was silence while the nurse listened to a distant voice. I used those moments to race back down to the basement level. I had no idea where Annie's friend would be going. I hoped there was a room somewhere on the lobby floor with a coffee and probably a soft drink machine. I barely made it back to my hiding place when a figure dressed in white descended to the landing and opened the door to the lobby. I pushed back into the shadows of the corner and held my breath while I waited for her to return and take the coffee back upstairs.

While I was waiting, I decided another cup of tea and maybe a midnight snack, even from a machine, would really hit the spot. I felt around in my pockets, but all I could turn up was the change from my ham sandwich. Fifteen cents wouldn't get me a stick of gum. I caught myself in the middle of a big sigh as the nurse returned balancing two cups and some cookie packets and made her way back up to the next floor. I followed quickly, thinking that no one else would be coming out for a while. I got almost to the landing before the door opened again.

"Damn it, Annie! Two sugars should be enough for anybody. Now before I go back down make sure there's nothing else you want. Salt? Pepper? A straw?"

She came back down the stairs mumbling to herself, "A brain?"

I huddled in the corner trying to keep from gasping for breath. Despite the cool temperature I was drenched in sweat. At least I could say I had done my aerobic exercise for the week. The nurse came back relatively quickly and was soon upstairs and out of sight. I peered out into the hallway and saw that the lights had been dimmed. Soft voices could be heard coming from around the corner, but I saw no one. Luck was with me—the stairs were just opposite Mabel's door. I quickly crossed the hallway and slipped inside.

I was grateful that Mother insisted Mabel be given a private room; I would have had a hard time explaining my presence to a roommate. A faint night light left most of the room in darkness, but I could hear soft snores coming from the bed. As I tiptoed closer, I could see that Mabel was sleeping peacefully. I checked her I.V. and saw that it had just recently been changed. The clear plastic pouch of saline solution that hung above her bed was full. I could be reasonably assured that we would not be disturbed until morning.

The bedside chair was a big comfortable recliner. I pulled it a little closer to the closet so that I could slip out of the chair and into a hiding place quickly before I gratefully eased my body into the soft, cushy seat.

CHAPTER TWENTY-SEVEN

The two cups of tea I'd drunk earlier woke me up at two in the morning. I had to pee in the worst way. I eased myself silently out of the chair and over to the bathroom. Just as I closed the door and was lowering my jeans I heard someone enter the room. I pushed the door open slightly. I heard some paper rustling and something tear. I strained closer to the door and got cross-eyed trying to get a glimpse of Mabel's visitor. Just at that moment the change fell out of my drooping jeans pocket and bounced with a loud metallic clink onto the tile floor.

"Who's there?" the visitor whispered urgently.

The jig was up. I zipped up my jeans and decided to brazen my way out of it.

I opened the bathroom door and yawned mightily. I held my finger up to my lips.

"Shhh. She's asleep. We don't want to disturb her rest, now do we?" I whispered.

I walked nonchalantly over to the man in the white coat. Even in the poor light I could see that he wasn't her doctor. And oddly enough, the man seemed to be even more nervous at finding someone else in Mabel's room than I was.

"Who, who are you?" he stammered.

"I'm a friend," I whispered.

I thought quickly and decided to go with most of the truth.

"Her husband had to go home to stay with the children. I offered to stay with Mrs. Jones during the night. Mr. Jones will be back in the morning. Is there something you need to tell him? I'll be glad to give him the message."

The more I spoke the more confident I felt. This turkey was definitely more ill at ease than I. The light was dim, but I could see his hands trembling slightly. The sheen of perspiration was visible on his wide cheeks and bald pate when he turned towards the night light. He was about my height but twice as broad. His resemblance to Porky Pig was uncanny. I tried to read the name tag on his jacket, but it was too dark. All I could make out was that the name of the hospital department embroidered on his jacket started with a large letter "P." I wondered if someone had thought Mabel needed a psychiatric evaluation. Surely not. But it was possible. She had been very upset.

Porky backed towards the door and further from the light as I advanced on him. "I'll come back in the morning when the husband's here. No need for a message."

He turned and was gone before I could assure him again that my presence was benign.

Now I really had to pee. I decided to get it over with before the nurse came to kick me out. I was sure Porky was headed straight to the nurse's station. Annie or her companion would be here any minute now.

I went about my business quickly. I wanted to be ready when an irate nurse came barreling into the room searching for my butt to kick down the back stairs. When no one appeared after a few minutes, I was curious. Cautiously I peeked out the door and down the hallway. Everything was quiet as a mouse. There was no sign of Porky or anyone else.

I tiptoed back over to the bed to check on Mabel, relieved to see that she was still sleeping. I turned to go back to my chair and crunched something with my foot. It was a paper sleeve from a syringe. How messy, I thought. I should complain to housekeeping. I picked it up and absently tucked it in my pocket.

I took up residence in my comfy recliner once again and tried to get back to sleep. The worst had come to pass—I had been discovered, but nothing had happened.

The dial on my watch was barely visible. So much for my beloved antique Rolex. All I could tell was that the big hand was somewhere in the vicinity of three o'clock. I had four hours plus or minus before I had to leave.

Fifteen minutes later I realized that there would be no return engagement of sleep for me tonight. I looked around for something to read, but we hadn't had time to get Mabel any magazines. The housekeeping department was remiss in some areas, but they had cleaned the room of any reading material from the prior inhabitant. Then I saw Mabel's medical chart on a metal clipboard at the bottom of her bed. I struggled with my sense of decency and Mabel's right to privacy for a minute or so until boredom won out. I grabbed the record from the bottom of the bed and took it into the bathroom.

For the next two hours I tried to read Mabel's medical record. Time after time I cursed my lack of knowledge. I was once again in the unpleasant situation of having to learn a foreign language, just as I had been when I first went to South America with Rafe. Somewhere in the back of my mind that thought rang a bell. Medical terminology was based on Latin and Greek. Spanish was Latin based. Maybe I should look again with that thought in mind. After a while I able to make some sense of the information before me by thinking in Spanish.

Mabel had borne six children in the last twenty-six years. She had been pregnant when she had married Apollo at age seventeen. Three months later she had given birth to a seven pound baby boy.

Before she was twenty, she'd had two more children. Another boy and a little girl. Both children had positional deformities of the right foot which had been corrected with orthopedic splints in their first six months. At age twenty-three she had two miscarriages and a very serious case of hepatitis from a blood transfusion. After that she had not gotten pregnant for fifteen years, even though she and Apollo had never used any birth control measures. That little bit of knowledge made me a trifle uneasy and I almost put the chart away. Almost.

Mabel was overjoyed when she found herself pregnant at thirty-five. Her new baby boy had no evidence of the foot problems of his older siblings, but the next two little girls did. Even though the couple loved children, they acknowledged that this last pregnancy was probably all they could handle. Dr. Edgar Baxter, who was Mabel's physician, felt they already had more than their share of children. He tried to discourage his patient from having her baby. She was forty-three years old. She had a heart murmur, another detail I was uncomfortable knowing. And Apollo had prostate cancer.

"Oh, God!"

I let it out before I knew it. I flicked the light off and opened the door a crack to listen. Mabel was still snoring softly. I sat in the dark for a moment and contemplated what I had just learned. I was savvy enough to know that cancer wasn't always a death sentence, but just the same, it had to be quite a burden—emotionally and financially. Dr. Baxter had urged Mabel to have an abortion. But she and Apollo, knowing that this child would be their last, resisted his pleas and opted to have the baby. From that point on, they began to have problems. Apollo needed to go to the Veteran's Hospital in Nashville three times a week for his cancer treatments. Mabel had to take on more housecleaning jobs to make ends meet. She got sick. The doctor diagnosed a severe allergic reaction to house dust and goldenrod and started her on immunotherapy. Three weeks later she had some vaginal bleeding. She was working in Morgantown at the time and went to the emergency room there. Much the same thing had happened then as she was going through now. She had spent the night in the hospital and then gone home to bed for two weeks. Dr. Baxter reported at her next visit that the baby's heart tones were strong and the fetal ultrasound was within normal limits. Everything was fine except for her allergies. He resumed treatment, and as of her last office visit two weeks ago, she had improved. She was five months pregnant

The Ob-Gyn who had admitted her tonight had dreadful handwriting. I looked at his notes from every angle, even upside down, before I could decipher the fact that he had no idea what was causing her premature labor and bleeding. If he had known, I thought cynically, he would probably have written in big bold letters. I was slowly but surely losing my faith in the medical profession.

The rest of the chart was mostly lab reports and nurse's notes. There was no mention of a mental evaluation having been ordered, although one nurse had mentioned that "the patient was anxious and distraught." The doctor must have decided to call in a specialist after reading that.

I had been up for over twenty hours by this time, and the sleep I had sought to no avail earlier was threatening to take me unawares. Standing up was a chore because my knees and shoulders were cramped and stiff. I hobbled out of the bathroom like an old woman.

It was still dark outside. I had a couple of hours to sleep before pulling off my disappearing act. I opened the miniblinds so the sun would wake me at dawn and lay back to relax.

Mother shook me awake at ten-thirty. Cassie and Mabel were laughing at me as I struggled to my senses. I wiped the sleep from my crusty eyes and the drool from my cheek.

"Um, uh, oh," was all I could manage.

"Good morning, Mom. How's the sleeping beauty?"

"Don't tease your sweet momma, child. She's been watchin' out for me all night long, and I really appreciate it."

"You're right, Mabel. I'm sorry, Mom. Here, I'll get you a hot washcloth. You can wash the sleep off."

"Never mind," I mumbled. "I'll come to the bathroom."

I tried to get up, but my entire body refused to cooperate. The whole of me was one big aching muscle. I took the hot cloth from Cassie and wiped my eyes and face. By the time I had finished, I felt somewhat more awake. She then presented me with a nice hot cup of tea, which made me feel even better.

"Thanks! You're an angel, Cassie. How are you feeling Mabel?"

"The cramps are gone, and I think everything is all right. The doctor's coming any time now, and I hope he'll let me go home. I surely do miss my own bed."

By the time I finished my tea I could stand up. I stretched until I heard things popping. Mother offered me a comb with a disapproving shake of her head. I tried to run it through my unruly curls but they were too tangled. I did borrow a bit of lipstick, however. When I tucked my shirt back in my jeans, I was ready for the day.

"How about some breakfast?" I inquired hopefully.

"It's almost eleven, dear. Why don't we wait and see if Mabel's doctor is going to dismiss her. We don't want her to have to stay here a minute longer than necessary. When we get home I'll fix you a nice lunch. Maybe an omelette with mushrooms and onions?"

"Ummm, okay," I reluctantly agreed. "How come nobody minded that I was here, Mabel?"

"I don't know, Miz Paisley. I woke up and saw you sleeping in the chair. When the nurse came in I told her you were my friend. She didn't seem to care. I guess folks have family stay with them all the time."

"Upfhh," I grumped, thinking of the uncomfortable hours I had spent waiting in the dirty stairwell when I could have been up here in this cozy chair all the while.

Mabel's doctor had gone off duty, but his partner came in shortly before noon. He read her chart and asked us to leave while he examined her. He came out in a few minutes and told us all was well and we could take her home. Mabel had to be on strict bed rest for at least two weeks. He asked if she had a regular doctor. When we told him Dr. Baxter had more or less retired, he gave us his card and directions to his office in Morgantown. Cassie kindly volunteered to take her to the appointment in fourteen days.

She and I helped Mabel get dressed while Mother waved her magic wand in the business office. Cassie brought the car around, and I followed the nurse as she wheeled her patient down to the exit. For a moment or two I had a sense of *deja vu.* Only a few months ago, I was leaving this hospital the same way. I tried to shake the sleepytime cobwebs from my head. There was something I needed to know before we left, but for the life of me I couldn't think of what it was. The thought eluded me until we had taken our patient home and helped tuck her back in bed. Porky Pig! I had forgotten to ask the doctor about the psychiatric consultation he had ordered for Mabel.

CHAPTER TWENTY-EIGHT

I tried not to act like a spoiled child but it was hard going for the next two hours. After we took Mabel home and made sure she was comfortable, Mother sent us to the one remaining pharmacy to fill Mabel's prescriptions and to the grocery store to fill her pantry. Mother wanted to make sure Mabel and her family had everything they might need. Apollo would be more or less confined to the homestead with Mabel in bed and the three little ones to care for. Cassie, who loved the children, immediately offered to take them to the movies one afternoon and to the park at the lake on the weekend in order for Apollo to catch his breath.

By the time we headed for home it was late in the afternoon and everyone seemed to have forgotten my breakfast. As my blood sugar fell so did my ability to remain affable and pleasant. After I made a particularly nasty remark to a driver who tried to turn in front of me without a signal, Cass took notice.

"Crabby, are we? Did we forget to fill your tum-tum, hummm?"

"Don't get smart with me, sister! I'm a fiend when I'm feeling sorry for myself and right now I think I'm just about the most pitiful person on earth."

"Here, Mom, have a Tootsie Roll. I snagged one out of a machine at the drug store."

"Umm, thanks! And where is my omelette? Where are the fresh mushrooms?"

"It's after lunchtime now, Paisley, dear," admonished Mother. "You don't want to ruin your supper. I have a beautiful tenderloin marinating in this divine oriental . . . "

"Divine my hind foot! All I've eaten since yesterday's piss-poor lunch was a miserable little ham sandwich that would leave a mouse starving and two cups of rotten tea. Feed me!"

"No need to raise your voice, Paisley. It's so unbecoming. And foul language makes you sound like a stevedore. You must never forget that you are a southern lady. You do, after all, have to set a standard of behavior for your daughter."

"Oh . . . my . . . God!"

"And blasphemy is definitely . . . "

Instead of turning into our drive I headed downtown. I pulled into the drive-through window at the Dairy Queen and ordered a super-duper serving of fat and salty grease. I licked my chops and enjoyed every minute. Mother kept up her dissertation on my failure to set a nutritional example for my offspring during my entire meal. To show her that I had heard every word, I circled the Dairy Queen again and drove back around to the window. I placed an order for a large hot fudge sundae with cherries, whipped cream, and nuts. I wolfed down that little delight to the tune of my being an ungrateful daughter who has no discipline.

"Just one thing, Mother. You forgot to mention that I'm an unfit maternal role model for Aggie."

"Go ahead, my dear, continue to make fun of me. You'll be sorry one day."

And, of course, she was right. God planned it that way. Mothers always get to be right. I wondered when it was going to be my turn. I was a mother, too. And I was thankful for that because it was Cassie who held my head as I threw up all night.

Around two in the morning, when my salty, greasy meal was just a bad memory, I told her about my nocturnal adventures in the hospital.

"So who do you think he was?" she asked.

"I have no idea."

"It was awfully late for a consultation."

"You're right, hun. I hadn't thought of that. I was so busy trying to explain my own presence I forgot that at three in the morning, he was out of place as well."

We were both snuggled down in my cozy queen-sized bed. It was one of those beautiful fall nights when you could leave the windows open to hear the crickets and shiver delightfully under the quilt when an occasional cool breeze entered the room.

"Let's see," Cassie mused sleepily. "'P' stands for psychiatry, psychology, physical training . . . "

"I think they call it 'rehab,' now." I raised up on my elbow to ask, "Is there any more ginger ale?"

Cass hopped up and poured some ginger ale over my melting ice cubes.

She slid quickly back under the covers and warmed her cold feet on mine.

"Brrr! It's getting cooler. Don't hog all the quilt."

She continued her litany of "p's."

"Phototherapy . . . "

"Try again," I chuckled in the midst of a deep yawn.

"Pharmacy . . . "

"Cassie!"

She jumped out of bed in alarm.

"What is it? Do you need to throw up again? I'll get the basin."

"No! No, you guessed it! I should have thought of it myself. Of course! He was from the pharmacy. Bring me my jeans."

"Please."

"Please, bring me my jeans."

Cassie retrieved my jeans from the heap of dirty clothes I had abandoned on the floor when I felt my stomach rebelling against my eating habits. I fished around in my pockets.

"Rats!"

"What, Mom?"

"I forgot to pick up my nickel and dime from the bathroom floor." I dug deeper down. "Oh, here it is."

I produced the paper syringe sleeve I had found in Mabel's room last night. We turned the bedside light up and examined my find.

"What's so exciting about that? I imagine people from the pharmacy come into sick people's rooms with needles all the time," she said.

"Not to administer medicine all by themselves, they don't. You should know that, Miss Candy Striper."

"You're right, Mom!"

She sat up and gave me a high five.

"A pharmacist would never give anyone medicine, much less an injection. Only doctors and nurses can do that. Anyone else would get in major trouble."

"That's right. And do you notice anything else about my little treasure?"

She picked up the paper and examined it closely.

"It smells funny." She gingerly took another sniff. "Smells like a barbecue."

"It smells like a fire. Like a fire that burned down a certain doctor's office a week ago."

"Wow!"

"Quite."

Another dose of Pepto-Bismol set my innards straight, and I was able to fall asleep around three o'clock. I was afraid this late night stuff was getting to be a habit. This last week had been murder on my sleeping patterns. It would catch up with me sooner or later. Cassie shook me awake at seven.

"I simply cannot believe this!" I shouted angrily. "I stay up until three for days on end trying to help you and your boyfriend, and you won't let me sleep late, ever! You're in real trouble, Missy!"

Cassie whispered softly and urgently, "Mom, please keep your voice down. Ethan just called me. He's escaped from jail. He wants me to meet him tonight and help him get out of town."

I sat up and stared at her in disbelief. He was headstrong and determined to do things his own way, but I had a hard time believing Ethan McHenry was a complete idiot.

"Why in the blue-eyed world would he do something so incredibly stupid?"

"I don't know, Mom."

Cass shook her lovely head in misery. She was shivering and I realized the room was very cold. The windows were still wide open and the temperature had dropped significantly during the night. I pulled her in bed under the quilt and held her close.

"And why," I continued angrily, "would he try to involve you in something that could get you into serious trouble with the law?"

"I guess you were right, Mom. When you said he was a maverick, I mean. This is a very foolish thing to do, isn't it?"

"Yes, my sweet. He just signed away his rights to having me for a happy mother-in-law."

Cassandra sat up and looked me straight in the eye.

"Mom, let's not go there right now. Okay?"

"Okay," I agreed grumpily.

I was of half a mind to call the police and turn the silly jackass in. I had lost too much sleep and given up too much time and energy on him. I could put a stop to things right here and now with one phone call.

Cassie read my mind as usual.

"And we aren't going to turn him in either, agreed?"

"But, Cass . . . "

"But nothing, Mom. Ethan had a reason for doing what he did. I'm sure of it. He asked me to trust him and I do."

"Still?"

"Well . . . yes."

"You don't sound absolutely certain. You know you might go to jail if you meet him tonight. If you help him get away and he's convicted, you most certainly will serve some time. Are you willing to accept that?"

"Mom, he sounded so desperate." Her voice was hoarse with anxiety. "He said it was a matter of life and death. He's sure his life is in danger."

"Oh, Cassie! That's absurd! Andy Joiner put Ethan in Teddyville to protect him."

"All I can do is tell you what he said. And I believe him. At least I believe that he believes it."

"Good grief!"

"Are you coming with me?"

"Me? Where?"

"To meet Ethan tonight, or actually early tomorrow morning."

She raised her head up and looked at me again. Her dark eyes were shining with unshed tears. Her fresh young face was clean and without a trace of makeup. Cassie was always in motion. It wasn't until moments like this, when she was still, that the full reality of her beauty hit me. It always amazed me, even though I was her mother and saw her every day. The most amazing thing of all was that her face was only a mirror to the beauty within.

I knew I would go with her to meet Ethan, and so did she.

"Where?"

"He said to meet him where we had our first kiss."

"Ah ha! And just where was that? I've always wanted to know."

"Over in the field beyond the lake. Near where we found our Christmas tree last year."

"*Au bois!* What time?"

"Two-thirty in the morning."

"Okay, then let's get busy."

She looked at me quizzically.

"I thought you would want to go back to sleep. It's going to be a long night."

"It's going to be an even longer day. Hop up! We've got a bunch to do."

CHAPTER TWENTY-NINE

Aggie was waiting patiently outside the bedroom door for her mistress. Cassie slipped a pair of my sweatpants and a sweater on over her pajamas to take the puppy for a morning walk.

I deliberated over whether or not to tell Mother about our plans while I showered and dressed. Finally, I put it in the back of my mind. After all, I had all day to mull it over.

My stomach felt normal again and I was hungry for breakfast. I knew better than to ask for anything more than "a middle-aged woman's fare" after last night. Mother was probably on her high horse about my stomach proving her right. But she surprised me with a lovely bowl of oatmeal topped with yoghurt and honey.

"The phone rang early this morning, but I was too sleepy to answer. Do you know who it was dear?"

"Eh, no." Lie numero uno. I felt my nose growing longer.

"Mabel called a little later. She asked if we could come by for a moment."

"Surely she doesn't need anything from the grocery?" I answered somewhat irritably.

"Paisley, that's unkind."

I felt like a rat, a rat with a long nose.

"I'm sorry. You're absolutely right. I'm a naughty brat and I behaved like a rotten two-year-old yesterday. Forgive me?"

I stood up and planted a quick kiss on her cheek. She smiled and patted me on the head. I was forgiven. I stopped and admired the trim figure she cut in her navy blazer, blue-and-white striped shirt, and grey slacks. The red and yellow Ralph Lauren silk scarf at her throat was a perky touch.

"You look very nice this morning. All dressed up for something special?"

"Miss Lolly Parsons called earlier and asked me to come over for a visit."

"Wow, you're really in demand today. What's the occasion?"

"Honestly, I have no idea, Paisley. I'm very curious myself."

Cassie came stumbling in the back door with Aggie barking and dancing around her feet. Her hair was tousled and the color was high in her cheeks.

"Gran! Mom!"

"Close the door, dear, and please don't slam . . . "

The sound of the door slamming set Aggie to barking again.

"Never mind, dear."

Mother's sigh was full of resignation. I knew she was certain that neither Cassie nor I would ever grow up.

Cassie sat down and struggled to get her breath.

"There are policemen all over," she panted. "There are two cars at the bottom of the drive and two men in front and two or three out back. We're surrounded!"

"Oh, my God."

Once again I had visions of myself growing old behind bars.

"Well, I never! This is simply ridiculous. I cannot have my home invaded. Hand me the phone Cassandra. I'm calling Andy Joiner. I hope he has an explanation for this intrusion."

"You don't need to call, Mother. He's coming up the walk."

I grabbed Cassie by the arm and whispered urgently in her ear.

"You haven't heard from Ethan. Act surprised and run out crying when he tells us!"

"Gotcha!"

Mother watched our performance with unveiled curiosity, but she had no time for questions. Chief of Police Joiner was already knocking on the back door. Mother turned with quiet dignity and smiled at him through the glass panes before she got up slowly and let him inside.

"Good morning, Andy. To what do we owe this pleasure?"

"Now, Miz Sterling, you know . . . "

She quickly cut him off. Mother hated being approached in a blustery way.

"Calm down, Andy. It's not good for your blood pressure."

"Look here . . . "

"Excuse me, Andy, but we are having our breakfast. Would you care to join us? When we've all finished, then perhaps we will be able to give you our undivided attention."

He knew when he was licked. Mother's home was her castle, and she was decidedly the queen.

"Ah, just a cup of coffee, if you please."

He laced the coffee Cassie gave him with a heaping spoonful of sugar and a generous dollop of fresh cream. I had to give it to Cass. She was all sweetness and light.

"Cinnamon bun, Mr. Joiner?"

"Why, yes, thanks. Cassandra have you heard . . . "

"Andy, please, you'll spoil your digestion," chided Mother. "How are Constance and the girls? We stopped in at the bakery last week, but I didn't see them."

Joiner looked miserable. I was hard put to keep from laughing. He was getting redder by the minute. He choked down the cinnamon bun in two swallows and took a swig of coffee that was obviously still too hot to drink. I got happier and happier as I watched him struggle to swallow the burning liquid. *Surround my Mother's house, will you,* I thought. *She'll fix your wagon!*

177

Cassie cleared the table and made a special task of wiping up the sticky crumbs that Andy had dropped. All the while she gave him an running exhibition of her most dazzling smiles. When she was finished she sat back down next to me in preparation for the next act.

"Now, Andy, dear," invited Mother, tell us the reason for your very early morning visit."

She was good. She even made him apologize.

"I am sorry about the hour, Miz Sterling, but you gotta understand that I'm just doin' my job."

"And what job would that be, Andy?"

"Why, uh, protecting you."

I couldn't resist. Mother was having all the fun.

"From what Chief Joiner? Have the Martians landed?"

I wasn't as daunting as my mother. He didn't mind staring me down. I wished I had kept my mouth shut.

"Ethan McHenry has escaped."

Cassie jumped up right on cue. She screamed loudly in Andy's ear and ran from the room. It was a bit overdone, I thought, but it got the correct response. Andy shook his head to stop the ringing in his ears. "I guess she didn't know."

Mother hadn't move a muscle. I couldn't tell if she had known about Ethan or not.

"Why, of course, not!" she affirmed. "It's preposterous even to suggest such a thing. I'm sure that young man has better manners than to involve a young woman of my granddaughter's caliber in such a sordid affair."

Coming from Mother, it sounded perfectly reasonable.

"I guess you're right," he admitted sheepishly. "He did seem to be very fond of her, and I guess you could call him a gentleman. Especially now that we know he didn't kill Hayes."

"What?" I was astounded. "Why didn't you let him go sooner? Did you at least tell him he was cleared of murder?"

"That's just the thing. I ordered the deputy to fetch him from Teddyville in the prison van. The Hayes girl told her aunt she wanted to speak to me this morning. The aunt hinted that she was gonna take back her story about being raped. I was hoping I could give the boy the good news in person. Doc Baxter went on ahead to give him a standard prerelease physical so he couldn't make any claims later about abuse or anything. When the guards took McHenry to the prison hospital to meet the Doc, he got away somehow. We're still not sure how he did it."

"But if he's done nothing wrong, why are you looking for him? Why are you camped out here?"

"Paisley, this is a whole new ball game. Now he's wanted for jailbreaking. He also managed to slug one of the guards so that's assault. We gotta bring him in again."

"Well, I can assure you, Andy, that you will not find him skulking around here. I imagine he's half way to Atlanta by now."

Joiner wasn't going to be dismissed quite as easily as Mother hoped.

"Just the same," he insisted, "I'll leave some of my men here. If you don't mind, Miz Sterling. For your protection, of course."

"I'm quite sure we need no protection, but if you are adamant about it, there's nothing I can do. You are the law, until the next election, of course."

Mother gave him a very direct and meaningful look.

He cleared his throat and stood up. His face was even redder than before.

"Ahum, yes, of course, he mumbled. "See you later, M'am"

CHAPTER THIRTY

Cassie decided that she had recovered enough from her emotional outburst to drive us to Mabel's. I had to poke her twice in the ribs on the way to the car to keep her from laughing out loud in front of the watching policemen. When Andy had gone, I found her in my bedroom in a state of great hilarity. She seemed to have grown into my unfortunate habit of laughing uncontrollably under stress. Oh, well, I thought, it was better than crying.

As we pulled out of the drive, I noticed one of the police cars circle around to come after us.

"That bastard is following us!"

"Paisley, please."

Mother turned and looked out the rear window.

"Well, I'll be damned!"

"Like mother, like daughter," laughed Cassie.

"This is intolerable. I will not stand for it. Put the pedal to the metal, Paisley, dear. Let him eat our dust."

"You've been watching too many old movies, Mother. Besides, we're almost there."

The Jones' homestead was already beginning to give little hints to stress in the family. For the first time in my memory the grass on the five acres around the house was high and needed cutting. The fast-growing weeds were poking up along the picket fence in patches, and toys were scattered around the front steps.

"Looks like Apollo has his hands full."

"I'll send Billy out to cut the lawn this afternoon. He won't mind. He thinks the world of Apollo."

"Great idea, Mother. From the looks of him I don't think Mr. Jones is going to argue with you."

Apollo was standing at the open door with his youngest on his hip and the other two at his knees. The children looked like they were glued in place. Their eyes were big and frightened. Something was wrong.

I parked quickly and jumped out of the car.

"Apollo, is Mabel . . . .?"

He smiled tiredly, "She's fine. Don't worry about her. The baby's fine, too. He's been kicking up a storm."

Apollo stood aside and ushered us in the house. I wouldn't say it was in shambles, but it was obvious that the woman of the house was out of commission.

Mother and Cassie stayed in the living room with Apollo and the children for a moment to hand around some games and puzzles we brought for them, but I was anxious to see the patient.

Mabel was sitting up in bed working on some mending. The color was back in her cheeks and she looked one hundred percent better. She put her work down and smiled up at me.

"Oh, it's good to see you, Miss Paisley. Thanks for coming. Sorry for the bother."

"You look great, Mabel. How's the soccer player?"

She smiled and patted her middle. "If he's this active when he's born, then we're in big trouble!"

Apollo came in the bedroom and went around to the other side of the bed to sit beside his wife. That's when I noticed the window on the other side of the bedroom had been forced open. The lock was hanging loose and the screen had a big hole in it.

"Apollo! What happened? Did you have a break in?"

"That's why we called you, Miss Paisley. We didn't know whether or not to call the police." He looked down and studied the bed quilt with great interest.

"Why wouldn't you call them?" I asked in surprise.

"Yes indeed," agreed Mother, as she entered the room and heard our conversation, "you simply must call them. It's about time they chased after a real criminal for a change."

"Well, we heard on the radio this morning that Miss Cassandra's young man had escaped from the prison in Teddyville. You all have been so kind . . . there's no way we would cause you any more trouble."

"Oh, Apollo, Ethan wouldn't have tried to break into your house. He would never endanger you or Mabel. That's something I'm sure of," I insisted.

"Then who could it have been?" asked Mabel. "I didn't see a thing. It was too dark, and Apollo was sleeping with little Isaiah. He's frightened because I've been sick, you know. Anyway, I heard a sound and looked up and saw a man climbing in the window. He almost got inside. I started screaming and Apollo come running in and scared him away."

"By the time I got outside, he was gone. I never seen where he come from or where he went," admitted Apollo with a shake of his head. "We didn't hear no automobile, that's why we thought it might have been young McHenry. They said he escaped on foot."

"There's no way Ethan would do such a thing. It must have been just a plain thief."

I tried to convince them of that fact, but I was beginning to think something entirely different myself.

"Apollo, you look like you could use some help," said Mother in an attempt to change the subject. "I'm sending Billy Bennett out here this afternoon. He's got some free time until my back field has to be cut. I'm sure he be more than happy to take care of your lawn and maybe help some with the animals."

He raised his hands in protest, but she was insistent. "Never mind arguing with me. You know me too well for that."

Mabel laughed, "I told him this morning when he brought me breakfast in bed that he was gettin' properly henpecked."

Her husband looked at her fondly, "There ain't nothin' wrong about bein' henpecked if you're pecked by the right hen."

CHAPTER THIRTY-ONE

Since Mother didn't know how long she would be at Miss Lolly's, Cassie and I decided to take her back home so she could take her own car and not have to worry about us. We said goodbye and headed towards town. The police car stayed persistently behind us at every turn. I wondered if one would follow Mother, too.

"Damn! He's on my tail tighter than a tick."

"Want to have some fun, Mom?"

"Sure. Tell me how."

Cassie looked back at the policeman trailing us in the squad car. "Turn down West Market Street and pull into the gas station on the corner.

I followed her instructions exactly. The car behind us followed me.

"Now pull into the car wash."

"But Watson doesn't need . . . "

"Just do it, Mom, please."

She unbuckled her seat belt and got up on her knees to see out of the rear window. Her eyes were sparkling with mischief.

"He's right behind us. This is going to be great!"

"I hope so, we're about due for some fun. What now?"

"I'll run in and pay for the wash. But wait for me to drive inside, okay?"

She was in and out and back in two seconds flat. We pulled slowly into the entrance of the car wash until the red light turned on. Water and soap started raining down in great quantities on Watson's roof.

"It's so hard to see. Wait a minute."

She crawled quickly over the seat into the back and peered out of the rear window.

"Yes!" she shouted. "He's pulling around to the exit of the car wash on the next street over. That's where he'll wait for us. It's on the other side of the building. The schmuck will never see us leave. Wait a sec, Mom, and then back out fast and go the other way."

"But won't it hurt something? I mean, those brushes are huge. We could get stuck."

"We can wait until the rinse cycle. The brushes will go up then. I'll tell you when."

We waited for a moment in delicious anticipation.

"Now! Now! Back out now, Mom!"

I threw Watson into reverse and screeched out of the car wash. One of the big revolving brushes started descending, but we got out from under it just in time. We flew out of the gas station flinging soap suds and water in our wake. Cassie was laughing hysterically in the back, but I was too busy trying to see through the suds on the windscreen to share in the hilarity.

"Turn on the windshield wipers, for God's sake!" she laughed.

"Oops! I should have thought of that. I must be getting old."

Cassie climbed back in the seat beside me. She was wiping tears of laughter from her eyes.

"You'll never be too old for anything, Mom. That's what's so great about you."

"Just remember that when you have to roll me to one of your capers in a wheelchair."

"Any time, Mom, any time."

She settled back down in her seat and buckled her safety belt.

"What now?" she asked. "It's your turn."

"I've been thinking."

"That's another thing I love about you, Mom. You're just like Winnie the Pooh. You think and think until you've thunk it through."

"Seriously, Cassie, remember the other night-time intruder in Baxter's office?"

"The mysterious arsonist?"

"Exactly! I think it was Dr. Edgar Baxter himself."

"Doc Baxter? But why would he set his own office on fire? For the insurance?"

"I don't think so. I'm not sure why, but I believe he was trying to destroy evidence."

"Evidence of what? He hasn't done anything wrong, has he?"

"Let's go ask him. Are you up for it?"

"Wahoo! Lay on, MacDuff!"

Thirty years ago, Edgar Baxter and his wife Julie built a lovely home on fifty acres of rolling farm land between Rowan Springs and the lake. Julie had been a fine arts major in college, and she was an avid collector. The large modern cedar shake home was a series of boxes on many levels, with lots of windows to let in light from all directions. Julie hated artificial light. "It changes one's perception of colors," she had once told me. "I like to see things as they were meant to be, not as they appear under the glare of one hundred watt bulbs."

As we came closer to the big house on the hill, I realized that Winston Wallace had made a poor attempt at copying this imposing structure when he had designed his office. He must have either admired, or envied, Edgar Baxter a great deal.

I was startled for a moment as a police car suddenly appeared behind us with siren blasting and lights flashing.

"Damn! We didn't lose him for long."

"Is that for us, Mom? Does he want you to pull over?"

"I don't . . . No! Look, he's pulling in front. He must have been called to an accident. Good riddance! I was wondering how we were going to be able to talk to the doctor in private."

The car in front of us sped away and then braked in the distance and turned into the driveway leading to the big house on the hill.

"For pity's sake. What's he doing that for?" I wondered. "Great! Now we'll have to explain why we brought along our little escort."

"Do you think Dr. Baxter will talk to us with the police here?"

"All we can do is try, hun."

We followed the police car into the driveway and up the hill. We were not the only visitors Edgar Baxter had that day. The asphalt apron in front of his garage was full of vehicles, including an ambulance. One of Rowan Springs' finest came over to my window as I pulled up to park.

"'Fraid you'll have to leave, Miss. There's been an accident. This here is an investigation."

"But, Officer, I'm a friend of Dr. Baxter. Perhaps I can help."

"Can't nothin' help him no more, if you get my drift. Now turn around, please, and go back where you came from."

I was stunned. This morning I had convinced myself that Edgar Baxter was the mastermind behind a lot of the weird things that had been going on. Mother hadn't seen him enter his office the night it burned down because she left to answer a call of nature, but I was positive that he was the one who had walked down that dark hallway and set the fire. There must have been incriminating evidence in his office that he needed to dispose of. He had to have something to do with Ethan's mystery. Why else would he have refused to talk to a colleague from the Centers for Disease Control? That was a big opportunity for a doctor from a small town. He might have gotten his name on paper in a famous medical journal. Now he was dead, and my theory was shot to hell.

"Oh, my," breathed Cass. "This will really upset, Gran. She liked that old man"

I struggled to extricate Watson from the tangle of cars in the driveway without scraping any fenders. That would be a bummer. A fitting end to my morning.

"Hey! Hey! Stop that car!"

I heard the shouting over the sound of the engine and looked in the rear view mirror. Andy Joiner was running after us.

"Terrific! First he sends a cop car to follow us and now he's doing it on foot!"

"I think he wants you to stop, Mom. Better do it before he has a heart attack. I don't think he's really in shape to run much further."

"Let's see," I teased.

"Oh, Mom, don't be mean."

"Yeah? And what if he tries to pin Doc Baxter's 'accident' on your little friend Ethan."

"Then, I guess we'd better stop and let him tell us what happened."

"Oh, well," I sighed, "you may be right. Let's see what he wants."

I pulled Watson over to the edge of the lush green lawn and turned off the engine. Andy Joiner lunged against the side of the car and leaned heavily on my door while he caught his breath.

"P . . . aisley," he panted, "c . . . can you please come back up to the house?" He took a deep breath. "Maybe you can help us with something."

"Sure thing, Chief!" I grinned wickedly at him. "Always delighted to cooperate with the powers that be."

He gave me a sour look and turned to trudge back up the hill.

"Want a ride, Chief? You look a little out of shape there. Be glad to give you a lift."

He made an obvious effort to try and pull in the little pot belly his wife's good cooking had encouraged over the years and doggedly climbed the steep drive while I slowly drove beside him

"Mom, give the poor guy a break," whispered Cassie.

"Shhh! You had your idea of fun. Now I'm having mine."

CHAPTER THIRTY-TWO

Andy recovered from his exertions while I parked the car. His color was still high, and he was sweating like a horse, but he managed to maintain his dignity in front of the other officers.

"We can enter the house through the garage," he said stiffly, as he pointed the way. "Follow me, please."

Andy's polite demeanor made me ashamed of the way I had teased him. He kept up a running conversation as we entered the house. I missed most of what he said while I stared in awe at the beautiful paintings Julie Baxter had obtained since I had last been a guest in her home. The walls of the long hallway leading from the kitchen to the main part of the house served as a sort of minor art gallery. A series of skylights overhead opened up the narrow passage to the bright sunlight. The space was filled with the brilliant colors of paintings hung all along the expanse. It was a dazzling spectacle.

" . . . perhaps the young lady would like to wait here with Officer Harley."

"Do I have to, Mom?"

From the grim look on Joiner's face he wasn't going to change his mind.

"I guess so, Cassie. I'll be right back."

I hadn't heard what Joiner was saying as we entered the house, so I was not at all prepared for the horrible sight of Dr. Edgar Baxter sprawled across his big walnut desk with a large ragged hole in his head and brain tissue leaking out across his blotter.

"Uhhh . . . My Lord! Oh God, I didn't know."

Andy came from behind and supported me as I backed up and sat down heavily in a big leather armchair. Blackness washed over my vision for a moment, and I found it hard to breathe. My thoughts scattered, searching desperately for something trivial, something other than the scene of violent death confronting me.

I finally managed a deep breath and sat back in the soft comfort of old leather as my vision cleared. I found myself thinking that this was just the sort of chair I had always wanted for the library on the farm. I wondered absently where Edgar, or maybe Julie, had found it. I put my hands palms down on the seat next to my thighs to push myself deeper into the enfolding leather. As I moved back, my fingers brushed against what felt like a glass tube. I gently folded it into my palm, hoping Andy hadn't noticed.

"Are you all right, Paisley?"

"What? Oh . . . I guess so."

Andy crossed over to a small table in the room and poured me a glass of water. As soon as I was sure he wasn't looking, I put the glass vial in my pocket. When he turned back to me, I took a sip from the glass of water he offered, then wet my fingers and rubbed my temples.

"I was just . . . I didn't know about . . . " I stammered, feeling the sting of tears in my nose and throat.

"I guess you didn't hear me before."

He knelt on one knee in front of me and examined my face carefully.

"Do you need to leave? You don't have to stay, you know."

I patted his big shoulder gratefully and then blew my nose on one of the tissues he offered.

"I'm sorry I made you run up the hill. It was mean of me."

He laughed. It was a big booming laugh, and somehow it cleared the room of ghosts. The lifeless body that had once been our dedicated family doctor had become a pitiful and gruesome object, but one I was finally able to deal with.

"What happened to him?" I asked in a voice that was still a little shaky.

"Well, from the looks of him I would say he's a goner," he answered sardonically

The memory of Joiner huffing and puffing up the driveway gave me a moment's pleasure. Apology be damned!

"I would agree," I responded with careful dignity. "The question was meant to be how did it happen?"

"We found a shotgun on the floor beside the desk. It would appear that it was the murder, or maybe even suicide, weapon."

"You think he might have killed himself? But why? Was there a note? There always has to be a note."

"Whoa there! You're way ahead of us. I don't have access to a whole lot of forensic science here in Rowan Springs. The state folks are sending down some specialists to help look for things like powder burns and bullet angles. We'll have to wait until some of those tests come back to say much more."

"Andy, you don't fool me. You may be a country cop now, but you used to be a big city detective. You've seen a lot of murders. The story around town is that's why you moved your family here three years ago—to get away from all the violence. I'm sure you know more intuitively than any fancy forensic specialist can tell."

He stared at the discarded flesh and bone that used to be Edgar Baxter. He hadn't known Edgar Baxter as well as my mother had—as a trusted physician and friend. To Andy, the body in front of him was just the focus of another crime scene.

"And just why should I share that intuitive knowledge with you?" he asked politely.

There wasn't a trace of the old country-boy accent he sometimes affected in his voice.

It felt weird grinning in a room that was beginning to stink of death, but nevertheless, I gave him a big one.

"You don't have to, but I think you want to. You are as fascinated by violent death as I am. That's why you became a policeman in the first place. You may have moved back here because of Constance and the girls, but you still share my morbid curiosity about the criminal mind."

"Or the reasons why decent, normal people become criminals," he added.

"Exactly!"

"I've heard you're as cunning as your mother. Are you giving me a snow job?"

"Maybe."

He laughed again. This time I joined in.

"Well, I can tell you that we didn't find a note. The shotgun is a fancy collector's item which shouldn't be hard to trace and . . . Are you sure you're all right? You still look a little pale."

"I'm fine now, really. What did you want to ask me? Why did you bring me here in the first place?"

"Under . . . well, underneath the body we found a laptop computer. There were no identifying marks on it, but a disc inside had several chapters and some notes for a novel. The author is Leonard Paisley?"

I tried to get up, but Andy gently held me in the chair.

"Believe me, Paisley, this is as close as you want to get."

"Edgar Baxter was the one who stole my computer? I can't believe it."

This wasn't a part of my theory at all. I never figured the town's leading physician for a sneak thief.

"Why didn't you report the theft? That little piece of plastic and technology must have cost you a pretty penny. And a work in progress, with all your notes? That can't be unimportant to you either. Why didn't you call it in?"

I couldn't tell him the truth, not just yet, anyway. And I couldn't think fast enough to tell a lie that would sound like the truth. I fell back on that ancient weapon of southern womanhood: I pretended to swoon. I'm sure Andy didn't fall for it, but he had no choice. He called for someone to help him carry me outside to the car. Cassandra ran alongside us, her eyes wide with alarm.

"My Mom, is she all right?"

I moaned loudly to announce my pretended return to consciousness.

"She'll be just fine. Just let her get some fresh air. And here . . . "

The icy cold water was totally unexpected. Andy had dumped a big soft drink cup of the stuff over my head. I came up gasping, cursing, and damning the man for getting in the last word!

"She's fine. You can take her home now," he said to Cassie with a huge grin. "Tell her we'll call if we need anything else. And here . . . " He handed her a computer disc. "Here's her book. We'll need to keep the laptop for a while but there's no reason for her not to have the disc. I know how much it means to her."

Cassie helped her poor dazed mother into the car and hopped into the driver's seat.

"Get me out of here now!" I whispered, trying not to move my lips.

Cassie turned startled eyes on me, "Mom! You're all right!"

"Move it on out!"

"Okay! Okay!"

CHAPTER THIRTY-THREE

As soon as we were down the driveway and out of sight I sat up and shook the ice and water out of my hair, giving my daughter an unexpected cold shower.

"Mom!" she protested.

"I'm sorry. Damn, damn, and double damn! I'm going to get that man if it's the last thing I do."

"Joiner?"

"Yes!"

I fished around between the seats and found some old napkins from the Dairy Queen. I patted my face and shirt as dry as I could until the paper disintegrated into a sodden mess.

"What happened to Dr. Baxter? Did he have a heart attack?"

"I'm afraid not, Cassie. Andy Joiner says it looks like he shot himself." I didn't tell her that I had my own doubts about calling it suicide, or that the shotgun looked all too familiar.

"Oh, how horrible! Then you must be right! Dr. Baxter's the one responsible for all the dead babies. I can't wait until we tell Ethan that we've solved his mystery!"

I didn't interrupt her litany. I couldn't. My teeth were chattering too hard.

"Do you want to go home and change?"

"No, I'll be okay. Just turn on the heater. I'm freezing."

I huddled in front of the heater vents. By twisting and turning I exposed as much wet fabric as I could to the warm air. By the time we got back to town, I was as dry as I could get. My hair was a different story. Auburn curls stood up and out in every direction. I had never looked more like Raggedy Ann.

"Nobody will take me seriously looking like this," I moaned.

"Which nobody do you have in mind, Mom?"

"I have no idea," I admitted. "Somebody with a lab that can tell me what's in this little bottle."

I pulled the small yellow-capped vial I had found in Edgar Baxter's house out of my pocket.

"What is it and where did you find it?"

"I don't know what it is. I found it tucked in between the cushions of a wonderful leather chair."

I held the vial up to the window and squinted. I could see nothing in the colorless liquid but tiny little black dots. "You know anybody with a lab around here, or even a junior chemistry set? Anybody with a microscope?"

"Ethan told me that the extension service of the state agriculture college out on the Teddyville road has a pretty decent lab. He went there several times. I went with him once and met the guy in charge, Barry Sedmonds. He's really nice. If I thought you would go for a man with a huge grey beard who wears overalls all the time I would have introduced you earlier.

"No time like the present. I'm sure to make a fantastic impression myself."

"Let's go then!"

The local extension service was the place that farmers in Lakeland County came to analyze the soil on their land. They also brought in all kinds of creepy crawlers to find out what was eating their corn, or sorghum, or fescue. I had never had a reason to visit before, and now I was sorry. It was quite a lovely place.

The small low-lying buildings were set unobtrusively on several beautifully green and verdant acres of everything that can be grown in this part of the country. A roadside stand selling big red tomatoes and Indian corn and green beans was an advertisement for the expertise of the farmer scientists. Each one of the little white buildings was festooned with trellises of climbing roses, morning glories, and scarlet runners. It was a beautiful and calming sight. I almost forgot why we had come.

"Wow, Mom, did you see those tomatoes? Gran would love to have some, I bet. And let's get some to take to Mabel."

"I'm hungry," I realized. "What time is it?"

"Almost four o'clock.

"Gee, how time flies when your having fun."

Cassandra drove to the end of a neat one-lane gravel road behind the buildings. From the back, I could see that they were actually greenhouses. The glass was covered with shutters which could be moved about on a series of rolling tracks built on the eaves of the roofs. It was an ingenious plan for getting most of the sunlight during winter months.

"Barry's office is in the last building. I'm sure he has a microscope. But be prepared, Mom. He's a little bit of a loon."

"All my best friends are loons. He'll fit right in."

Cassie parked Watson as far off the narrow road as she could. We got out and walked across the gravel to the little building.

"Are you sure he's here? I don't see any more cars."

"He doesn't have a car. He says they aren't environmentally efficient. He's here. There's his bicycle."

"Oh," I said under my breath, "He's one of those sorts of loons."

But as soon as I met Barry, I realized he was a loon after my own heart.

"Cassandra the beautiful! Welcome back. I'm delighted to see you. Where's your good-for-nothing Romeo?"

The big man in red plaid flannel and vast amounts of denim

ushered us into the warm and earthy-smelling confines of the green-house. His beard did resemble steel wool, but when he brushed past me to secure the door, it felt as soft as goose down.

"All my babies are going to sleep," he explained as he shut the door carefully and pulled a heavy sheet of plastic down over it to prevent any possibility of a draft. "I don't want them to catch a cold," he said, as he gestured towards the plant beds extending back the length of the greenhouse.

The big man turned and looked me up and down.

"I'm supposing you're Cassandra's famous mother, Paisley Sterling. I would say sister, but I'm hoping you're not that young because she is a mere child. You want to have dinner with me Friday night? I'm fixing venison spaghetti. I may not be Robert Redford but I have a terrific personality." He leered comically at me as he continued, "And you, my sweet Paisley, have enough good looks for the both of us."

I laughed. I couldn't resist his effervescent smile and bright green eyes. They were the youngest part of him. I judged his age at about forty something. He was still firm and athletic, and the face behind the beard was smooth and unlined. The only wrinkles he had were laugh lines around those terrific eyes.

"Sorry, Barry—about the lack of introduction, I mean," Cassie offered in a somewhat distracted voice. I could tell she was surprised that Barry didn't know about Ethan's escape. "This is my mother, Paisley DeLeon."

"Then you're married?" He looked at Cassie and back at me and blushed an indecent red. "Oh, of course you would be, you're her mother. Oh, well, never mind. Next time around, next life."

He busied about and found two rickety old three-legged stools and pulled them up to his lab table for us.

"What can I do you fer? As my maiden uncle used to say."

"Mr. Sedmonds," I started.

"Barry, please," he insisted as he put one big hairy paw on my arm.

"Barry, I found this at the scene . . . somewhere this morning, and I'm really curious as to its contents. At first I thought it was water, but if you look really closely you can see the tiniest spots of something in it. I was hoping you would let me borrow your microscope."

I put the little bottle with the yellow cap on the lab table in front of him. He sat back in surprise and almost fell off his seat.

"Well, there's no mystery here. I'm sorry I can't pretend and play the role of all-powerful scientist, but this is just too simple."

"It is?" asked Cassie.

"Sure is, honey," he answered.

"Then what is it?"

"Haven't you ever been to an allergist?" he asked me.

"Sure, just last week. I had some poi . . . "

"Well, then you must know that this is the weakest dose of an allergen. Most allergy docs I know have the same system. The yellow tops are for the first immunotherapy inoculations, and they go on through a series of stronger extracts. Those are in the same bottles topped in green, blue, and red. What are you allergic to?"

"Nothing, I guess. I had . . . "

"Dust mites! That's what gets me—the little buggers. Damn dust mites make me about sneeze my beard off. I had to have shots for dust mite allergy for three years! Twice a week for three years! Can you imagine?"

"Well, I don't . . . "

He grabbed the little bottle.

"Let's see if we can tell what this is in here."

Cassie was laughing. I had to smile. The man was a tornado in blue denim.

"You're right, my sweet lady! There is the tiniest of somethings in this bottle," he said, turning back from his microscope. "And I would hazard a guess that this is an allergen for Goldenrod."

"Goldenrod?"

"Yes! Because it has an artifact."

"Artifact?"

I was beginning to sound like an echo.

He slammed the bottle down on the table and barreled past me in the confined space again. This time I could swear he pinched my buttocks. I gave a little jump and Cass looked at me quizzically. This was no time to get on my feminist high horse, I decided. I was brimming over with excitement. I had the feeling that this bear of a man was coming close to solving Ethan's problem.

Barry came back down the narrow aisle of the greenhouse carrying a long stalk of grass with small yellow flowers on the end. He was obviously in the throes of scientific excitement because he forgot to pinch me again. He shook the flowers vigorously over the lab table. Cassie immediately started to sneeze.

"See?" he gestured towards Cassandra with the flowers. "Yon damsel is allergic to Goldenrod. As a good mother, you would naturally take her to an allergist."

He leaned across the table and glared at me. "Why haven't you, by the way?"

"She never . . . "

"The doctor would start her on a series of allergy shots made with a natural extract of the very plant that was giving her nasal passages fits."

When he slammed the yellow bottle down on the table again, Cassie and I both jumped.

"Naturally, he would start with the yellow-topped bottle since it is the weakest strength and progress over a period of months to the strongest. After a year or two of this magical treatment she would find that her allergy to Goldenrod was no longer. She could go out and roll in the stuff and be sneeze free." He sighed, "Ah, modern medicine."

"What's the artifact?" asked Cassie.

"Ah, there's the rub," he boomed. "For the last year, all of the Goldenrod in our fair state has been infected with a rust." He saw our questioning looks and explained. "A rust is a plant fungus. It invades like a virus and before you know it—poof!"

He slammed his fists down and we jumped again. I decided I might have to smack him if he did it one more time.

"You can ask anybody in the allergy business. Goldenrod treatments have been put on hold."

"Why?"

"Because, dear lady, no one knows how the plant rust will affect the patient. And it cannot be eliminated from the plant extract. Not with absolute certainty, anyway."

I tried to remember some of my college botany.

"You said this rust was a fungus?"

"Right!"

"Then it has spores."

"Exactomundo!"

"Then it can spread."

"Give the lady a gold star! And that's just why nobody wants to take a chance on using it for allergy therapy. It could theoretically carry another disease from patient to patient."

He looked at me with those emerald eyes, "That's just theory, you understand. But enough of a possibility to halt treatments for a while until we can come up with a nontoxic fungicide that's specific to this particular rust. I don't know where this little yellow bottle came from, but whoever made it could be in big trouble, because it's full of fungal spores."

"Have you ever heard of Goldenrod causing abortions?"

"Where in damnation are you all getting this information? That happened so long ago, and yet, you are the third person to ask me in the last three years."

"Edgar Baxter was the first?"

He looked at me with unveiled admiration.

"Beauty and brains, too," he sighed. "What a winning combination."

CHAPTER THIRTY-FOUR

Before he let us go on our merry way, Barry Sedmonds fixed us the best tomato sandwich I ever had. He even washed his hands first.

Cassie backed Watson out of the one-way drive behind the greenhouse like an expert. We were well on our way again when I realized that we had not been given another police escort. I mentioned it to Cassie.

"Maybe Joiner forgot."

"In the words of your Confederate great-granpappy, 'Forget hell!' I think he's pretty sure we're not going to meet Ethan during the daytime. He'll be back at the farm tonight with reinforcements."

The mood of the town seemed a bit somber as we drove through on our way home. There was a huge white silk bow of mourning tied to the one remaining post in the rubble that had been Dr. Edgar Baxter's office. The few people out on the street were gathered in small conversational groups. I don't think I was wrong to imagine they were discussing the old man's life and death. Mother would be sad, too. I hoped I was wrong about Edgar Baxter. It would be nice if he could rest in peace.

I had left the little yellow-capped bottle with Barry. He was going to make an official analysis of the contents, including the spores. He had been dying of curiosity, but had the good manners not to ask me where my little find had come from. I promised him that after this was over I would take him up on his dinner invitation. I would fill him in on all the details over tiramisu. The mascarpone cheese, he promised, would be made with milk from his very own goats. I guessed I was up for it. At the very least, it would be interesting to observe Mother and Barry in action. She and Cass would come with me. He said I would need chaperones to curb his unbridled lust.

My being right all the time never ceased to amaze me. The circular drive at Meadowdale Farm was full of police cars. The sleek Bentley convertible belonging to Horatio Raleigh was parked closer to the house. Horatio was most likely trying to spirit Mother away from the plebeian clutches of the law by taking her to some exclusive place down by the lake for dinner.

Right again!

"I simply cannot leave the children, Horatio," she insisted as she took another sip of the excellent *chenin blanc* he'd brought as an enticement.

"We're not exactly children, Gran. I'm over twenty, for God's sake, and Mother's almost . . . "

"Never mind what I am almost. Cassie is right, Mother. Go and have dinner with Horatio. We'll be perfectly fine here."

The late afternoon sun was still warm as it filtered through the wooden slats Mother had lowered over the screen on the back porch to give us some privacy from the watching eyes of the local cops. I stretched back in the comfortable chaise lounge and took two more long sips of the wonderful wine.

"Some day you're going to have to educate me on the whys and wherefores of buying wine, Horatio," I said.

"Glad to my, dear. I always said to your dear late father that the bottom of that unused cistern out in the side yard would make the most perfect wine cellar. It's even shaped like an amphora. That's what the ancients kept their . . . "

I dozed off as Horatio continued his lecture on wine and Greek civilization. Cassie awakened me when she rescued the empty wine glass I was about to drop on the sandstone floor.

"Sorry, Mom," she whispered. "I didn't mean to wake you up."

"Why should you stop now?" I grumped as I cleared the sleep from my voice. "How long . . .?"

"About an hour and a half is all. And you weren't even snoring." She smiled and patted my head. "You must feel very rested."

"Yeah, terrific. Rarin' to go."

I turned over and shut my eyes again. "Let me have just a few more minutes . . . "

"Mom, it's almost eight o'clock. We have to meet Ethan in just a few hours and we haven't even made a plan yet."

"Horatio got rid of Mother for us. That was our biggest problem. The rest is a piece of cake. Now let me sleep."

"Sorry to disappoint you, but our biggest problem is in the kitchen preparing dinner. She refused to leave us, and Horatio won't leave her. Now we have the two of them to contend with."

"Piss!"

"No. Lobster bisque with artichoke crostini. But you were close."

Cassie hated lobster almost as much as artichokes.

My daughter warmed up chicken noodle soup from a can while the rest of us marveled over the smooth texture and delicious taste of the bisque. I chomped delicately on crostini as I invited some more information from Horatio's seemingly endless storehouse of knowledge. This time I wasn't interested in the ancients. I wanted gossip.

"What are people saying about Edgar's death?"

He paused in his pursuit of a choice bit of lobster and patted his lips delicately with one of Mother's monogrammed linen napkins. She had decided that our being the object of a police stakeout called for a formal occasion.

"Edgar Baxter was an old and dear friend of mine and your Mother's. In fact," he continued, "of almost everyone in town. For years, he and Julie were the leaders of the young social set until her rather unfortunate, er, habit, began to make her shun the public eye."

"I always thought if Julie had only consented to adopt a baby she and Edgar would have been so much happier," Mother sighed. "What a waste! A lovely young woman and a truly fine man. It's a tragic ending to such glorious possibilities."

I pondered over that statement for a moment as I finished my soup. Mother was right. Since my return to Rowan Springs, I had come to realize that it was only in little towns like this that one could see the complete play of a person's life acted out. In Manhattan, life was played out in short segments. You knew people for sporadic periods of time only, and certainly never from birth to death. A little town was a stage for the entire scenario of one's life. In Rowan Springs all the players were known—only the ending was in doubt. You just had to sit back and wait for the curtain to come down and the critics to descend. Then you could decide if the play was worth the effort of the sixty or seventy years of its production.

"What did Miss Lolly want, Gran?" asked Cassie, as she scraped artichokes off her crostini.

"I almost forgot! She gave me one of Ethan's 'tiny little records' as she called it. Apparently you and your mother didn't fool her for one second when you removed his computer last week. Her gardener found the disc under the stairs in the rhododendrons. One of you must have dropped it as you were leaving."

"Cassie did."

"I'm sure it was you, Mom."

"Anyway," continued Mother, "she was delightfully conspiratorial about it. She had all the blinds pulled down. She even asked me if I had been followed."

"Had you?" asked Cassie and me together.

She looked at us questioningly. "Why, of course not! Andy Joiner would never dare to impugn my integrity by suggesting that I would have anything to do with rescuing your young man."

"I imagine the dear old thing sees herself as quite the Jessica Fletcher," suggested Horatio. "I do recall her looking somewhat like a young Angela Lansbury when I was a boy and . . . "

I interrupted when an errant thought struck me. "Horatio, I almost forgot! Who's in charge of the pharmacy at the hospital?"

He took a sip of wine and pondered for a moment. I am quite sure he didn't need to ponder at all; he simply wanted to create a dramatic pause.

"Miss Teresa Downs. She has been there for at least twenty years."

I was disappointed. The identity of Porky Pig remained a deep dark mystery.

CHAPTER THIRTY-FIVE

Mother was just about to put the torch to the bananas and rum in her silver chafing dish when the phone rang. It was Barry.

"I can't believe it, honeychile, but I got robbed! Somebody broke in the greenhouse and made off with your little bottle!"

"Gosh, Barry, are you all right?" I asked, although I couldn't imagine anyone trying to overpower that mountain in blue denim.

"Oh, my heart! I knew you cared!" he laughed. "No, I'm fine, darlin.' I was back in the office." He paused for a minute, "I have to 'fess up 'cause I'm so smitten by you. It was my fault. I'm afraid I left the door unlocked."

I could almost hear him blushing.

"That's all right, Barry. I shouldn't have burdened you with something that could have possibly been evidence in a police investigation."

"Really? That important, huh?"

"I'm afraid so."

"Then I guess the analysis I did on the contents would be pretty important, too?"

"Oh, Barry, I do love you! What is it?"

"I was right the first time. It is Goldenrod, and it does contain fungal spores of the rust we've seen for the last year. Funny thing, though—it's twice the strength of the usual first treatment allergen. Somebody could be in big time trouble for making that little cocktail."

"Barry, you don't know how much I appreciate this. But I have to warn you—you could be in danger for just knowing that. I'd feel so much better if you'd stay with a friend tonight."

"You, maybe?" he breathed deeply and dramatically into the phone. "All night long?"

"Not me," I laughed. "Somebody with a gun. And don't ride anywhere on that bicycle of yours. Get your friend to come and pick you up in a car. Or better still, a truck." I remembered his size and added, "A big truck."

Cassie was waiting like a vulture for the fancy banana dessert. I bequeathed her my share and begged to be excused. I had some more telephone time to put in. When I explained that I needed to call my agent, Mother willingly agreed. She loved Pamela Winslow. She was everything I was not, including a lesbian. But that was one little fact Mother willingly overlooked in her admiration of Pam's style, panache, and wardrobe.

We had been college roommates for four years. It was Pam who had suggested I become a writer after Rafe disappeared and I needed to get a job to care for my little daughter. With her helpful introductions, I was able to launch a career as a successful writer of children's books which lasted for nearly a decade. And when the kiddies tired of me, she had been the one to suggest that I write mysteries under the *nom de plume* of Leonard Paisley. I still wasn't exactly one hundred percent happy about that. There had been several times during the last year when I had wanted to murder Leonard so I could take all the credit for his popular novels—the ones I worked so hard to write.

Pamela answered on the first ring, but she obviously wasn't expecting a call from me.

"Oh, drat!"

"Well, hello to you too, Pam."

"I'm sorry darling, but it's this damn water heater. This was such an adorable penthouse. I just couldn't pass it up, but it does have its own personality. And tonight of all nights it's being extremely anal retentive about the hot water. I was hoping you were the plumber."

She sounded so pitiful. I tried not to laugh, but I couldn't help it.

"Go ahead, sweetie! Have your fun at my expense. I'm sure you've had your hot shower today."

"As a matter of fact, I can't remember, Pam. This has been one hell of a day and the night is still young."

Her voice got very quiet. "Oh, do tell, darling, a new man, have we? Does my sweet Cassandra like him? Tall, dark, and handsome, humm?"

"I hate to disappoint you, but no, there's no new . . . well, yes there is!"

Just for fun, I decided to give her a bit of misinformation.

"He is tall. About six four I would guess, and he weighs about two fifty. He has a grey beard and vibrant green eyes. He asked me out to dinner."

I knew this bit of news would travel from one side of Manhattan to the other in the space of twenty-four hours.

"How delicious, pet," she breathed. "I've been hoping you could have some really good sex!"

I chuckled, "Not sure about the sex yet, but the menu sounds interesting."

I could hear her rustling about on her desk.

"Not to change the subject, love, but Leonard owes me some chapters. You promised them almost a month ago. What's going on? How many do you have ready?"

She was all business now. I struggled to keep up with her. I should have thought to turn on Ethan's computer so I could read the floppy disc Andy had returned to me. I could not remember for the life of me how many chapters of our latest tome I had completed before my laptop was stolen.

"Just give me a sec while the computer warms up."

I twisted around and grabbed the disc from the coffee table where Cassie had left it.

"Ah, let's see. Okay. I have a synopsis and thirteen, no fourteen chapters done."

"And that's translates into how many words?"

Pamela was very interested in the word count. I always teased her about that. I cared what the words were, she cared how many. I went to the document info tab and let it do the counting for me.

"Twenty-five thousand, one hundred and fourteen words to be exact. That's odd."

"What dear? Sounds perfectly fine to me. Get those off to me tomorrow at the latest, please. I have a luncheon Monday with a new editor. He's hungry, and you know I'm always looking out for Leonard's interests."

"Not to mention your fifteen percent!"

"Don't be crass, darling. Kisses to the munchkin and that divine mother of yours."

"By the way, Pam, just out of curiosity, what's so special about tonight?"

"You're too young to know, babe, too young to know!"

I hung up the phone and stared at the computer screen. I was puzzled over the numbers the computer had brought up on Leonard's latest. I was very consistent about my writing. I never used an outline. The number of pages and chapters formed the backbone of my books. Each page held about two hundred and twenty words, and each chapter had approximately eight pages. Fourteen chapters should have added up to a little over twenty-four thousand, six hundred words, not over twenty-five thousand. I must have been seriously verbose in the last one or two chapters.

I scrolled down the pages. Everything was fine until I got to chapter twelve. Sure enough I had written eleven pages instead of the usual eight in that chapter. I paged back to the beginning and quickly scanned thorough it. It had been a while and I couldn't quite remember exactly what I had written.

Cassie came loping in with Aggie dancing around her heels.

"Brought you the last banana, Mom. They're scrumptious."

"No thanks. 'A full mongoose is a slow mongoose.'"

"What?"

She plopped down on the red chintz sofa. Aggie pounced up on her stomach and started licking her chin.

"Don't let the puppy lick your . . . !"

"No, the thing about the mongoose. What's that all about?"

"Rikki Tikki Tavi. Don't you remember your Kipling?"

"No, but I remember Garcia Lorca, and Isabel Allende, and . . . "

"Cassie!"

She jumped up from the sofa causing Aggie to scramble around trying to keep her footing on something or somebody. The dog failed to gain purchase and fell to the floor with an angry growl and a disgusted look on her furry face.

"What's the matter?" asked Cassie, her eyes wide with fear.

"Baxter! He left a suicide note hidden in Leonard's twelfth chapter!"

"Oh, my God!"

She tripped over the angry snarling puppy in her attempt to reach my side.

"Pull up that chair," I pointed to my grandmother Howard's dainty little rocker. "Here, I'll turn the screen around so we can both read it."

"Shouldn't we call Gran and Horatio?"

"Do you want to wait?"

"No!" she responded impatiently.

"Well, neither do I. Besides, let's find out what he said first. Gran might insist that we call in Andy Joiner. If she does that, our plans for tonight will be shot to hell."

"Oh, I hadn't thought of that. Thanks, Mom, for putting Ethan first."

"Just remember that on visiting day when you have other things to do."

I scrolled quickly through the pages to see how much Edgar Baxter had written within Leonard's text. There seemed to be two and a half pages of odd, sometimes rambling sentences, all without standard punctuation or any capital letters.

"Seems very strange. Do you think he was drunk or on some medication?" asked Cassie.

"Could have been. Or maybe nothing mattered any more, least of all the rules of grammar. And remember, he had no computer in his office. He probably couldn't type."

We read quickly thorough the old man's hasty notes. It was difficult to get the meaning without periods or commas, but essentially he was making a strained confession without any apologies for his actions:

"my darling lovee juliia died an lef me al alone she who wold hav b en the most lov inm other had nown to lovf andnoento leave behinfor med to lov ei am alone I hav a missionnow to mak sertann only those who shold an deserve to bar the infAnts old a ndpoor and foolish with foul genes and c roooked souls and eevil heartts canno long caRry seed"

"Spooky!" breathed Cassie.
"Shhhh, I'm trying to read."

"none lissened to me I spok to them and inthhhhheir prided they laufed at my gpod c onsul theyh angered med an d so they lost the right to c hoolsz researxc h fvoujnd the goldednrod and and"

"I'm getting a headache. Mom, you read and tell me what the crazy old fart said."

"Umm, he does sound a bit off. I wonder why no one ever noticed?"

"I always thought he was a bit medieval, but that's a long way from being crazy enough to start your own plague."

"You want me to try and decipher some more of this?"

"Please! You're the detective—detect!"

"He seems to have discovered the same information Ethan did about Goldenrod." I went on reading so I could explain it to Cassie. It seemed that when Baxter decided that he was going to play God, he approached an allergist—my allergist—in Morgantown, and had him make up several batches of allergen. When he kept asking for stronger extracts, the allergist became suspicious and started asking questions. Baxter then had to bypass him and find another source so he could continue to give the extract to his patients. He used a series of three injections which he would prescribe for the women under the guise of folic acid and prenatal vitamins.

The first shot was twice the strength of the regular Goldenrod allergen and would put unusual stress on the fetal heart. The second, even stronger one, brought on bleeding from the placenta. The most concentrated extract, the third and last, would cause deep contractions of the uterus and expulsion of the fetus.

He only used his "special therapy" a few times that first year, but then he began seeing more and more families who didn't, to his mind, deserve a baby. His Goldenrod treatments increased. So did his need for the allergen.

Something went terribly wrong during the last fourteen months. Even those fortunate mothers he had deemed worthy of bearing children began to miscarry. When it happened time and time again, he panicked and closed his practice to obstetrical patients. The abortions continued. Baxter felt that he had brought about a plague. He had no choice. He sentenced himself to die.

The night Cassie and I had gone to Wallace's office, Edgar Baxter had gone also. He went to find the records of his maternity patients who had gone to Wallace when he closed his own practice. He wanted to find any evidence against himself and destroy it as he had, or thought he had, destroyed his own records in the fire.

He heard our voices just in time and hid in the examining room where Winston had surprised me and Cassie. He found Wallace's shotgun, which I had left on the examining table, and decided to take it with him. He had never owned a gun. Wallace's fancy weapon seemed the perfect instrument for his own demise. When we stayed at Winston's until dawn, and his last attempt to tie up loose ends failed, he decided to go ahead and use it. He hoped the gods would judge him for his intentions rather than the results. Again, these were his own words.

"That's it? No, 'I'm sorry.' No, 'Gee, I guess I played God and went a little too far?'" asked Cassie.

"Doesn't look like it."

"What a creep!"

"I think he was insane," I responded sorrowfully.

My daughter was still too young to understand that minds are fragile things. She had no patience for a very good and decent old man who had cracked after years of seeing too much suffering and death. I wished we could have helped him before it was too late. We might have stopped him before he went into his mental cave and unleashed the monster. He was gone now, but the monster was still with us—maybe forever.

Cassie went back to the sofa and rescued her banana. Aggie was trying her best to lick it out of the bowl.

"Crazy as a bed bug, that's for sure!" she said shaking her head as she shared her dessert with the puppy.

"No, I think he was one of the walking wounded," I continued. "Completely insane but able to function in the normal everyday world without calling too much attention to himself. Maybe it happened slowly after Julie died. Or maybe it even happened after his surgery."

"Nuts! He was nuts—plain and simple."

"No, Cassie, there was nothing plain and simple about the insanity of Edgar Baxter. He thought he was God. His divine mind mulled over the ability of each and every woman to care for her child. His decision was absolute, his actions terminal. He was the one who gave life and took it away."

"Wow! The ultimate power trip."

"There's only one thing," I added. "He made mistakes."

"What?"

"Underestimating Mabel and Apollo, for one."

CHAPTER THIRTY-SIX

"Have you finished your telephone call, Paisley, dear?" Mother preceded Horatio into the library. "We thought perhaps you and Cassandra would like to join us for coffee."

Horatio put the heavy silver tray on the table between the two sofas. Cassie plucked Aggie off the cushions to make room for the four of us and dropped the puppy on the floor quickly before she could bite her. Aggie didn't like being displaced. The big comfortable sofa in front of the fireplace had become her throne.

"Well, my dears, what's new on the mystery front?" asked Horatio as Mother poured his coffee. "Have you proven the innocence of Cassandra's young man?"

He took a sip and peered intently over the rim of the dainty porcelain cup.

"Do you have him hiding under your bed?" He winked broadly as he continued, "I heard this morning that he escaped from Teddyville in the wee hours."

"He's not under the bed, yet, Horatio," I sighed. "But you and Mother might as well know, Cassie and I are meeting him later tonight."

"Did you plan this foolishness, Paisley?" demanded Mother sternly.

I shook my head in response.

"Did you Cassandra?"

"Well, sort of," answered Cassie guiltily.

She busied herself with pouring her own cup of coffee. She hardly ever drank the stuff and certainly not with five teaspoons of sugar

"Aha!" Mother nodded her elegantly coifed head so hard a tendril of snow white hair escaped from her French twist.

"The early morning phone call. The one I was too sleepy to answer. You little devils! You've known all day long, and yet you still haven't seen fit to tell me."

"I'm sorry, Mother," I lied. "It was for your own protection. I didn't want you to become involved in a potentially illegal situation."

"Ha!" she laughed ironically. "Like that ever stopped you before, my dear."

"Well . . . " She had my number. I couldn't think of anything to say.

"You should be ashamed of yourselves," she chided. "When are you meeting Ethan and where? And," she continued, "don't lie to me any more, Cassandra. It's very disrespectful." Mother glared at me in fury. "Your mother should have taught you that."

I squirmed in my seat like a child while my mother reprimanded me. I felt like I was in kindergarten. Suddenly Horatio started laughing. Mother turned on him with her eyes blazing. He choked and sputtered.

"I'm quite sorry, my lovely Anna," he croaked. "But you are so fearsome! You would have had General Patton quaking in his boots."

He smiled fondly and kissed her on the cheek in appeasement. "Thank the good Lord you were not my mother. I might have missed out on all the naughty fun."

"Gran's not that bad, Horatio, honest!"

Mother sniffed haughtily, "No need to try and butter me up, Cassandra. The damage is done."

"Okay," I sighed. I knew it was time to come clean. "How about we trade you all the information we know for some much needed assistance later this evening?"

Mother's eyes sparkled with merry excitement. Once again she had manipulated us with Machiavellian expertise. The woman who was furious at us one moment ago for engaging in nefarious undertakings was now quite ready to listen to our adventures.

I let Cassie start. I had some quick thinking to do. Horatio Raleigh was one of Rowan Springs' leading citizens. He was also a businessman with a lucrative commercial enterprise. I didn't want to compromise him in any way. I stopped Cassie when she got to the tale of the car wash.

Horatio was laughing heartily, "Don't stop, my dear, please. The thought of our grave and somber Chief of Police being outwitted by a mere slip of a girl is much too delicious."

"I'm sorry, Horatio," I apologized, "but I am too fond of you to relate anything more in your presence."

He raised one white eyebrow questioningly. I was being reprimanded again but in a much more subtle way.

"I'm glad you have the decency to blush, my child," he said softly. "You speak to me as though I were a stranger instead of someone who has had intimate and loving ties to this family for three generations."

He took pity on my discomfiture and patted my hand with his beautifully manicured one. "There's nothing that could happen under this roof that I would not be proud to be a part of," he assured me.

"How about over this roof, because that's how we're going to elude Joiner's men when we sneak out to meet Ethan."

"Marvelous!" he said with admiration. "I was wondering how you were going to pull it off."

Since he had declared himself to be in for the long haul, we confessed everything. I explained about our trip to the extension farm, and the startling information we had learned from Barry. Horatio already knew about him.

"Ah, yes, Dr. Bartholomew Sedmonds."

"Doctor?"

I was sorry to hear there was another medical doctor mixed up in the case. I was even more sorry to hear that Barry was the doctor.

"Yes. Sedmonds has a Ph.D. in microbiology."

I breathed a sigh of relief as Horatio went to explain.

"Very esoteric specialty, as I remember. Something about mushrooms."

"Fungi?" asked Cassie.

"Exactly! He's a world renowned expert. We should be proud to have him here in our midst. Even if he is a bit peculiar."

"He should fit right in," I mumbled.

"What's that, dear?"

"Nothing, Mother. He asked me out for dinner," I added to placate her.

"Oh, how lovely, dear!

"Venison spaghetti. You and Cassie are invited, too."

"How charming! I simply cannot wait!"

"Yeah, me, too," I grumped. But I had to admit I was just the tiniest bit excited by the prospect of seeing Barry again. It was hard to forget that warm infectious laugh and those wonderful green eyes.

By the time we had finished relating all of the day's events, including the suicide of Edgar Baxter, Mother and Horatio were exhausted and depressed, and Cassie and I were high on caffeine and adrenaline in anticipation of our next adventure.

"Ethan will probably be hungry, dear. Shall I fix some sandwiches for you to take?"

"No, Gran. He said he had someone who could put him up for

the day. I'm sure he's had nothing to do but eat and sleep. He'll be fine. Thanks anyway."

"Why couldn't that 'someone' get him out of town? Then he wouldn't have to involve you and your mother." asked Horatio.

"I honestly don't know," answered Cassie. "I'm sure he would have made other arrangements if he possibly could have."

"You can still make those sandwiches if you want to, Mother. As a matter of fact it's a great idea. I was wondering how we could distract those cops while we make our escape. If you don't mind, you and Horatio can serve them coffee and something to eat while we play monkey on the rooftop."

"Terrific idea, Mom!" Cassie laughed. "I know you'll slip at least once and yell something nasty. Maybe if they're eating and talking with Gran and Horatio they won't hear you."

"I'm as surefooted as . . . well, maybe you're right," I admitted. "And don't forget Aggie. She's sure to hear us up there and make a ruckus. Feed her something also."

"Just make sure it's not jelly beans," hooted my daughter.

CHAPTER THIRTY-SEVEN

Mother was always able to cure herself of depression by cooking. Horatio picked up on her mood, and in no time at all the two of them were laughing and talking as though Edgar Baxter had not shot a big ragged hole in his head. It was a perfect example of the fittest surviving. I firmly believed the first tool of civilized man was not fire or some silly old sharp rock, but his unique ability to enjoy a sense of humor.

I sat and listened to them for a moment so I could sneak a finger full of Mother's wonderful pimento cheese when she wasn't looking. I was sorry now that I had abandoned my dessert to Cassie. My stomach was warming up to all the possibilities in the kitchen. Cassie poked her head around the corner and caught me as I was stealing another swipe of p-cheese.

"Remember Mom, a full mongoose is a . . . "

"I know, I know," I sighed.

"The food is ready, Paisley. Just let me know when you want me to serve it to the men outside."

Mother looked worried for a moment. "I do hope you know what you're doing."

"Relax, Mother, it's a piece of cake."

I looked around to see if Cassie had left. "By the way, do you have any of that cake . . .?"

"Mom!"

"Coming Cassie!"

I gave my concerned little mother a quick hug.

"We'll be fine, you'll see. This mess will be straightened out in no time, and everything will be back to normal."

"Normal?" she laughed. "What's that?"

I smiled, "Point well taken."

Cassie and I dressed in black jeans and dark sweaters. The sweaters would come in handy. The evenings were getting chilly even though we hadn't yet seen the last of September.

"Put on an extra pair of socks, Cassie. We'll walk across the roof in our stocking feet. We'll have better footing that way. Tie your sneakers around your waist by the shoestrings. We can put them on once we get down on the ground."

"Sounds like you've done this before!"

"Your Aunt Velvet and I did this almost every night in the summertime. Granpa Sterling would have been furious if he had known we were traipsing about on his roof, but lucky for us he was partially deaf. And Grandma Sterling either didn't hear us or pretended not to, because she never said a thing."

"How come you never told me?"

"It's dangerous! Do you think I want my one and only precious duckling cavorting about on a steep roof two stories off the ground?"

"Who says I haven't?"

I sat down hard on the floor and looked up at her.

"Have you, Cassie?" I asked, astounded.

"Let's see how good I am at cavorting. That may answer your question."

I shook my head in amazement as I pulled on a second pair of thick athletic socks. I had always thought Vel and I had just been very clever with our nighttime activities and that's why we weren't discovered. Now I realized that maybe our grandparents just never imagined we would do such a thing.

Cassie turned off the light in her bedroom, and I ran back to mine to do the same. Mother was to tell anyone who asked that her daughter and granddaughter had already gone to bed.

I stood in the darkened dining room just outside the kitchen and whispered loudly to get Mother's attention.

"Don't look, Mother, just in case somebody's watching. Pretend that you are talking to Horatio. Cassie and I are ready to leave. You can start serving the food anytime."

"Good luck, darlings," she whispered back while smiling brilliantly at Horatio.

"Thanks!"

Cassie and I hurried through the dark house and up the stairs to what used to be the second floor. For the last fifty-odd years it had been an attic. For some mysterious reason the previous owners decided to lower the roof. They also boarded up the windows and doors on the top story. There was no rhyme or reason for what appeared to be a rather hasty and haphazard job.

At one time there was speculation in town that something terrible had occurred in one of the upstairs bedrooms—something so terrible, it was rumored, that the people who lived there wanted to erase the very space in which it happened. I did know that the story was common knowledge around town. Chief Joiner would believe that the only exits from the house on Meadowdale Farm were on the ground floor. He didn't know what Velvet and I had discovered one summer night over thirty years ago.

"How do we get on the roof, Mom?"

"Aha! I thought you had done this before?"

"I always used a ladder."

"That's cheating," I chuckled. "Look around you," I said as we climbed to the top of the stairs. "What do you see?"

She started to turn on the flashlight, but I stopped her just in time. The logs were less insulated up here. Chinks of mud and limestone had fallen out over the last one hundred and fifty years, and even though the outside was covered with wood siding, I was afraid the light might shine through in places to give us away.

"Ugh, I can't see a thing, but I just walked thorough a spider web."

"Stand still a moment and let your eyes adjust to the dark."

We stood side by side in the big dark hallway of the old house. Up here with the old logs exposed, it was easier to imagine what it might have been like to live in a log cabin. Of course, this was a monster of a log house. Some of the older folks in town swore it used to be a way station for travelers on the trail to the Mississippi and further west. Others claimed that it had been the frontier residence of a wealthy merchant from Chicago who came out here for his health and had the bad luck to die the first winter. He left the house, they said, to his three children, who each refused to give their share to the others. All three had lived here together until they died of old age. The story was told that they died within days of each other after almost sixty years of spiteful, jealous sibling rivalry.

"This place gives me the spooks!" exclaimed Cassie. "What am I supposed to be looking for?"

"Light. Look for the moonlight. That's the way out."

I felt her turn around in the dark and peer in all the corners.

"There's no . . . oh wait, the chimney! You climbed out the chimney!"

I grinned in the dark and grabbed her hand. "Let's go!"

The last time I had climbed up the big brick chimney, I was only fourteen years old. I was considerably larger in width and length now than I'd been then, and suddenly I wasn't sure I could make it. It would be extremely embarrassing to have to call the fire department to come and pluck me out like a cork from a wine bottle.

"Uhhffff!"

"Uhhfff, is right! Quit knocking soot down in my face, Mom!"

"Shhhhh!"

I paused to get my breath and wipe the sweat from my eyes.

"I told you to wait until I was up and out before you started climbing. We're not even sure this can be done. It's bad enough for one of us to get stuck. The two of us crammed in here like sardines would make us the laughingstock of Rowan Springs for the next three generations."

"Then you should have let me go first," she complained. "I'd rather be stuck in this dirty chimney with you than wait alone in that creepy old attic."

I looked up and saw that by some miracle I was almost at the top. I felt around for another purchase in the rough handmade brick as I called softly down to my daughter.

"Hey, guess what? We're almost there."

In just a few more minutes, we had both made it up and out of the chimney. We lay spread-eagled on the warm shingles and breathed deeply of the cool fresh air. I looked up at the harvest moon.

"Wow! It's beautiful!" whispered Cassie. "It looks so much bigger up here."

"I thought you had been up here before?"

"No, Mom, not this far up. I was just trying to get your goat. You and Aunty Vel are the only ones who ever did this at night before. Now I can see why you did."

She rose up and looked down into the yard. "It's like the dreams I used to have of flying!" she said softly. "I feel so free."

"Let's hope we stay that way. Come on, follow me. And be as quiet as a mouse."

We crept over the rooftop in our stocking feet until we reached the place where the original log structure ended and the modern renovation began. Here the roof was flatter and easier to traverse. That's when I slipped.

My ankle turned under me as I was hurrying along the roof over the dining room. Fortunately I was out of sight of anyone down below when I fell and rolled head over heels until I fetched up against the flue over the kitchen stove.

"Mom? Are you all right?" whispered Cassie urgently.

For a moment I couldn't answer. The breath was knocked out of me. And then I heard voices down below. Mother and Horatio had decided to entertain the law on the back porch.

"Damn!" I said under my breath. But I forgot that Cassie had bionic ears.

"What?"

"Shhhh!"

I crawled back up the roof and pulled her along behind me until we reached the old part of the house again. We huddled down next to the chimney while I explained our problem.

"I forgot to tell Mother and Horatio to take the food out front. It's not their fault. I didn't explain our escape route. I meant for us to climb down to the lower level, hang off the side porch roof, and jump off into my night garden. But if we did that we'd be clearly visible to anyone sitting on the back porch. Now what do we do?"

"We do what I used to do," she laughed.

"What's that?"

"Climb down the tree next to my bedroom."

"Gosh, I never thought of that! Clever child, Cassie!"

"Follow me, Mom."

Unlike the chimney, Cassie's tree had grown in the last few years. The limbs reached up to the exact height of the second story roof. We took a moment to slip on our sneakers and then stepped off the roof into the protective canopy of leaves. We descended slowly and carefully until we had almost reached the bottom.

"Head for the orchard when you reach the ground," I whispered. "We can hide under the trees until we get to the beginning of the lane where the undergrowth is still thick and bushy. They'll never see us from the house."

We jumped down from the lowest tree limb and hugged the trunk for a minute to make sure no one was watching. Cassie went running toward the orchard, and I followed close behind. We paused to catch our breath under the cherry tree, then waited for the moon to go behind a cloud before we zigzagged across the orchard to the entrance of the lane.

"We did it!" laughed Cassie as she collapsed against me. We both fell down in a heap on a bed of leaves.

"I can't believe it worked."

"Of course it worked, Mom! It was a great idea. Are you sure Leonard didn't help?"

I grinned. "Maybe just a little bit."

CHAPTER THIRTY-EIGHT

We were almost an hour ahead of schedule, but Cassie was anxious to see Ethan, so we didn't waste a minute while we were on the flat even ground of the lane—we ran. We would have to be more careful crossing the field to reach the lake where we were supposed to meet him. The hay was almost waist high, and the ground was soft and loamy. Moles and groundhogs burrowed for hundreds of feet around the shore line. It would be easy to step into a hole in the dark and break an ankle.

Still, it was a beautiful night. The sky was clear with only a few fleeting clouds across the moon. I could even see the fuzzy white edge of the Milky Way as it reached across the heavens. The wind rustled softly through the leaves and the tall grass and carried the scent of wild honeysuckle from the vines along the fencerows. We started nervously as a hoot owl called to his mate from the top of the hickory nut tree on the hill, and then laughed together as we walked on.

"Gosh, I wish we had a tent. We could bring it back here and camp out."

"Not me!"

"Mom! You used to go camping with me two or three times a year when I was a Girl Scout in San Romero. I thought you loved it. You always had fun."

"I'm glad you thought so. That was the whole point. I did it so you could do it.

We were pretty short on leaders. Not many pampered Latin mothers wanted to take off their high heels and risk snake bite and God knows what in the jungle. I wanted you to have the experience. And we did see some pretty neat things. Remember the anaconda?"

"Wow, do I!"

"Shhhhh, did you hear something?"

As I hunkered down in the tall grass, I found myself wishing we had taken the long way around the edge of the field instead of walking across the middle. In the bright moonlight we were sitting ducks for anyone who might be watching.

"Get down," I urged. "Let's crawl the rest of the way."

"Don't you think that's a bit silly? I didn't hear anything, but if somebody is out there they saw us a long time ago when we started across the field. Crawling on our hands and knees through this grass isn't going to get us anything but chiggers and ticks."

"Oh, well," I sighed as I stood up. "I guess you're right. Leonard is going to have to get a lot better at this clandestine nighttime stuff."

"We've done pretty good up until now, Mom."

She looked at her watch. She had a Timex with a dial that glowed like a beacon in the dark.

"It's only ten minutes till one-thirty."

I laughed. Cassie had always told time that way. It was almost a direct translation from the Spanish.

We reached the edge of the field and walked along the fence for about two hundred feet until we came to a place where we could crawl under without snagging our clothes.

Cassie led the way as we crept through the underbrush of thicket that we used to call the jungle. My father had built a tree house here for Velvet and me when we were children. He had not used any nails. His building supplies were the vines and limbs of sassafras and young willow that grew near the lake. When we played here every day I knew this wild area like the back of my hand. My hand was a lot bigger now. Cassie was closer to childhood, and she used to play over here, too. I let her take the lead.

Pounding footsteps echoed the heart-shaking sound in my chest as we surprised two deer drinking at the water's edge. We held on to each other for a minute in fear.

"Whew! Bambi almost ran over me!" I gasped.

"Yeah," laughed Cass. "That would be a switch—like man bites dog."

"There's the big cedar tree up on the hill. Isn't that where we're supposed to meet Ethan?"

"Where *I'm* supposed to meet Ethan, Mom."

"Whatever do you mean?"

"Don't get funny on me now, please, Mom. Ethan doesn't know you're coming. He asked me to meet him alone."

"Cassie, I can't allow you to . . . "

"Mom, I have to see him alone first," she insisted. "I promise I'll call you after I explain everything. It won't take long."

"Okay," I agreed grudgingly. "But don't call, whistle. You know how to whistle, don't you? You . . . "

"Yeah, yeah," she laughed softly. "Henry Bogart and all that old movie stuff."

"Humphrey," I corrected. "Be careful!"

I squatted down next to a big fallen tree stump and watched as she picked her way around the shore of the lake. As more clouds covered the moon it got harder and harder to see her tall, slender figure. After a while I lost sight of her altogether.

I tried to read the fading dial on my watch and cursed at it for its lack of brightness.

"Damn Rolex! Damn attempt at conspicuous consumption. I'm getting a Timex like Cassie's."

But I knew I never would. Rafe had given me this watch on our first anniversary. It would be buried with me.

My knees were getting stiff, so I struggled up and moved over to sit on a stump. I was almost past caring whether Joiner or his men were watching us. This was probably one of the stupider things I had ever done. My beloved daughter was somewhere on the other side of the lake in the arms of a suspected rapist and murderer, and I had allowed it. Hell! I had engineered it. What kind of mother was I? Damn! Why didn't she whistle?

And then I heard it—sweet and pure over the little lapping sounds of the water against the shore. My baby was fine and dandy!

My knees creaked and popped as I pushed myself off the log and set out across the rough path around the lake. In places, the underbrush grew out past the water's edge, and my feet slipped in wet mud and algae. My toes grew numb as my sneakers filled with cold water. The wind picked up, and I shivered as it blew across the lake and found the moth holes in my sweater. I wished for a jacket and wondered if Cassie needed one, too.

"Enough of this nonsense," I mumbled crossly. "Sneaking around in the dead of night, hummpff." And then I laughed, "Henry Bogart!"

Poor little Cassie knew so much, but she was definitely missing some important facts of popular North American folk culture. Someday we would have an old movie marathon. I would find all of the great oldies, *The Thin Man, To Have and To Have Not, Frankenstein.* She had seen *Casablanca,* I was almost sure. But, *The Uninvited,* now there was a scary . . .

I heard the whistle again. It was much closer. I pulled my right shoe out of the mud and grimaced in disgust. I hated being uncomfortable, and I was rapidly reaching that stage. I was cold and wet and . . . The high-pitched scream finished it off for me. Now I could add "scared" to my list.

"Cassie, I'm coming!" I shouted, as I stumbled the rest of the way around the lake.

The big old cedar tree stood tall and dark against the white face of the moon. It was up on a hill overlooking the rocky spillway where the lake overflowed into a creek below.

As I got closer, I could see Ethan sitting at the base of the cedar. He was leaning back against the trunk with his legs stretched out in front of him. His arms hung limply from his upper body, and his head sagged on his chest. He looked like a discarded rag doll. Alarmed, I ran up the hill and fell on my knees in front of him gasping for breath. I raised my head as I struggled to breathe and saw the white face and pale bald pate. It wasn't Ethan after all. It was Porky Pig. And he was dead, dead, shot in the head.

CHAPTER THIRTY-NINE

My mind went all fuzzy for a moment. I sat down hard on the cold damp ground. There was something very important I had to do, but for the life of me I couldn't remember what it was. And then clarity returned and with it the overwhelming fear that something really, really, terrible had happened to Cassie.

I struggled to get up, but a cramp in my thigh held me down. I kneaded the muscle as hard as I could to restore the circulation and winced as the pain ebbed and flowed. At least I could still feel pain, I thought, as I examined Porky's body while I waited for the cramp to subside. He was wearing jeans and a plaid flannel shirt, and he was barefoot. That was odd, I thought, especially since the bottoms of his feet were white and clean.

After a minute or two, the cramping pain degenerated into a burning ache. I crawled awkwardly to the bottom of the big tree. I couldn't bring myself to touch the body, but I wanted to see the wound in the middle of his forehead. It was odd—not round and circular like a bullet hole—but more like an "x" with only one leg.

"It's from an arrow."

The deep voice scared the shit out of me. I scrambled wildly, flailing my arms and one good leg as I tried to get up and run. A heavy body descended on mine and a big rough hand covered my mouth.

"Don't scream," the man whispered harshly. "We're expecting a visitor. Mustn't frighten him away."

I briefly struggled against the superior strength, then sagged back in exhaustion against his chest. Metal buttons from his overalls poked through my sweater and scratched the tender skin under my shoulders.

"Barry!" I squeaked through his fingers.

I felt my own body relax against his big strong one in relief. Thank God! Sometimes a woman, even an independent woman like me, just really needs a big strong man. I figured this was one of those times. I tried to turn in his arms.

"Be still!" He whispered angrily.

I was confused. He was supposed to save me and Cassie. But how could he do that if I couldn't tell him that she was in danger—that I had heard her scream?

The big hand tightened painfully over my lips. I could smell him now. His clothes held the fetid odor of old perspiration. I smelled unwashed soil and something else, the coppery stench of blood. I gagged. My stomach heaved as I came to the distinct realization that Barry wasn't here to rescue me and Cassie after all. He was the one we needed to be rescued from!

He held me so closely that I could feel his muscles tighten with impatience. His hot breath filled my ear as he swore softly.

"Damnation, where is that skinny bastard?"

Ethan! He was waiting for Ethan. Suddenly I was filled with an overwhelming curiosity. Amazingly enough, it gave me the strength I needed. There was no way I was going to lie here like a weak whinny wisp and maybe even die before I found out just what was going on. And where was Cassie? That last thought gave me the strength I needed for action. Especially since it came at a moment when Barry relaxed his grip just for a second.

I whipped my body like an eel on the end of a fishing line. With my free hand I pulled off my wet muddy sneaker and slammed it hard across the hand over my face. At the same time I kicked him in the crotch with all of my might. He gasped loudly in pain and let go of me. I jumped up and stomped him viciously in the face with my other muddy sneaker. Then I took off running.

He was right behind me. I heard him crashing through the thicket like an angry bull—snorting and cursing. He must have decided catching me was more important than lying silently in wait for Ethan. I ran.

I made it to the top of the hill and stood there for a moment as I caught my breath, knowing that my silhouette made me a perfect target against the moonlit sky. Then I remembered the triangular hole in Porky's forehead and Barry saying, "Arrow." I jumped with reckless abandon off the top of the spillway and onto the sharp rocks below.

Pain shot up through my one bare foot as I landed heavily. I turned to look behind me and saw the huge figure of Bartholomew Sedmonds standing on the spillway above. He raised his arms and screamed in rage.

"You bitch!"

I took off. The rocky stream meandered down through the field and beyond. The water was shallow now—only ankle deep—but during the heavy summer rains it became a small creek. At places, the bank was as high as my head and I couldn't see over it. I had no idea where I was, and I was getting tired. Barry would catch me soon. I couldn't go on much farther.

Suddenly the stream bed disappeared altogether. I fell heavily over the last big rock into the soft grassy meadow. I lay there panting—certain that I was a goner. Barry was right on my heels. He would be here any moment, but I couldn't run any more. I rolled over on my back and prayed for Cassie while I waited.

Something grabbed me around the waist and pulled me down into darkness. This time the hand over my mouth was firm but gentle and the voice in my ear was full of love.

"Oh, Mommy, Mommy, thank God you're okay!" cried Cassie softly.

"Shhh, he's coming," warned Ethan.

I heard the big man's footsteps as he ran past the cave mouth and on through the grass in the meadow beyond. Ethan released his hold on me as he whispered another warning.

"He's bound to come back. He'll soon realize there's no place out there for you to hide, and he'll come back looking for us."

"What'll we do?" cried Cassie. "We can't go up. He'll see us!"

"Then we'll just have to go down," decided Ethan.

"Down where?" I croaked.

I was still out of breath and on the ragged edge of exhaustion.

"Down through the cave," he answered.

I looked around me in the darkness. This was no cave, it was just a big hole in the ground, and I told him so.

"What do you think a cave is?" he laughed. "Follow me."

Ethan squirmed and turned until he was headfirst in the hole. His bony knees bruised my ribs as he pushed and pulled himself down deeper. Soon all we could see of him were the soles of his shoes.

"Mom? Do we have to?" asked Cassie tremulously, as she stared into the dark pit below.

"I guess we have no choice, pumpkin. Follow that man."

It was easier for Cassie and me to turn around, but pushing and pulling along the dark rocky walls of the narrow passage was terrifying. I wasn't aware that I had any phobias—spiders, maybe—but the terror I felt in that dark confined space beat anything I had ever experienced before. I'll take a Latin American revolution any day over a damp, narrow underground cave.

Just when I thought I would lose my mind in the darkness, the walls widened and the going got easier. In places it was actually possible to quit slithering like a snake on my belly and crawl on my hands and knees.

Abruptly, the cave opened into a large underground cavern. Even

Ethan was taken by surprise. He tumbled out of the narrow passage to splash headfirst into the natural spring basin below. Cassie and I followed in quick succession.

The water wasn't deep, but it was clear and very cold. All three of us came up gasping.

"Brrrrr! Oh, my God, I'm freezing. Mom, are you okay?"

I squirted half a pint of spring water out of my mouth so I could reassure her.

"Just hunky-dory! As a matter of fact, I don't know when I've had so much fun."

Ethan laughed a big booming laugh which resounded off the walls of the confined space. I looked around and realized that it wasn't dark any more. Everything glowed with a faint green light.

"Where's that light coming from?" I asked Ethan.

He was, after all, an expert on caves. Weren't we just the lucky ones to be trapped down here with an expert, I thought cynically.

"Phosphorescence. This water has tiny little animals that glow when we brush up against them. They give off that faint greenish light."

"Little green animals? Ethan, get me out of here," squeaked Cassie.

"Relax, honey. They won't hurt you. Even if we weren't here the fish would cause them to give off light by their swimming action."

"Fish? What kind of fish? Big fish?" she asked in a scared little voice.

"Maybe, but don't worry. They're blind."

"That's it! I've had it. Blind fish, green animals, suitors with murderous intent. Damn it all!" I shouted.

I splashed clumsily over to the rock ledge that ran around the pool and pulled myself painfully up until I could throw one leg over the edge. Slowly, I managed to lift my whole body up. I lay there panting and feeling as vulnerable as a beached whale.

"Watch out for snakes," warned Ethan.

"Don't you understand?" I croaked. "I, Paisley Sterling DeLeon, no longer give a shit."

Cassie waded over to my side, She reached up to rub my shoulders.

"Poor Mommy, you're so tired," she acknowledged. "But I love you. And when this is all over we'll sit out on the patio and laugh while we're telling Gran all about it. You'll see, everything will be okay."

She sounded so grown up, so authentically mature. She sounded like me. I should be the one to tell her those things. The world was all upside down, and we were inside and should be out. I started laughing. I laughed for a while and then I cried. When I was finished, I felt much better.

"Well," I hiccoughed. "That's over with. What's next on the agenda?"

During my little emotional outburst Ethan had climbed up on my ledge and pulled Cassie up beside him.

"I guess we wait down here until morning and then go back up and get some help. Find the police and . . . "

"Wait, aren't you hiding from the police? Maybe I forgot something in my delirium, but didn't you escape from prison last night? Aren't you 'on the lam' as they say in jailhouse parlance?"

Ethan let out a big heartfelt sigh before he answered me.

"I guess it's time for me to explain some things."

"Ethan, you don't have to explain anything to me," said Cassie.

"The hell he doesn't!"

"You're quite right, as usual, Mrs. DeLeon. I do have some explaining to do. Especially to you, Cassie. First of all, let me thank you both for standing by me when I gave you so little to go on. And out of curiosity may I ask why you trusted me so much? Was it woman's intuition?"

"Yeah, I got great woman's intuition!" I snorted. "I almost fell head over heels for that mountain of murderous muscle in overalls."

"Barry Sedmonds. Yes, he is quite likable," admitted Ethan. "He had me fooled, too."

"Yeah?" I asked. "I bet you weren't wondering what he'd be like in bed."

CHAPTER FORTY

Ethan might not have had my lusty thoughts about Dr. Sedmonds, but he had trusted him implicitly. He had gone straight to Barry for help when he escaped from jail.

"Then you were there yesterday afternoon?" asked Cassie.

"Not yet. I hadn't made it to Rowan Springs. You have no idea how far twenty-five miles is when you're on foot. And it was fairly easy for me. I had spent so much time in the hills and valleys around here that I knew exactly how to travel across country. I knew all the shortcuts and how to avoid the police roadblocks. I got to the experiment farm a little after dark. At the time I thought it tremendous luck because Sedmonds was just getting ready to leave on his bicycle. He saw me coming and opened up the greenhouse. I was totally up front with him before I went inside. I told him I had escaped from the police and needed a place to hide. He seemed quite willing to let me in. Now I know why."

"And why is that, Ethan?" I asked.

"Sedmonds is the brains behind everything. I thought it was poor old Doc Baxter. He's the reason I ran away from Teddyville in the first place. When they told me he was coming to give me a prerelease physical exam I panicked."

"Why? What could the poor old thing do to you?"

"Shut him up, Cassie. Right Ethan?" I asked.

"That's right, Mrs. DeLeon. Shut my mouth, as you say here in the South."

"Very funny! And as long as we're stuck in this cave together you might as well call me Paisley. Save the formalities for later."

He laughed again, "Okay, Paisley. But you're right. There are at least a dozen ways he could have made sure I never left Teddyville alive. I did a lot of thinking during those eight days I spent in jail. I was pretty sure Baxter was responsible for all the abortions. I thought that was the answer to everything." He ran a big hand thorough his hair and scratched his ear. "Boy, was I wrong!"

"You mean there's more to this?"

"You bet, Mrs. . . . er, Paisley."

"What, Ethan?"

"Drugs, Cassie. A big-time drug operation under the guise of normal agricultural experimentation."

I was flabbergasted.

"At the county extension farm? That's what Barry was up to? I thought he was a famous scientist—a something-or-other in fungus."

"He is. His background is impeccable. Someone at the CDC even recommended him to me as a resource when I was planning my trip. He studied at Stanford and Texas A&M. He even did a stint as associate professor at The University of Mexico. I think that's where he got the idea."

"Idea for what?" Cassie asked as she scooted closer to Ethan.

The temperature in the cave should have been even, but our wet clothing was lowering our body temperatures. I was tempted to scoot closer too, but I didn't.

"For growing a stronger, more prolific strain of certain mind-altering drugs."

"Marijuana?" I was disgusted. "All of this running and killing and hiding is about a few joints?"

"Not exactly."

"Then please explain it to me because I am righteously pissed!"

"Cannabis . . . " he began.

"In English if you don't mind," I interrupted irritably.

"The flower of the female marijuana plant has a resin which is extremely potent. That's what hashish is made of. Barry was growing a special strain of the female plant in his greenhouse. He had a highly sophisticated grafting process going on, which I would expect from a scientist of his knowledge and expertise."

I had to smile. Even after the man had tried his best to kill us all, Ethan still admired Barry's scientific mind.

"The hashish he was growing was like nothing we've ever seen before. It would be worth millions in the drug market. And he could have named his price for the process."

"Is that what caused the abortions? Hashish?" I asked.

"No, Paisley, I'm sure it was Goldenrod, or rather the fungus growing on it. The spores from the plant rust spread the abortifacient from one patient that Baxter had inoculated to other pregnant patients in his office. A microscopic airborne spore is hard to spot, especially if you're not looking for it. Sedmonds might have suspected what was going on, but he didn't care. It could even have furthered his study in a bizarre kind of way. He's trying to make a name for himself by developing a natural universal fungicide. I think that's why he got into the drug business. He really needed the money. Funding for his kind of research is notoriously scarce. Barry's been operating on a shoestring for years. He hunts for most of the food he eats, and he doesn't even own a car. That's why I had to call you to help me get out of town."

"Okay, about that, Ethan," I inquired a bit tersely. "Why didn't you just ask to speak to Chief Joiner? Why couldn't you tell him what you've told us? Why involve my daughter?"

"I honestly didn't know who to trust, Mrs. DeLeon. I've only been in Rowan Springs for nine weeks, and so far I've discovered that one of the town's leading citizens is a murderer and another is a drug dealer. The only person I knew for sure that I could trust was Cassandra."

"Okay," I admitted, "I'll buy that. But I still have a lot of unanswered questions. For one thing, who in the hell is Porky Pig?"

"Who?" asked Ethan.

He was no actor, and the surprise was written all over his face.

"The dead guy under the cedar tree, or didn't you see him? I thought that's where you were supposed to meet Cassie?"

"I never got that far, Mom. I met Ethan on my way around the lake. We, eh, we said 'hello,' and then I whistled for you, or rather Ethan did. I couldn't pucker."

Ethan laughed heartily until a blushing Cassie poked him in the ribs with her elbow.

"Well, I couldn't. For whistling, anyway," she grinned. "We didn't see any dead guy, but Ethan said he saw Barry walking away from the big cedar."

"That's why I had to find Cassie before she went up the hill. I didn't know what Barry would do, and I couldn't take a chance."

"And what about the poor old woman? Am I expendable? Is that why you whistled again, so I would walk into Barry's trap and draw his attention away for you to make good your escape?"

"Mom!" chided Cass indignantly. "First of all, Ethan only whistled once. I guess Barry heard and knew it was some kind of signal. He must have whistled again to see who would come running."

"But . . . "

"Wait! And second of all, we were coming back to find you when I fell off the spillway."

"Oh, Cassie . . . "

"Just one minute, Mom, I haven't finished. And third of all, how can you possibly think I would ever abandon you . . . " Her voice broke as she burst into tears.

"Cassie, darling! I'm sorry. Please forgive me."

"She's right, Mrs. DeLeon. We were coming back to get you when Cassie fell. I climbed down to get her. By the time we had started to climb back up, we heard you running towards us with Barry right behind. I grabbed Cassie and we headed towards the meadow and the mouth of the cave. I found it two weeks ago when I was out here alone." He held out his wrists. In the dim green light I could see faint white lines where the deep scratches had been.

"I fell in the hole. I got scratched trying to get back out again. It's a lot harder when you're loaded down with equipment."

"Speaking of scratches—what did you have to do with the Hayes girl?"

"Nothing," he denied vehemently. "The only time I ever saw her was the night of the festival. She attached herself to me at the street party. She wanted to dance. The girl was very insistent. I could tell she was drunk, and I tried to get away without making a scene. I'm afraid I wasn't too successful. She was furious. She spat in my face and screamed that she would make me pay."

"Well, that she did. I believe you, Ethan," I assured him. "I don't think that comes as a surprise. I've been somewhat impatient with you during these last two weeks, but that has nothing to do with my belief in your innocence."

I stopped a moment and listened.

"Does it seem noisy in here all of a sudden?"

Ethan turned and looked around at the hole we had fallen through like Alice. A slow but steady stream of water was trickling from the opening of the cave into the basin below.

"Oh, my God!" he exclaimed. "It's raining!"

"What's the big deal?" laughed Cassie. "It can't rain in here. And we couldn't get much wetter, anyway."

Ethan turned a white and frightened face to us.

"You want to bet?" he asked. "We've got to get out of here while we still have a chance!"

"What the hell? What's going on, Ethan?"

His fear was infectious. I felt the hairs on the back of my neck coming to attention.

"This cave is the lowest one in a system of limestone caverns that runs from one end of the whole valley between Rowan Springs and Morgantown. It's part of a still greater system of caves in the state. The biggest one is Mammoth Cave which is about a hundred miles from here."

"What's that got to do with us?"

I still didn't get the reason for his anxiety.

"All of the ground water from the valley above will flow down to this point. During a heavy rain this cave will fill up in a matter of minutes. We'll drown, that's what."

"Why can't we just go back out the way we came?" shouted Cassie.

The sound of the water pouring in the pool had increased so that I could hardly hear her. Ethan pointed to the rush of water now tumbling from the cave mouth. As we watched, it grew steadily into a small waterfall.

"IT WOULD WASH US RIGHT BACK OUT AGAIN, THAT"S WHY!" he shouted.

"WHAT ARE WE GOING TO DO?" screamed Cassie.

The water in the pool was rising rapidly. It was almost over the ledge we were sitting on. We stood up and huddled together. The water crawled slowly upwards and covered our feet and ankles. Ethan pulled our heads together so we could hear each other.

"We only have one hope," he told us. "This cave is connected to all the others in the system. There must be an outlet in the bottom of the pool. If we dive down to the bottom when the cave is almost full, we'll be pushed out by the pressure of the water above. There's a pretty good chance we'll come out into another bigger cavern or maybe into an open spring somewhere in the valley."

Cassie was trying to keep from crying, but she couldn't stop her lower lip from quivering uncontrollably. I knew if I hugged her she would dissolve into tears. As much as I wanted to hold her, I could not let myself. Instead, I whacked her on the rump as hard as I could. Her surprise and anger were instant and genuine. I had not spanked her since she was four years old.

"Mom! What . . . ?"

"Get mad, Cassie! Get good and mad."

I knew she could be an Amazon when she was angry.

"I'd rather see you drown here like a rat than marry this sorry son-of-a-bitch."

That worked. She raised her head and opened her mouth to rip me to verbal shreds. Ethan saw what I was trying to do and smiled a big slow smile.

"Save it for later, Cassie!" he said. "No time now! The water's almost up to our hips. When it gets to Paisley's waist we'll take three deep breaths and hold the fourth. Then we hold hands and dive. I'll pull you down to where the opening should be. By that time, there ought to be enough pressure to force us into the next part of the system— wherever it is. I wish I had explored these caves before." He gave us a wry smile. "There's no time like the present!"

As the water approached my waist, we held hands. Cassie gripped mine a little more firmly than necessary. Under other circumstances, I would have groaned in pain. But hey, I got what I wanted. She was standing tall and strong. A few broken carpals was a small price to pay.

"BREATHE NOW!" yelled Ethan. "OKAY! ON THE COUNT OF FOUR, WE GO!"

I had barely taken in my last big breath when Ethan jumped feet first off the ledge and pulled us down after him. The current pulled and turned us down and down towards the bottom of the pool. At first we moved slowly, like a runner in a bad dream. Then suddenly we were caught in the outer edge of a swiftly moving vortex. Cassie's grip on my hand slipped. My fingers were so numb from the pressure of hers squeezing mine that I couldn't hold on. As the spinning swirling current sped up, Cass and Ethan were swept away from me, and I was all alone. I tumbled head over heels in an upside-down tornado of pale green water. My other shoe was torn from my foot. My sweater and jeans followed as I turned and spun faster and faster like Dorothy and Toto, only I wasn't headed for Kansas.

I said my prayers. I prayed desperately that Cassie and Ethan would be safe. And I asked God to forgive me for all my sins. There was no time to enumerate them. I didn't have that long to live. Everything was getting dark. My body no longer had the strength to fight the current. I pulled my arms up and crossed them over my breasts. It was the last conscious act I made.

EPILOGUE

"Venus rising from the sea," laughed Mother. "That's what Mavis Madden said she looked like."

"My word," expounded Horatio. "To see the lovely Paisley Sterling popping up in the middle of Big Spring Park in the altogether . . . What a sight to behold! Thank goodness that young man had a camera."

"Hummpf! Yeah, we wouldn't want to deprive the world of any opportunity to humiliate and ridicule me. God forbid the picture should not have appeared on the front page of the weekly paper. And my so-called best friend, Pamela Winslow, made sure it was on CNN so the whole world could laugh at me."

"Not to mention the entire congregation of the First Baptist Church, Mom. That was the funniest," added Cassie.

"What in the hell were they doing having a Sunday School breakfast in the rain, anyway?"

"It wasn't raining when they started at sunrise, Paisley, dear. The storm came up very suddenly. No one was prepared for it."

"You can say that again! My head is still spinning from that roller coaster ride through the cave."

I pulled myself up to a more comfortable position.

Mother and Horatio Raleigh were seated side by side on the

window seat in my bedroom. Cassie was sitting cross-legged at the bottom of my bed. Occasionally I saw two of each of them. I said so.

"Dr. Wallace says you have a mild concussion, dear," explained Mother. "I'm sure you'll be fine in a few days."

"Great! And I'm supposed to trust that quack with my precious brain?"

"Give the poor man a chance to redeem himself, my dear," pleaded Horatio. "He convinced Andy Joiner that Mr. Hayes' death was accidental. The daughter finally admitted that he fell on his own gun in the act of chasing her. She was running away after a particularly severe beating. Miss Hayes has no idea why she put the blame on Ethan, but I do. He was a symbol of the world that had turned its back on her." He shook his handsome white head in dismay. "Poor child."

"Where is Ethan?" I asked. "I have a lot of questions remaining for that young man."

"Mom, I told you. He's already gone back to Atlanta," answered Cassie.

"Back?"

"Yes, I told you this morning."

"I can't remember," I worried.

"Short-term memory loss, my dear. Wallace warned us it might happen as a result of the concussion," said Horatio. "It won't bother you for long."

"Lord, I hope not! I have a book to write. By the way, how come I can remember all the bad stuff?"

"Winston said you might. He explained that amnesia is selective. There may be parts of your memory intact and big holes in the rest," explained Mother.

"Well, humor me then and repeat some things you may have told me that I cannot for the life of me recall."

"Shoot, Mom."

"Who was Porky Pig, for one thing?"

"I'll take that one, my dear," offered Horatio. "Alvin Vanover was the pharmacist, or actually, the son of the original pharmacist who shared the office with Edgar Baxter. He was something of a disappointment to his father. Young Alvin flunked out of several schools and generally played the prodigal son. When his father died, Alvin returned and took over the family business. The whole town was relieved because we depend on a good, reliable druggist. We thought we had one. None of us knew that he had a nice little black market drug business going on the side. For a price, he was perfectly willing to slip anyone an extra bottle of Valium, or almost anything."

"I mention Valium because that's what got poor, lovely Julia Baxter on the road to addiction. Edgar knew she was depressed, but because she had quit begging him for drugs, he thought she was getting better. After her death, he was furious when he discovered that she had circumvented him. He vowed to get even with Vanover. Imagine how he must have felt when the allergist in Morgantown refused him, and he had to depend on his enemy for the Goldenrod extract. I think he must have gotten great satisfaction from burning down the building and putting Alvin out of business. The fire also eliminated the spores that were spreading the abortions. The plague was eliminated, but Edgar didn't know that."

"Is that when Porky, er, Alvin hooked up with Barry? When he lost his business?"

"Ethan thinks it was earlier than that, Mom. He said Barry found out about Porky's sideline somehow, and he blackmailed him for his client list. The idea was that people willing to pay a fortune for Valium would fork over for marijuana and hashish, too. They both knew what Doc Baxter was doing. And they didn't care. Alvin was never very careful when he made up the extract for Baxter. When Barry warned him about the fungus, he ignored him and kept up his production. Doc Baxter went kind of crazy when all the babies started dying. He thought he had brought about a plague that would end the human race. He was ultimately responsible, of course, but it was the fungus that was spreading the abortions. Of course, as Ethan says, he wasn't working on all four cylinders in the first place."

Horatio took over the narrative. "Edgar was past caring what people found out about him. Vanover, however, still had a vested interest in remaining a free man. He knew that Baxter had a patient who had received one dose of the extract only. He had to make sure she got the rest of the series. Otherwise he might get caught."

"How's that, Cassie?"

"According to Ethan's medical theory, the extract goes straight to the fetus. If the baby dies and is aborted, there is no evidence. If the baby is carried to term, the extract can be found in the placenta and cord blood. He had to make sure that Mabel aborted."

"Mabel!"

"That's right," she continued. "Mabel was the patient that got away. Alvin tried to inject her that night you saw him in the hospital and later on when she went home."

"Is she okay?"

"Don't worry, Mom. She's fine and so is the baby."

"Okay, I think I got all that straight. But why did Barry kill Porky? I thought they were partners in crime. They seemed like such a nice couple."

"My dear, Paisley, it's so good to see your sense of humor returning."

Horatio patted me gingerly on the knee as he explained, "Dr. Sedmonds decided that Alvin Vanover was a liability. Sedmonds had his eye on fame in the scientific community. He was quite capable of discarding the hashish trade when he had achieved enough recognition to bring in grants from reputable universities. He needed few creature comforts, but he had an overpowering ambition. He knew that Vanover would never agree to close down their highly lucrative commercial enterprise. So he 'offed' him, as they say in the flicks."

"And why carry his body to the big cedar tree and dump him? That's one sight I really would like to forget."

"Ethan told Barry that he was going to meet me there, that's why, Mom. He was going to pin the murder on Ethan, then kill him to 'protect me.' But when Ethan discovered the hashish growing in the greenhouse, he took Barry's bicycle and got there first. He managed to head me off, but you . . . "

"Hummfp! I remember all that! But why shoot him with an arrow? That's a bit off the wall isn't it?"

"Exactly," she laughed. "Before Ethan learned Barry's big bad secret, they spent some time together. Ethan admired the hunting bow Barry had hanging on the wall in his office. They compared hunting stories. That gave Barry the idea. He knew he could count on someone coming forward afterwards to give evidence that Ethan had hunted in Africa with a bow and arrow."

"Speaking of someone—what about Ethan's mother? Did he ever contact her to explain this mess?"

"Mommy, can we discuss this in private?" whispered Cassie.

"Er, ahem, Anna, my dear, I find that I am yearning for another piece of that delicious French apple tart. Do you think we might . . . ?"

"Come Horatio, let's leave our ducklings alone for a while."

Mother leaned over and kissed my slightly banged-up forehead. She smiled down at me.

"Don't talk too long, dear. You must get some rest. You've been through quite an ordeal."

I waited until they left and turned to my daughter, who appeared to be totally unscathed, thank God.

"Speaking of ordeal, what happened to you and Ethan in the cave?"

"Ethan protected me, Mom. He kept me from getting as banged up as you are. And he also managed to pull me out in the spring above the park. We were just climbing down the hill when we saw you make your rather spectacular appearance."

"Oh, God," I groaned. "Naked as a jaybird in front of the whole town!"

"Just the same, Mom. I was never so glad to see anyone in my whole life."

She untangled her long legs and crawled up to give me a hug.

"You're all so calm and collected," I marveled. "I take it that means Dr. Bartholomew Sedmonds is safely behind bars?"

"Teddyville has a new inmate. Andy Joiner caught him trying to get away in Porky's car. He isn't a very good driver," she laughed.

"Okay, what's this about Ethan's mother? What did she do?"

"That's just it!" complained Cass. "Ethan never gave her a chance to do anything. That's why I turned him down."

"Turned him down?"

"Yes, I turned down his proposal of marriage."

"When did he have time . . . ?"

"That last computer disc Miss Lolly found was a letter to me. He was outlining all the reasons why we could live happily ever after."

Her voice broke and she buried her lovely face in my shoulder.

I let her cry for awhile. I could tell she had almost cried herself out. This was just the tail end of her heartbreak. When her shoulders stopped shaking, I asked her the question that was foremost on my mind.

"Why did you turn him down, Cassie?"

"Family!" she hiccoughed loudly. "He has no concept of family. He's a loner. He would expect me to be as self-contained as he is. I could never do that. I could never shut you out of my life, out of my problems, like he did his mother. I wouldn't want my children to grow up that way. My family is the most important thing in the world to me. It has to be that way for my kids, too."

"Oh." I couldn't think of anything else to say. Once again my daughter had overwhelmed me.

"Enough about me," she sniffed. "Are you really feeling better? By the way, Pam called to make sure you were all right. She said to remind you that Leonard's book is long overdue."

"Leonard? Who's Leonard?"